The Flimsiest
Evidence . . .

"Hold on. Let me get my purse and I'll come with you."

"Like hell you will! You're gonna stay right here and work. That's what I hired you for, remember?"

"But how do you know the police will even let you in to see Sterling Wyatt?"

"Don't worry, sweetheart, I'll see him. I got connections." Jackson stopped by the desk and looked at Jillian's job application. "Does Wyatt know you as Jillian, or Miss Fletcher?"

"Neither one," Jillian said. "Everything happened so fast yesterday, we never had the chance to exchange names."

"Just two ships passing in the night?"

"I told you, it wasn't anything like that. We didn't have time to—Wait, I know! Tell him, the girl with the . . ." She blushed and took a deep breath. ". . . the girl with the raspberry see-through bra . . ."

# THE TALL DARK ALIBI

## Carol Jerina

CHARTER BOOKS, NEW YORK

THE TALL DARK ALIBI

A Charter Book/published by arrangement with
the author

PRINTING HISTORY
Charter edition/April 1988

ISBN: 1-55773-035-0

Charter Books are published by The Berkley Publishing Group,
200 Madison Avenue, New York, New York 10016.
The name "Charter" and the "C" logo are trademarks
belonging to Charter Communications, Inc.

PRINTED IN THE UNITED STATES OF AMERICA

10  9  8  7  6  5  4  3  2  1

# ACKNOWLEDGMENTS

I wish to thank the following people for being so courteously helpful and informative.

Officer Gary Dietrich, Garland Police Department

Homicide Investigator Linda Erwin, Dallas Police Department

Millie Moore, Millie's Rose Patch Florist

Billye M. Johnson, E. R. Volunteer, Plano General Hospital

*To Eileen Fallon,*

*who was at the right place,*
*at the right time,*
*and thought of me.*

*Thank you,*
*C.*

# THE
# TALL
# DARK
# ALIBI

# CHAPTER 1

Tuesday, April 22

Why were some days worse than others? Jillian wondered. Days? In her opinion, the whole darn month had been sour.

She shifted her shopping bag to check her wristwatch, and winced when she saw the time. Twenty minutes to two. She should have been at her desk forty minutes ago instead of fighting her way through a herd of lunchtime shoppers. No doubt about it, only a miracle would save her from Miss Shaw this time. The old witch had threatened to fire her the last time she'd come in late.

Regretting the loss of her job, and the monthly paycheck that she and the local department stores thrived on, Jillian muttered, "Scratch that one."

"Where does it itch?" a deep voice asked behind her.

Jillian whirled around and stared almost levelly into the tall man's smoky-gray eyes. He had the kind of sexy good looks that would have made any woman's heart flutter. But not hers. Not today.

"Buzz off, pervert."

"Hey, you're the one with the itch, sweetheart. I just offered to scratch it." He shot a quick glance over his shoulder, then looked back at her and grinned.

1

Jillian narrowed her eyes and glared at him. "If you don't go away and leave me alone, I'll call a cop."

"Whew! You ought to have a license for those baby blues of yours, honey. They're lethal weapons."

"Why me?" Jillian grumbled as the light finally changed. "Why do the weirdos always pick me?"

"You work around here, or just slumming?" the stranger asked, following her out into the street.

"Ignore him," she muttered loud enough for him to hear. "Maybe he'll go away."

"Not me. I see something I like, I go after it. Persistent, that's me."

Jillian groaned, and gnashed her teeth. She wouldn't say another word to the idiot, because talking to him only made matters worse.

"The most persistent one of the litter, Momma always said. There were twelve of us, you know. Six of each. One great big happy family. You know something? I bet you're the kind of lady who likes kids."

Jillian stepped up onto the curb and increased her speed, wanting to get as far away from the creep as possible. A few feet farther down the sidewalk, she glanced out of the corners of her eyes. She didn't see him, and believing she had lost him, she heaved a sigh of relief. Now if she could only get to the office before—

"Anybody ever tell you, you got real sexy hips?" the stranger asked, falling into step beside her. "Breeder's hips, Momma would call them. Nice and round, you know, but not too wide."

Ignoring him obviously wasn't doing any good, she realized. If he hadn't gone away by the time she reached her building, she was going to sic the doorman on him. The doorman was built like a professional weight lifter, and probably hadn't had a good workout in a while. Throwing this jerk out on his can ought to be adequate enough exercise for him.

"Say, it's only about one-thirty," the stranger said, "and I got nothing else to do this afternoon, what do you say you and me go get married and have a couple of kids?"

Jillian came to an abrupt stop in front of her building and pivoted sharply. "All right, buster, you asked for it."

The stranger grinned crookedly. "Is that a yes?"

"Just wait and see," Jillian said, then turned to the doorman. "Excuse me. Would you please call the police and have them come pick up this—this asylum escapee? He won't leave me alone."

"Is that right, mister?" the doorman asked the stranger. "Are you bothering her?"

"Me, bother her? Of course not," he said. "I've asked her to marry me and have my kids—I call that a meaningful relationship."

"Meaningful relationship!" Jillian said, appalled. "We met at the corner not more than three minutes ago."

"I don't know about you, sweetheart," he said, stepping closer to her, "but three minutes is meaningful enough for me."

"Look," said the doorman, "why don't you two love-birds talk this over between yourselves and just leave me out of it? With two ex-wives, I ain't exactly an expert on marriage counseling."

With a groan, Jillian shook her head. "I haven't got time to stand here and argue; I'm already late as it is." Then to the doorman, "Don't let him follow me. Please!"

"Swear to God, miss," the doorman said, "he makes one move to get past me, I'll break his arm."

"Thank you," she said sincerely.

"But, honeybun, you can't do this to us," the stranger cried out as Jillian hurried toward the bank of opened elevator doors. "Think of what it'll do to the children!"

Jillian pushed the button for the tenth floor and slumped against the wall as the elevator doors closed with a hiss. She knew in an instant where she'd made her first big mistake— she'd gotten out of bed this morning. She'd made her second mistake in trying to shop on her lunch hour. Every maniacal woman in town had been at Sanger-Harris, hunting for bargains at the store's lingerie clearance sale. Never in her life had she seen so many panty girdles being tossed around. But running into the good-looking creep— now that topped them all. Nothing else could possibly go wrong. Nothing.

A little bell pinged and the elevator stopped moving. When the doors opened, Jillian took off at a dead run. She ran straight into the man waiting to get on. Her purse sailed off in one direction and the strap on her shopping bag snapped, sending its contents across the floor.

"Are you all right?" the man asked after a moment.

"What?" Jillian asked stupidly, feeling herself drown in the depths of his warm, concern-filled brown eyes. Why was it that only the men got long, thick lashes, and women didn't? Blinking, she gazed past him at the ceiling behind his head. "Is it my imagination, or are we lying on the floor?"

"Oh, I'm so sorry," he said, and quickly moved aside. "It's not bad enough I knocked you down, I have to try and smother you as well. But I guess that's what I get for being in such a hurry." He stood up, then helped Jillian to her feet. "You are all right, I hope. Nothing's broken?"

"No," Jillian said.

"No, you're not all right, or no, you are?"

"No, I mean, yes, I'm fine, but you've got it wrong," Jillian said. "You didn't run into me. I ran into you."

"Pardon me?"

"I should be apologizing to you, not the other way around."

He smiled, and Jillian felt her heart do a double somersault in her chest. An angelic Adonis right on the heels of an oversexed pervert—there was some justice in this world after all.

"There's no need for you to be so polite," he said, glancing away from her. "I know it's all my fau— Oh, look at your, uh, your things."

Jillian did, and she felt her cheeks turn as red as her new hot-pink bikini panties hanging from a ficus limb, right next to her new raspberry see-through bra. Her ivory-lace teddy hung by its strap on a doorknob across the hall.

"I went shopping instead of eating lunch," she said, scurrying to pick up her things. "I shouldn't have spent so much money, but Sanger-Harris was having this big sale, and I—"

"Is this your garlic press?"

"Yes. Just, uh, drop it there in the bag."

"A pasta maker! You won't believe this, but I've always wanted to get one of these. Right now, my mouth's watering at the thought of homemade fettucini Alfredo. How difficult is it to make?"

"I wouldn't know; I just got the machine today," Jillian said, cramming the last of her flimsy underwear into the torn shopping bag. "The sales clerk at Sanger-Harris told me that if I used the recipes that came with the maker, and followed the directions carefully, I wouldn't have any trouble at all."

"Really." The man turned the pasta-maker box in his hands until he came to the price sticker. "Is this all it cost?"

"Well, it was actually twenty percent cheaper than that. They didn't put the discounted price on the box."

"Hmm, I may stop by there and get one for myself," he said, handing the box to her. "Did they have very many left?"

"Oh, yes, lots."

The man looked at Jillian and slowly smiled. Jillian looked at him and felt her knees begin to wobble. Then a bell pinged, the red arrow pointing down flashed above the elevator door, and both of them blinked.

"Well, I have to be going," the man said, backing slowly toward the opened doors. "This turned out not to be a wasted trip, after all. It's been, uh, nice running into you."

"Same here," Jillian said.

As the doors closed, she released a long, wistful sigh. Now that was the kind of man you took home to meet the folks. Tall, handsome, thoughtful, considerate—and he was normal!

"Oh, my God!" she said, cringing when she suddenly remembered the time. She grabbed her shopping bag and purse and raced down the hall to her office.

Two hours later, Jillian sat with her bare feet on the edge of the coffee table, her television blaring unnoticed in the background as she studied the classified ads. One interesting job possibility caught her eye and she circled it in red ink. Then she made a face and, shaking her head, crossed it out again. It sounded too much like the job from which she'd just been fired. Living on unemployment for a few months was more preferable than working for another company that hired its accounting managers from the Nazi S.S. school of tact.

The telephone rang, and Jillian leaned across the sofa to answer it.

"What are you doing home this time of day?" asked a familiar voice. "You sick or something?"

"That's close enough. I got fired."

"No kidding!"

"I wish I were," Jillian said. "Want to come up and cry over a cup of tea with me?"

"Sure. We'll be up in a sec. 'Bye."

Jillian cradled the receiver and stood up. She barely had time to cross the room when a heavy knock sounded at the door.

"You really got fired, huh?" Vinnie asked, bending his knees as he entered her apartment.

To look at him now, with his muscles bulging beneath his T-shirt as he carried his hefty eighteen-month-old son on his shoulders, one would never suspect that Vincent de Marco was also known as Mad Man de Marco in the wrestling ring. Around his wife, Janine, and their little boy, he was a pussycat, but put him in a pair of skimpy tights, get him psyched up, and he could put the fear of God into anybody.

"At the rate Vinnie Junior's growing," Jillian said as she closed the door, "it won't be long before he's carrying you around on his shoulders."

"Forget the kid, what about the job?"

"It's like I told you—I got fired."

"Didn't they even give you two weeks notice?"

"No."

"Why not?"

"I was late getting back from lunch again. If it hadn't been for that pervert, I'd have—"

"Hey, back up to the pervert! You mean, some dude put the make on you and they fired you anyway?"

"Yes. It's a shame too, because he was kind of sexy looking, but—listen, come on back to the kitchen and I'll make us some tea. It's too long a story to tell standing up."

"Where you hiding Rusty?" Vinnie asked as he trailed after her.

"I'm not hiding him anywhere. He's taking a nap in the middle of my bed. Don't worry, Junior'll be okay."

"I'm not worried about the bruiser here; I was thinking about your poor dog."

"You're sweet, Vinnie, but Rusty doesn't deserve that kind of consideration," Jillian said. "You'd think an animal his size would be a good watchdog, but he's not. At the first sign of trouble, he runs and hides under the bed."

Over tea, Jillian told Vinnie about the two men she had encountered, the latter leaving a more positive impression than the first could ever do. "When I finally got into the office," she said, "Miss Shaw was waiting for me with steam coming out of her ears. She ordered me to clean out my desk—which I did while she hovered over me—then she personally escorted me to the door. Guess she was afraid I'd steal the company secrets, or something."

"You, steal? That's a laugh. If I were you, I'd have punched the old broad's lights out."

"This may come as a surprise to you, Vinnie, but some of us don't express ourselves physically quite the way you do. Although I will admit that it did cross my mind. I worked in accounting, for Pete's sake, not research and development; there was nothing for me to steal. Honestly, those people are paranoid—no, they're certifiably nuts about keeping everything a secret. No one but the company president, and maybe a few of his head engineers at the main office, know what anybody else is doing. Sometimes I even wonder about them. The more I think about it, the more I realize how much better off I am being completely free of that place."

"Any idea what you're gonna do now?"

"Get another job, what else? I have to eat."

"Eat!" Vinnie Junior cried and pounded his little fist so hard on the table that it rattled the cups and saucers.

"Geez, why'd you have to go and mention that for, Jill?" With a groan, Vinnie got to his feet and hoisted the baby onto his shoulders.

"Eat!"

"All right, all right, we'll go eat. Gotta keep up his weight," Vinnie said. "Can't afford a bench-press on what

Janine makes as a dental hygienist, so I make do with Junior here."

As they headed toward the door, passing in front of the television, a commercial ended and the afternoon news update began.

"I got a match over in Fort Worth this weekend, but Janine'll be home—if she doesn't decide to go to her mother's. Let us know if you need anything, okay?"

"Don't worry about me. By this time tomorrow, I plan to be gainfully employed again."

"Doing what?"

Jillian shrugged. "I'd like to get another accounting job; that's what I'm qualified to do. But heck, I'm not proud. I'll do secretarial work if I have to. One thing I do know, though—I'm not working for another big company."

"To hell with the benefits, right?"

"You got it."

"Eat!"

"All right, Junior, we're going! See you later, Jill. Let me know how it goes."

"I will. 'Bye." With a smile, Jillian closed the door.

". . . discovered the mutilated body of socialite Amanda Strickland," said the news-update announcer. "Eyewitnesses at the scene informed authorities that they heard an argument last night between Miss Strickland and her fiancé, Sterling Wyatt. And today at approximately one-thirty, it is believed that Wyatt returned to Miss Strickland's North Dallas apartment, where he brutally attacked and killed her. The reason for his actions are unknown to us at this time, but criminal psychologist, Dr. Albert Blackburn, has consented to—"

Jillian shuddered, and turned off the set. A socialite murdered in affluent North Dallas, and an accountant unemployed in trendy East Dallas—this didn't seem to be a good day for anybody.

# CHAPTER 2

Jillian stood on the corner of Market and Ross, staring at the five-story building across the street. She glanced down at the paper in her hand and double-checked the classified ad. This was the correct address, all right, but it looked more like a typical West End warehouse/restaurant than an office building. Six unloading bays marched down one side of the first floor, while the other hugged the fenced-off railroad tracks. At the end she now faced, a pair of green canvas awnings sheltered the plate-glass windows of a French restaurant. Above the building's main entrance, a large sign announced that limited retail and loft space was available, and offered a telephone number to call for those who were interested.

With a resigned shrug, she started across the street. A lot of changes had been and were being made in this part of town. Changes for the better, in Jillian's opinion. Dallas had a bad habit of tearing down old buildings and replacing them with glass and steel monsters. In this instance, however, some young creative types were restoring these structures—once warehouses and manufacturing concerns—on the outside, and converting the interiors into restaurants, boutiques, and offices. Even the crumbling streets and sidewalks had been repaired. Now red bricks skirted the one-way streets that were lined with trees, flowers, hard-wood benches, and outdoor cafés.

As she entered the five-story building, Jillian smelled the distinctive aroma of new wood, paint, and freshly baked bread. The restaurant's chef was obviously already at work, getting ready for the lunchtime crowd, she decided, catching sight of the freight elevator.

"Oh, terrific," she muttered, stepping inside the massive, cagelike conveyance. Buttons she knew how to push, but how did you operate this thing? Why hadn't the owner replaced it with a newer, easier-to-run model?

A metal plate on the left-hand side of the elevator bore a list of instructions. She read through them once, found them easy enough to understand, then proceeded to follow them, step by step. She rolled down the outer wooden bars, closing herself in, then grasped the mechanism's lever and slowly moved it to the right. Instantly the elevator began to lift.

Three minutes later, after a very bumpy start-and-stop ride, Jillian stepped up and out onto the fifth floor. The trip itself had taken less than a minute. She'd spent the other two trying to get the elevator floor and the building floor to meet evenly. Deciding she would never succeed, she simply gave up.

A short walk down the carpeted, high-ceiling corridor took her to 501, the suite number listed in the classifieds. Weird office building, she thought, eyeing the solid metal door and the door-bell button beside it.

She pushed the button, but couldn't hear a buzzer or a bell go off inside. Thinking that it might be broken, she rapped her knuckles on the door, but no one answered. Well, she decided, desperate people sometimes have to do desperate things. She twisted the knob and the door opened.

"Hello?" she called out as she entered the office. "Is anybody here?"

The cavernous room was easily fifty feet long with a twenty-foot-high ceiling. It didn't look like much of a business office in Jillian's opinion. In fact, it looked more like a half-empty apartment. To her far right an iron staircase rose in a tight spiral up to a glass-brick wall; a green metal file cabinet and an old rolltop desk with a swivel chair occupied the alcove beneath it. In the center of the bare hardwood floor, two unmatched sofas faced a long coffee table covered in newspapers. A big-screen TV hugged the far wall of windows, while a round table and three chairs separated the living area from the kitchen.

"Hello!" she said again, more loudly.

"Be down in a minute," came a man's voice from the upper regions of the loft. "Coffee's in the kitchen—make yourself at home."

"Thank you, but I don't want any coffee. I'm here about the— Uh, you are the one who advertised for a secretary-bookkeeper, I hope."

"Yeah, I am. You interested?"

"Yes, very."

"Okay," the voice said somewhat distractedly. "Well, look, why don't you go ahead and fill out an application. You know—your name, address, phone number, zip code, and any other stuff you think I might need to know. There ought to be some paper on my desk; just write it all down. I'll be with you as soon as I get this thing fixed."

By the looks of it, Jillian thought as she crossed to the alcove, this job would be a far cry from her last one—not nearly as regimented, that was for sure. Whether that was good or bad, she didn't yet know. The guy upstairs might well be the personnel manager currently doubling as the maintenance man, but he was no secretary-bookkeeper. The mountain of paper covering the desk told her that much.

As she searched through the debris for a clean sheet of paper, she unearthed, among other things, an uncashed check for three thousand dollars, made out to one Jackson Fury; an electric bill two months overdue; a letter from a Mrs. Tyler Winslow, thanking Mr. Fury for his generous donation to the society's worthy cause; and a personal invitation to "Bubba Jack," asking him to *please* try and make it to Sissy and Chuck's wedding on the fourteenth of February. Considering that it was now the end of April, Jillian decided she could safely assume that "Bubba Jack" hadn't made it to Sissy and Chuck's wedding. Oh, this man needed help, all right—in the worst way imaginable.

Finding a clean sheet of paper, she sat down in the squeaky chair, pushed some of the debris to one side, and began composing. At one point, she gave a momentary thought to leaving before Jackson Fury, or whoever the guy upstairs was, finished repairing whatever it was that had broken, but a latent sense of compassion held her back. With a mess like this, he really did need her. Almost as badly as she needed him.

Halfway through composing the application, Jillian heard the heavy tread of feet on the iron stairs behind her.

"Got that shower drain finally unclogged, and— Well, I'll be!"

She finished scribbling, then turned around with a bright, friendly smile, intending to impress the socks off her would-be employer. Instead, she froze at the sight of the pervert she'd met the day before.

"Yes, Virginia," he said, grinning like a demented idiot as he stretched both hands out wide, even the one holding a dripping plunger, "'there is a Santa Claus!'"

"Oh, my God." Jillian's bright expression melted into one of horror. As he started moving toward her, she slowly got to her feet. "Oh, my God!"

"You've come home to Daddy, sweetheart, just like I knew you would."

"I—I didn't know—" Jillian said, stumbling into the

center of the room and away from him. "If—if I had, I—I would never have— Oh, my God, let me out of here."

"But, baby cakes, you can't leave now. What about our meaningful relationship? What about all this?" Turning slightly, he made a wide-sweeping gesture that encompassed the room, and gave Jillian a clear view of the snubnosed revolver clipped to the back waistband of his tight, faded jeans. "Just say the word, and it's yours. Me along with it, of course."

"No," she said, her fear more obvious than ever. "No, uh, thank you very much, but I—I really must be going."

Jackson noted the look of terror on her face and sobered instantly. "Hey, what's the matter?" he asked, taking one step toward her.

"No! Y—you stay away from me!"

"Okay, okay!" He threw up his hands and backed away. "Just settle down, all right?" A brief pause, then, "Look, I know we didn't get off to a very good start yesterday, but if you'll let me explain—"

"No, I—I just want to go. Please, let me leave."

"Not until you've heard me out."

Jillian watched him toss the dripping plunger aside, and saw his hands drop toward his hips. Believing he was going for the gun, she inhaled a sharp, frightened gasp.

"Hey, cut it out, lady. I'm not gonna hurt you."

"Uh-huh. I'll bet that's what Jack the Ripper said."

"Jack the— Just what the hell do you think I am, anyway? No, don't answer that. I already know. A perverted sex maniac, right?"

Feeling faint, Jillian managed a weak nod. "Only you've got a gun instead of a knife."

"This?" Jackson whipped the revolver out of its clip holster. "You're afraid I'm gonna—"

Jillian released a bloodcurdling scream and dove to the

floor behind the littered coffee table. "Don't shoot me. *Please*, don't shoot me!"

"Jesus Christ," Jackson said with a groan. "Hey, look up here just a minute." Jillian didn't move a muscle. "Come on. Just uncover that pretty head of yours and look at me."

Shaking all over, Jillian timidly did as he ordered and was surprised to see the small gun dangling in midair, the butt held between his thumb and first two fingers. She watched him slowly straighten his arm and drop the weapon onto the sofa.

"See?" Jackson said. "All gone. The big bad gun is all gone now."

Jillian's first and only thought was to get away from the creep as quickly as possible. She rose to her feet cautiously, making certain that the length of the coffee table remained between them. "Th—that's very considerate of you, I'm sure. But what's a maniac—I mean, a *man*—what's a *man* like you doing with a gun?"

"Oh, yeah," Jackson said with a slow nod, "we sure as hell did get off to a bad start. Look, honey, I'm not a maniac. For your information, I'm a private investigator."

"A what?"

"A private investigator. I carry that gun"—he pointed to it—"because I have to. In my line of work, I sometimes use it to protect people."

Jillian stared at him in disbelief for a moment, then jerkily shook her head. "Uh, no offense, but I don't believe you."

"It's true. Here's my license, see for yourself." Jackson dug a leather wallet out of his hip pocket and flipped it open to show Jillian his state-issued investigator's license and gun permit.

"Okay, so you're a private investigator. But that still doesn't explain about yesterday."

"Yesterday?"

"Yes, yesterday. What was it, your day off, or something?"

"No, I was on a case. Well, sorta."

"Oh, so while you were on the case, sorta, you had some time to kill and decided to go out and harass a woman—me!"

"Look, I'm sorry about that, but somebody was tailing me. Making a move on you seemed like the best way to shake him."

"You did a lot more than just make a move on me, buster!" Jillian said, a wave of hot rage washing away the last of her apprehension. "You cost me my job!"

"How'd I do that?" Jackson asked, his face twisting into a stupid frown.

"You made me late getting back to work and I got fired—that's how!"

"Oh. Well, hey, no big loss, right? You got yourself another one."

"What are you talking about?"

"That's what you came here today for, wasn't it? To get a job? Well, you got it! You can see for yourself what a mess my office is in. Can't ever find a damn thing, and never seem to have enough time to get it all straightened out."

"You're not only a pervert, mister, you're crazy. I wouldn't work for you if you were the last—" Jillian abruptly broke off. Her blue eyes widened, and her jaw slowly dropped as a ruder, more horrifying shock registered in her brain.

"What the hell did I do now?" Jackson asked.

"My God!"

*"What!"*

"Th—they arrested him for murder."

Jackson stared at her for a long, silent moment. "Don't tell me, you got ESP and you're having a vision, right?"

"What vision? It's right there in black and white." Jillian

pointed down at the coffee table and the newspaper that lay on top. Below the bold front-page headlines was a grainy photograph of the late Miss Amanda Strickland, standing beside her fiancé Sterling Wyatt. "They arrested him for her murder, but he didn't kill her. He couldn't have."

"How do you know?"

"Because at precisely the same moment she was being murdered yesterday, he was halfway across town, lying on top of me!"

# CHAPTER 3

"Hey, wait a minute!" Jackson leaped forward when Jillian started for the door. He reached it the same moment she did and blocked her exit with his considerably larger body.

"Get out of my way," she said. "I've got to go to the police and tell them they've got the wrong man."

"You go to the police now, sweetheart, they'll laugh right in your face. I read that newspaper article. The police have got eyewitnesses who saw the guy leaving her apartment covered in blood."

"But he didn't do it!"

"How do you know? That's a lousy photograph. For all you know, it may be a completely different guy."

"It's not. Believe me, I could never be confused over a face like that."

"One you'd been intimate with, right?"

"Intimate!"

"Didn't you just say that he was lying on top of you? If that's not being intimate, I'd like to know what is."

"Not that it's any of your business, but we ran into each other. Literally! I was getting off the elevator as he was getting on, and when we knocked each other to the floor, he

landed on top of me. He even helped me pick up my underwear!"

"Your underwear," Jackson repeated with a deadpan
nod.

"And my pasta maker, and my garlic press," Jillian said
through clenched teeth. "Why am I even talking to a dirty-
minded pervert like you, anyway? I should be telling all of
this to the police."

"Hate to be the one to break it to you, honey, but they
won't buy it any more than I do."

"But it's the truth!"

"Maybe. Maybe not. Can you prove it?"

"Prove it!"

"Yeah. Did anybody else see the two of you run into each
other?"

Jillian thought for a moment, then shook her head. "No.
The hall was empty, but what's that got to do—"

"It's your word, alone," Jackson said gently, "against
some very influential eyewitnesses, sweetheart."

Only then did Jillian realize what he was doing—playing
the devil's advocate to make her see how foolhardy her
noble intentions were. "Oh, my God," she said. "And who
am I, right?"

"I'd say that's it in a nutshell."

With a defeated groan, Jillian turned away from the door.
She crossed to one of the mismatched sofas and sat down,
propping her elbows on her knees and cradling her head in
her hands. Moments later she looked up and found Jackson
sitting beside her on the arm of the sofa.

"What am I going to do?" she asked.

"Well, I've been thinking about that."

"You have?"

He nodded. "The way I see it, you can do one of three
things. You can, one, just forget you even met that guy, let
alone know he's innocent. Might be a little hard living with

yourself, of course, when they send him to prison. And they
will send him to prison, honey. You don't get a slap on the
wrist for butchering up a beautiful face and body like
Amanda Strickland's. Or, two, you can take a wild chance
and tell your story to the police. But my guess is they won't
believe you, and you'll end up making a complete ass of
yourself."

"You said I had three choices," Jillian said, feeling more
helpless than ever before, "but that's only two. What's the
third one?"

Jackson slowly grinned. "I was hoping you'd ask."

"Well, what is it?"

"Simple. If what you've told me is true, then your
Sterling Wyatt has gone and got himself framed. Looks to
me like you're gonna have to hire yourself a private
investigator."

"Me, hire a private investigator?" Jillian laughed, but as
the reality of what he suggested sank in, her laughter faded.
"Oh, my Lord. You mean hire you, don't you?"

"I'm between cases, and don't have anything else to do
right now—why not?"

"I'll tell you why not. I'm almost flat broke, that's why
not! Or are you telling me that you're willing to work for
free."

"Honey, honey," Jackson said in a deep sexy voice as he
ran a finger down her smooth cheek and slowly traced the
curve of her full lips, "everything's got a price. Even my
sevices."

Jillian leaped to her feet and slapped his face so hard that
it knocked him off the sofa and onto the floor. "You dirty-
minded creep! Believing I'd go to bed with you to pay
for—"

She started for the door, but as she stalked past Jackson,
he reached out and grabbed hold of her ankle. One clean
jerk of his wrist had her on the floor beside him, and in the

blink of an eye, she was on her back with him lying on top of her.

"Now you listen to me, sweetheart," Jackson said. "If anybody around here's got a dirty mind, it's you, not me. You may think I just made another move on you, but I didn't. We were talking about two completely different things."

Jillian opened her mouth to say something, but Jackson quickly covered it with his hand. "No. You're not gonna say one more word until I've finished. Nod your head if you understand."

With blue eyes narrowed into angry slits, she reluctantly nodded.

"Good. Now if this guy you met yesterday is the same Sterling Wyatt who's in the newspaper, and if he was with you instead of Amanda Strickland at the time she was killed, then like I said before, he's being framed for a murder he didn't commit. Ain't no way you can clear him on your own, because you wouldn't know where to begin. But I do. That's why I'm in this line of business. Are you with me so far?"

Jillian nodded.

"Terrific, we may be getting somewhere after all," Jackson said. "Now then—you're out of work and need a job, right? Well, I'm in the same boat. Sorta. I'm busy most of the time, and I need somebody here to take care of the paperwork end of this business. Somebody who knows what the hell they're doing, who won't get in my way, and who'll keep their nose out of my affairs. So what I'm proposing is that you work for me, and in return I'll do my damnedest to get this Sterling Wyatt of yours off the hook."

Jillian's eyes widened, then blinked in disbelief.

"Don't look so surprised, honey. We all gotta make trade-offs at one time or another. In this case, me more than you. Tell you what—I'll even sweeten the deal by paying you a salary. And you won't have to worry about getting my bill when the case is over. How's that sound?"

After a brief, thoughtful moment, Jillian nodded.

"Good," Jackson said, grinning. "Thought you'd see things my way."

Their negotiations supposedly at an end, Jackson still did not move off of Jillian. Instead, he grew very still, his grin evolving into an expression that clearly reflected his mixed emotions. A husky purr vibrated inside his chest as he stared into her dark-blue eyes. Jillian knew instinctively what he was going to do and realized she had to stop him, but he didn't give her the chance.

"Oh, what the hell," Jackson muttered, sliding his hand off her mouth and replacing it with his lips.

At the moment of contact, a powerful jolt surged through Jillian. Unbidden, the room started to spin. It grew fuzzier and fuzzier until it finally dissolved in blackness. She heard a provocative groan nearby, but with her eyes closed, she couldn't be sure if she had made the sound, or he had.

Wait a minute! What the devil was she doing with her eyes closed?

Good thing they were doing this on the floor, Jackson thought, ignoring the way Jillian's body stiffened beneath him. If he had tried to kiss her standing up, not knowing it would be this good, they'd have fallen for sure, and one of them might have been hurt. Of course, doing this with her in bed would have been a hulluva lot more— A sharp, unexpected pain brought Jackson's eyes wide open.

Jillian pushed the weak, pliant body off of her and got to her feet. She watched him curl into a tight ball as she rubbed her knee. "Geez, that hurt," she said.

Jackson shot her a surprised look out of one eye. "That's supposed to be my line," he said in a raspy voice.

"Just be thankful I didn't knee you harder. You'd be singing soprano, permanently."

An agonizing moment passed before Jackson attempted to sit up. "You realize, of course," he said, moving slowly, "that you just cut our chances of ever having children in half."

"Your chances maybe, Mr. Fury, but not mine. So help me, if you ever try that again, or even think about trying it, I'll sue you for sexual harassment."

"Guess this means you don't want the job now, huh?"

She stiffened. "Are you still offering it to me?"

"I may need my head examined—not to mention the old jewels," he said, levering himself onto the sofa, "but, yeah, I am."

"Well, in that case, I'd like to have it. But only on one condition."

Jackson thrust a hand into the air. "My word of honor—I'll never try anything like that again, so help me God. Not unless you're willing, of course."

"I'm not talking about that. I want it understood up front that my lunch hours are to be flexible. If I'm five, ten, or even thirty minutes late because of circumstances beyond my control, I don't want to be fired."

"You got it, babe. Anything else?"

"Well, now that you mention it, there is. I don't drive—at least not here in town—and your office isn't exactly within walking distance of my neighborhood. I'd rather not have to work late at night, but if for some reason necessity makes it impossible for me to leave at a decent hour, I'd at least like to know that I can get home in one piece."

"Asking for a chauffeured limousine's a bit much, don't you think?"

"I don't need or want a limo. A taxicab will do just fine. With the fare paid by you, of course."

"Flexible hours, and a free ride home . . . you'd better be worth it, sweetheart."

"Don't worry, I am," Jillian said.

"Yeah, well, we'll just see." Carefully Jackson stood up, reclaiming his revolver en route. "Since you're already here, we may as well get started."

"Believe me, you won't need that gun to help me sort through your files. Or were you planning on holding it to my head?"

"That's a thought," Jackson said, slipping the gun into its holster as he headed for the stairs, "but lucky for you it's not my style. No, I'll leave all the filing to you. I'm gonna go see a man about a frame-job."

"You're going to the police now?"

"That's what you hired me for, isn't it?"

"Well, yes, but— Hold on. Let me get my purse and I'll come with you."

"Like hell you will! You're gonna stay right here and work. That's what I hired *you* for, remember?"

Jackson left her staring at him as he climbed the stairs and disappeared behind the glass-brick wall. He reemerged moments later, zipping up a dark-blue Windbreaker.

"How do you know the police will even let you in to see Sterling Wyatt?"

"Don't worry, sweetheart, I'll see him. I got connections." Jackson stopped by the desk and picked up her handwritten application. "Does Wyatt know you as Jillian, or Miss Fletcher?"

"Niether one," Jillian said, crossing toward him. "Everything happened so fast yesterday, we never had the chance to exchange names."

"Just two ships passing in the night."

"I told you, it wasn't anything like that. We didn't have time to— Wait, I know! Tell him the girl with the"—she blushed, and took a deep breath—"the girl with the raspberry see-through bra sent you."

"Raspberry . . . see-through . . . bra?" Jackson swallowed.

"Listen, buster, you can just wipe that dirty look off your face right now. I wasn't wearing it; it fell out of the shopping bag along with—with some other things."

"If you say so." Jackson crammed her application into his Windbreaker pocket and headed toward the door. "Raspberry see-through bra. If Wyatt can't remember a thing like that, he's a helluva better man than I am."

Jackson stopped at the corner as the light flashed from WALK to DON'T WALK. He pulled Jillian's handwritten application out of his Windbreaker pocket, unfolded it, and grinned. Momma had always told him that good things came in small packages, but where Miss Jillian Fletcher was concerned, it came in big packages, too. A five-foot-eleven, black-haired, blue-eyed, one-hundred-twenty-pound package of pure dy-no-mite! Beautiful, intelligent, a bachelor's degree in accounting, and only twenty-three years old. Give her a few more years, and no man alive would stand a chance.

The direction of his thoughts changed when DON'T WALK flashed back to WALK. Shoving Jillian's application back inside his pocket, he stepped out into the intersection.

Sterling Wyatt, Jackson mused. Engaged to a woman like Amanda Strickland, the man probably had money coming out of his ears and a whole slew of attorneys waiting on the sidelines just to cover his parking violations. So if he was as innocent as Jillian claimed, his lawyers probably already had him out on bond.

When he walked into the Lew Sterrett Justice Center sometime later, Jackson discovered that Wyatt was still in jail.

"Any chance of me getting in to see him?" Jackson asked the surly looking city police sergeant.

"You trying to be funny or something, Fury?"

Damn, Jackson thought. The asshole was still holding a

grudge against him. Hell, it wasn't his fault that Thornquist was stupid enough to get demoted, but try and tell him that. Talking to a brick wall would be a lot easier.

"You know me, Thornquist," Jackson said, "I never joke about things like murder."

"So, what's Wyatt got to do with you? Or you with him, for that matter."

"I'm sorta working on the case."

"'Sorta' don't mean shit around here; you ought to know that, Fury."

"Okay, then I am working on the case. Now, can I see him?"

"Nope. His lawyer, Walter Collins, is in with him now. And Collins don't want nobody but members of his own legal staff or Wyatt's family to see him. He's got this thing about his client getting bad media coverage."

"All right," he said, "then let me talk to Collins."

"You just don't give up, do you?"

"Nope. Not when it's about something this important."

Thornquist shrugged. "It's your neck. Wait here a minute."

The sergeant disappeared behind a door, then reappeared a few minutes later and gestured for Jackson to follow him. Collins, a flustered man in his mid-fifties, sporting a western-cut suit and string tie, met them in the hall outside one of the interview rooms.

"This interruption had better be necessary," Collins said, wiping his balding forehead with a handkerchief.

"Trust me, it is," Jackson said.

"Just who the hell are you, anyway?"

"Jackson Fury." Jackson pulled a bent business card out of his Windbreaker pocket.

Collins took the card, glanced at it, then crumpled it up and threw it aside. "What in God's name do I need with a private investigator when I've got one of the biggest firms in the town working—"

"Believe me, you need me," Jackson said. "Look, do me a favor, Thornquist. Go breathe down somebody else's neck for a while. Collins and I have something we need to discuss in private."

"You carrying a gun?" Thornquist asked.

"I forgot." Jackson divested himself of the snub-nose and handed it to the sergeant.

Thornquist continued to stand there with his other hand held out. "Come on, Fury. Hand it over."

Taking a deep breath, Jackson lifted the leg of his jeans and removed the knife he wore strapped to his calf. "That's it," he said with an apologetic shrug. "I was in kind of a big hurry this morning and I only got half-dressed."

"You want a receipt for this stuff?" Thornquist asked.

"No, I trust you."

"Same don't go for me, Fury," the sergeant said, then turned around and walked away.

"Now just what the hell is all this about?" Collins asked. "I've got a client in there whose life is—"

"Not gonna be worth a plug nickel," Jackson interrupted again, "if you don't give my client a chance to clear him."

"Your client?"

"Yeah, my client. Look, you want to waste time standing out here talking about it, that's fine with me. But I think we'd get a lot more accomplished if we went inside and discussed this with Wyatt."

Collins eyed Jackson skeptically for a moment, then released his breath. "Hell, it doesn't look as though I've got much choice. Come on."

"After you."

Inside the room, Jackson found Wyatt pacing the floor in long, nervous strides. They guy was much better looking than his newspaper photo, Jackson thought. Blond, clean-cut, all-American-looking—just your typical boy-next-door, unjustly accused of murder.

Introductions were made, and they all sat down at the table; Collins and Jackson on one side, Wyatt on the other.

"I'm sorry, did you say Jackson Fury?" Wyatt asked. "I don't believe I recognize the name."

"No reason you should," Jackson said. "We've never met before. But you have met my client."

"Your client," Wyatt repeated, frowning.

Jackson glanced sideways at Collins, then he took a deep breath. "I was told that the two of you didn't have time to exchange names, but that you'd recognize—oh, shit!—the girl with the raspberry see-through bra."

Instantly Wyatt's worried frown vanished. His eyes grew wide as he swung around to Collins. "I told you!" he said. "Didn't I tell you?"

"Okay, then where the hell is she?" Collins said. "Why didn't she come herself instead of sending—" He broke off, and a look of comprehension crossed his face. Slowly he nodded his head. "Oh, now I get it. Money, right? Well, just how much does this mysterious client of yours think she's gonna get out of this?"

"Where she is, is my business," Jackson said evenly. "And she didn't come herself because I wouldn't let her. Until I know what's going on, what's at stake here, and who all is involved, I'm gonna make damn sure she keeps a low profile. This might rattle your cage, Collins, but my client is a lady. She'd be downright insulted if she knew you thought she was only in this for the money, when all she really wants is to save a man's life."

"Exactly the remark I was about to make," Wyatt said. "Any girl today who can still blush like she did is not the mercenary type."

"Shut up, Sterling. I'll handle this," said Collins. "All right, Fury, I apologize. But with my client's reputation, his future—no goddammit—with his life at stake, I've got a right to be cautious."

"So have I," Jackson said.

Collins studied him for a thoughtful moment and then nodded. "Yeah, I guess you do at that." He picked up his pen and poised it above his note pad. "All right, now that that's out of the way, let's get down to business, shall we? About this client of yours, Fury . . ."

# CHAPTER 4

The walk from his West End loft to the Lew Sterrett Justice Center had taken Jackson less than ten minutes, but the return trip took him twice as long. Tourists, executives, and office workers alike clogged the sidewalks and intersections as they hurried to and from lunch. Ordinarily he would swear and curse at the slow-moving pedestrians and in general be chomping at the bit, but not today. He ambled along the sidewalk, deep in thought.

Miss Jillian Fletcher, he decided, was either telling him the truth, or she was in cahoots with Wyatt and was lying to establish his alibi. One part of Jackson wanted to believe that she wasn't that kind of girl, but another more suspicious part of him strongly suspected that she was. One way or another, he would find out which very soon.

He heard the loud commotion the moment he stepped off the freight elevator. Moose was obviously back from the beauty shop. He envisioned a scene that would have made him smile were he in a different frame of mind. Knowing what he was about to do, however, what he had to do, he couldn't even work up a grin.

Pocketing his keys as he walked down the corridor, he wondered how Moose was taking to Jillian? Better yet, how was Jillian taking to Moose? One thing was certain; they'd either love each other on sight, or hate each other. With Moose, there was no happy in-between. Until you got to know her, she could be a little overwhelming.

Jackson opened the door and as he entered the loft he saw Jillian glowering down at him from the top of the spiral stairs. Squeezed together on the step below her were a uniformed delivery man and a pretty but slightly plump middle-aged blond that he'd never seen before. Guarding the foot of the stairs and sporting, of all things, a shocking pink bow around her neck was Moose.

At the sight of him, the Great Dane whined like a puppy and headed toward him, leaping over the boxes stacked in the middle of the floor. Jackson braced himself for her affectionate welcome. Moose skidded to a stop, reared up on her hind legs, and, resting her huge paws on Jackson's shoulders, licked his contorted face from chin to forehead as her tail whipped back and forth in delight.

"Yeah, yeah, I missed you too, baby." Jackson hugged the dog, patted her smooth, fawn-colored neck, then gently pushed her aside.

Not to be dismissed so easily, Moose whined again and thrust a paw against Jackson's leg.

"What the—" Jackson broke off, seeing Moose's shocking pink toenails. "Well, no wonder you're upset. You go off with Bruce to get a bath, and he brings you back gussied up like some little French floozy. Don't you worry, Moosie honey," he said, untying her bow and throwing it aside, "I'll give Bruce a piece of our minds. He won't do this again, I promise."

Moose's single, deep-throated bark echoed about the room.

"If you and that—that animal—don't mind," Jillian said, "we'd like to come down."

"So what's stopping you?" Jackson asked.

Jillian cleared her throat and shot a pointed look at the terrified pair below her.

"Hey, y'all aren't afraid of the princess here, are you?" Jackson asked. "She may be titled royalty, but she's just a lovable old mutt at heart. Aren't you, baby?"

Moose issued a soft "woof" as if she agreed with Jackson.

"How sweet," Jillian said, deadpan. "No offense to the princess, but I think Richard and Evelyn would feel better if you got her out of the way for a while."

Jackson eyed the cowering pair and then shrugged. "All right, if it'll make Richard and Evelyn happy."

Richard the delivery man didn't move a muscle until Jackson had led Moose into the kitchen. Then he stumbled down the stairs, grabbed his clipboard off one of the boxes, and raced out of the loft. Evelyn wasn't so silent. She started chattering a mile a minute as she wound down the stairs, her spike heels clacking on the iron treads.

"Milly never said one word about you having a dog here, mister. Dog, hell! That's a half-grown horse! What'd you do with it when she came to see you, hide it? You must have, 'cause I know she'd've told me about it. She knows I don't like animals. Oh, a little kitten, I can maybe take. Goldfish in a bowl, or a little hamster in a cage even, but a horse? And in an apartment this size? Ain't there a law against that in this town?

"Geez, if I'd known, I never would've come here in the first place. I'd've took my business to somebody else. I know Harry's two-timing me with that little cheerleader of his, but neither one of them's worth risking life and limb over. I'm the mother of two kids. What'd they do if I got myself eat up by an animal like that? It ain't like Harry's the type of guy who's gonna step in and take over. He's got more important things to do than worry about washing the kids' stinking sweat socks, or putting up with all their crap.

No, he's too busy playing pom-poms with his little cheer-leader.

"We come out here from New York—what, six, seven months ago?—thinking we'd like it. Harry and the boys took to it right away. What's here for them to hate? Harry's got his big important job, and his little cheerleader on the side. The boys got their weird friends. Weird? Cripes. First week we're here, all three of them come home looking like fags out of a man's fashion magazine. Shirts unbuttoned clear down to their zippers, and gold chains around their necks. But me? Hell, I'm from Brooklyn. Lived nowhere else for thirty-seven years.

"I ain't never gonna get used to this Dallas lifestyle garbage. Boots and cowboy hats I could maybe understand, but Harry and the boys look pure West Coast. I tell that to Harry, but does he listen? I even tell him I know what's going on with him and his cheerleader, and that I'm gonna divorce him and go back to Brooklyn. You know what he says to me? He says, 'Evelyn sweetie, loosen up a little. You give me my space, I'll give you yours.' Space, you know, like he's some rocket scientist or something. Hell, the jerk sells computer parts."

Evelyn reached the door and opened it to leave. "Well, I'm gonna give the shit-head all the space he wants. When I get back to New York, there'll be three thousand miles of space between us. And I'll tell you something else that Harry don't know yet. I'm taking the boys back to Brooklyn with me. Him and his cheerleader can pom-pom each other to death for all I care, but I'm gonna make damn sure my kids grow up in a decent environment."

Standing side by side, Jackson and Jillian winced as the loft door slammed shut.

"I think you just lost a client," Jillian said.

"Thank God," Jackson looked at her, then angled his

head toward the stairs. "Just what were you and Richard doing up there with Evelyn? Or should I ask?"

"This is your place," she said, "you're entitled to know everything that goes on in it." She picked up one of the boxes on the floor and carried it to the desk. "After you left this morning, I phoned in an order for some office supplies."

"Wait a minute. Is this gonna take long?"

"You want to hear what happened, don't you?" At his resigned look, she continued. "You didn't have any file folders, pens, pencils, paper clips . . . I couldn't even find a typewriter or adding machine. How do you expect me to balance the books without an adding machine?"

"You're gonna need all that stuff?"

"For starters, yes, if you want me to turn this into a real working office. But to get back to Richard and Evelyn—I let him in with the first load of supplies, then when he went out to bring up the second load, I had to, uh, go powder my nose. You know, it's going to be really inconvenient if I have to go upstairs every time I need to use the bathroom.

"Well, just as I finished going to the bathroom, I heard this loud barking down here. Someone—I don't know who because I didn't see them—delivered your dog, and then left. When I started down the stairs, Richard was running up behind Evelyn. We must have been up there for a good half hour before you got here. I tried to tell them that nothing would happen to them, but poor Richard and Evelyn were afraid they would get eaten alive."

"And you weren't?"

"What, afraid? Of course not. I like dogs. I even have one of my own. Rusty's not quite as big as what'sher-name—"

"Moose," Jackson said.

"Whatever. But he's not pint-size either."

"Actually her registered name is Princess Beatrix Hildegarde von Fury," Jackson said. "But I think Moose suits her better."

"Yes, I can see why." Suddenly Jillian threw down the manila folders she had just unpacked and whirled to face Jackson. "What on earth are we talking about Richard, Evelyn, and dogs for? Tell me what happened with Sterling Wyatt."

If she wanted to pull a fast one on him, she was going about it the right way, Jackson decided. The way she was acting, he could almost believe that she didn't know what was going on. Maybe she did, maybe she didn't. He would play along with her for a while, see how far she would go, and then go for the kill.

"Last time I saw Wyatt," Jackson said, "he was with his lawyer, waiting to be arraigned before a judge. Can't get out of jail until bail has been set."

With mounting curiosity Jillian waited for him to continue, but Jackson remained perversely silent, studying the different piles of papers Jillian had sorted. He noted the number of undeposited checks he had lying about, and the many phone calls, many from members of the female persuasion, that she'd taken in his absence. He dismissed the messages and focused on the checks. He hoped he wasn't overdrawn at the bank.

"Well, is that all?" Jillian's question held a note of irritation.

"No. I had a long talk with Walter Collins."

"Who?"

"Walter Collins. You know, Wyatt's attorney?"

"No, I didn't know, because you never mentioned his name," Jillian said. "What did he have to say?"

"Oh, this and that."

"Could you be a little more specific? 'This and that' doesn't tell me much."

"You want specifics? Okay. The three of us talked about

what the eyewitnesses had to say, what the detectives at the
scene reported, what the medical examiner found. Wyatt's
reason for being on the floor with you—that sort of thing.''

"The tenth floor," Jillian said.

"What?"

"He wasn't just on the floor with me, he was on the *tenth*
floor with me.''

"Yeah, I know," Jackson said with a slight sneer.
"Helping you pick up your underwear. You've already told
me that.''

"Why?"

" 'Cause you wanted to make me jealous?''

"No," she said, irritated by his side-tracking quip. "I
mean, why was Sterling Wyatt on the tenth floor at that
particular time?''

"He said he had an appointment to meet some guy. Guy
never showed, so he left.''

"Who was he supposed to meet? What was his name?''

"Taggart something, or something Taggart. I forget
which.''

"Garner Taggart?''

"Yeah, that's it. You know him?''

"Not personally," Jillian said. "Junior accountants don't
have much opportunity to rub elbows with company
presidents.''

"Oh, the head honcho, huh?" Jackson shook his head.
"It's a shame. Being the company president, he'd have been
a pretty solid witness for the defense if he could've backed
up Wyatt's story. Which he didn't.''

"The police questioned him?''

"Of course they questioned him; they don't read minds
for a living. Taggart told them he was out of town on
company business, and that he didn't know about any
appointment with Wyatt. Neither did his secretary. So that,

I'm afraid, puts your boy Sterling right back where he started. At square one. With you as his only alibi."

"What about those eyewitnesses?" Jillian asked, dismissing his snide remark. "And the detectives at the scene and the medical examiner? What did they have to say?"

Jackson turned away from the desk, and sidestepped the boxes stacked on the floor as he headed toward the kitchen. "Well, your Sterling Wyatt is the number-one suspect. All the evidence points directly to him, and nobody else." Moose trotted up behind him as he opened the refrigerator. Both examined the half-empty interior. Both groaned in disappointment.

"I'm starved," Jackson said, closing the door. "What do you say we go get something to eat?"

"How can you think of food at a time like this?" Jillian asked.

"Can't think at all on an empty stomach. Food seems to sharpen my wits. But I got nothing in there. What sounds good to you? Deli, Chinese, or pizza? Moose likes chicken chow mein, but seeing as how you're our guest, we'll let you decide."

"The only thing I can think of that would be even remotely appetizing at the moment is your head on a platter!" Jillian said. "Look, just forget about food, will you? Tell me what happened."

"Something to eat'll fix your low blood sugar and take the edge off your temper."

"I don't have a temper, and I am not hungry!"

"Yeah, you are. You gotta be; it's past two o'clock. I bet you haven't eaten anything since breakfast. And that was nothing but toast and coffee—no, tea, right?"

"How did you know th—" Jillian stiffened. She started to tell him that what she did or didn't have for breakfast was none of his business, but her growling stomach interrupted her.

With a soft, questioning whine, the Great Dane cocked her head, her ears perking to attention. Jackson leaned against the counter and grinned.

"Oh, all right!" Jillian said. "You win. We'll eat!"

An hour later, they sat on the floor, the coffee table between them littered with empty Chinese take-out cartons. Moose, having wolfed down three orders of chicken chow mein, now lay with her massive head on Jackson's thigh.

"*Now* can we talk?" Jillian asked.

"Sure. What about?"

"The case. Sterling Wyatt. What else?"

"Yeah, what else. I was kind of hoping you might want to talk about us."

"There is no 'us,' Mr. Fury."

"Then how about we talk about you and Wyatt."

"Excuse me?"

"Come on, honey, you can level with me. Lover boy's safely tucked away in jail; he won't know that you told me all about it."

"Told you all about what? And I have leveled with—" Sudden comprehension flashed across Jillian's blue eyes. Slowly she hoisted herself onto the sofa behind her. "You think that I'm covering something up, don't you? You think that I've been lying."

"Haven't you?"

"No! No, I haven't."

"That's what they all say."

"Until yesterday, Mr. Fury, I had never seen, let alone heard of, Sterling Wyatt. We met by accident, I swear we did. Good gracious, I didn't even know the man's name until I saw his photograph in the newspaper this morning."

A lazy grin tugged one side of Jackson's mouth. "You ever think of taking your act out to Hollywood, sweetheart? You're very good at it, you know."

"I'm not acting, and don't call me sweetheart," Jillian

said through clenched teeth. "I'm not, and God willing, I never will be. And for your information, whether you believe it or not, I'm not Sterling Wyatt's sweetheart either."

"Just what are you then? Some girl he picked up off the street and paid to alibi for him?"

"No, I'm just an ordinary person who wants to see the good guys win, and the bad guys lose." Jillian stood up and crossed to the desk where she retrieved her purse from the floor. "Sterling Wyatt is a good guy in my book. I don't care what the police think, or what motive they believe he had, or what proof they've got that points to him; he did not kill Amanda Strickland. But it's obvious that you don't believe or trust me. Well, that's okay. This is a free country, you can believe what you like. I'll go to the police on my own, and I'll tell them everything I know. And you, Mr. Fury, can take your warped sexist skepticism, and go straight to the devil."

Jackson experienced something like déjà vu as he leaped to his feet and rushed after Jillian.

"I believe you," he said, throwing his body against the metal door and slamming it shut.

"Get out of my way. I'm leaving."

"No, you're not. Not until I've apologized. I'm sorry, Jillian, but I had to find out if you were telling the truth. I don't like being set up as the patsy."

The anger Jillian had managed to keep under restraint suddenly boiled to the surface. "You've got some nerve testing me. I'm the one who should be testing you. Just what are you anyway?"

"I told you, I'm a private investigator. And a damn good one, too."

"With sordid little divorce cases, maybe. I don't doubt you're world-class when it comes to proving that a husband is cheating on his wife. With luck on your side, and if there's not too much mental work involved, you could probably even find a missing person. But when it comes to something serious, something very important, like proving a man is innocent of murder, chances are you—you don't know your ass from a hole in the ground."

"If that's what you really believe, then stick around and help me."

Jillian staggered back a step. "What?"

"Help me. Work with me on this one, Jillian." He saw her expression grow more startled and knew he'd played the right card. Of course he wasn't serious. His offer was just to throw her off guard. "Help me prove Wyatt didn't kill Amanda Strickland. Help me find the one who really did murder her."

"My God! You're serious, aren't you?"

"Deadly. Pardon the pun."

"But I—I'm an accountant, a secretary—a pencil pusher for heaven's sake. I don't know the first thing about solving a murder case, much less the ins and outs of investigating."

"No, but I do. I've been in this business for"—Jackson did some quick mental calculation—"almost ten years. Damn! It's been that long?"

"I suppose time flies when you're having fun."

"No, not 'til you're past thirty, then it's like mach two straight down hill." Jackson noted the fleeting look of indecision on Jillian's face. "So will you do it? I'll even apologize again if it'll help."

Jillian considered his suggestion for a long moment, then relented. "All right." Jackson visibly relaxed, and she added, "But I want to know everything that was said at the police station. Start at the beginning, and don't leave anything out."

"The very beginning?" Eyeing the gentle sway of Jillian's hips as she headed toward the desk, Jackson smiled. "Okay. As soon as I walked in the door, I had this sort of run-in with the desk sergeant. Thornquist is in charge of booking city prisoners, not the county's. The guy doesn't like me for some reason. I think it's because I got all the credit for collaring the guy he was after, and he got demoted."

"Fury, would you skip the bull do-do and get to the important stuff?"

"Bull do-do?"

"Yes, bull do-do." With steno pad and pencil in hand, Jillian returned to the sofa.

"Honey, my relationship with Dallas's boys in blue is not bull do-do. But then again, considering Thornquist, maybe it is at that."

"Fury!"

"The case, right. After I got past Thornquist, I had a long talk with Wyatt and Walter Collins—he's Wyatt's attorney."

"Yes, I know. You've already told me that." With mounting impatience, Jillian wondered if she had done the right thing by staying here. Jackson Fury was enough to give anyone ulcers. "And you've told me that you know what the eyewitnesses said, what the detectives at the scene reported, and what the crime lab found. Now just what did they say, report, and find, darn it!"

"You want this straight from the hip, huh?" All humor vanished from Jackson's voice.

"That's right. Straight from the hip."

"Okay. Amanda Strickland's neighbors swear they saw Sterling Wyatt leave her apartment at one-thirty yesterday. The same time you swear he was with you."

"He was with me. I wasn't lying."

"They say his raincoat was splattered with blood. A fact the detectives corroborated when they went to his house and found said raincoat along with a pair of driving gloves, also stained with blood, wrapped up in a plastic bag that was stuffed inside his garbage can. Lab tests proved that the blood type on them matches Amanda's."

"Wait a minute. When he was with me, he wasn't wearing a raincoat."

"Well, it was his just the same. Wyatt said he'd been wearing it the night before." At Jillian's puzzled frown, Jackson explained, "It seems he paid an unexpected visit on his fiancée the night before she was murdered. He found her with another man. From what he and the neighbors said, Amanda and this other guy were doing a lot more than just playing spin the bottle, if you get my drift."

"You mean, they were . . ."

Jackson shrugged. "Either that, or they had been. Or they were about to. Anyway, Wyatt got upset and made some loud threats. The neighbors swear they heard him say, and I quote, 'I'll see you dead first.'"

"Oh, no!"

"Oh, yes! Finding his fiancée with another man just three weeks before the wedding is a pretty sound motive for murder, I'd say."

"But he didn't kill her," Jillian said. "He couldn't have. It's not possible for one person to be in two places at the same time. Unless . . ."

"Unless what?"

Jillian considered her thought for a moment, then shook her head decisively. "No, that doesn't make sense at all. No man in his right mind would hire someone who looked like him to go out and commit murder. If he hired anyone at all, he'd make certain beforehand that the killer looked like the other guy. You know, the guy that he caught her with."

"Jonathan Northrop."

"Who?"

"Jonathan Northrop," Jackson said. "This'll get you— Northrop is Wyatt's business partner."

"His partner?"

Jackson nodded. "After they took Wyatt back to his cell, I found out from Collins that Wyatt and Northrop share equal ownership in one of the biggest land-development firms in Dallas. Second only to Trammell Crow's, it seems. Not only that, Northrop is married to Wyatt's cousin and he's the father of two kids."

"That's sick."

"No, that's open marriage, honey. And, by the way Northrop's wife behaved when the police questioned her, she knew all about his affair with the Strickland woman."

"Well, Northrop's the one who should have been shot, not Amanda."

"But Amanda wasn't shot. She was stabbed. With a big, sharp kitchen knife they found"—he thumbed his heart—"sticking out of her chest."

Jillian shuddered. "Oh, God!" Suddenly she stared straight at Jackson, her eyes growing round. "But if Amanda was killed with a knife, the police must have found fingerprints on it. Fingerprints that couldn't have been Wyatt's."

"Sorry, honey. No prints."

"What do you mean, 'no prints'? Didn't they—oh, what do they call it on TV? Oh, yeah! Didn't they dust for fingerprints?"

"They dusted, all right, but the only prints they found on the murder weapon belonged to Amanda's maid."

"Her maid?"

"Yeah. Evidently the lady comes in every day, except Sundays, to clean the apartment, do the laundry, and some light cooking. Or so she told the detectives who questioned her. But she swore that the last time she touched the murder weapon was when she took it out of the dishwasher and put it away in a drawer. The police believe her. They didn't have much choice after they found those bloody gloves in Wyatt's garbage can."

"Okay, then what about Northrop? Those gloves could have been his just as easily as they could have been Wyatt's. Northrop could have murdered Amanda, and then thrown them in Wyatt's garbage can to make Wyatt look guilty."

"The police thought of that. So did I. But Northrop's got an iron-clad alibi. Seems he was in a meeting with some pretty heavy-duty guys at the time Amanda was murdered. Shook him up when he heard what had happened. And besides, he didn't have a motive."

"He certainly did! He was playing around on his wife."

"Yeah, his wife. Not Amanda."

"Well, Amanda could have gotten pushy—you know, jealous. She could have told him that if he didn't leave his wife, she'd go to her and tell her what was going on."

"But his wife already knew."

"Oh, that's right. I forgot."

"You forgot about Wyatt, too. Amanda was gonna marry him in less than three weeks, remember? Why would she upset Northrop's little apple cart if she intended to go through with the wedding?"

"Don't ask me; you're the detective. I can't understand why she would even want to sleep with Northrop."

"Oh, come on, Jill, you're not that dense. Haven't you ever heard of sexual gratification?"

"Yes, of course I've heard of it. But she was engaged to Wyatt, for Pete's sake. And believe me, he's not chopped liver."

"Maybe he couldn't satisfy her. Maybe he's . . ." Jackson balanced his splayed fingers in the air.

"No, Wyatt is not gay. You didn't see the look on his face when he was lying on top of me in the hallway. I did. And don't you even dare suggest that he's bisexual, either. That man is straight."

Moose whined in complaint when Jackson suddenly pushed her head off his leg. Mumbling beneath his breath, he stalked into the kitchen, wrenched open the refrigerator door, and then slammed it hard. "Did he turn you on, too?"

"What do you mean 'too'?" Jillian asked.

"The way you're talking, you certainly turned him on. I just want to know if he turned you on, too?"

Jillian considered the question. "A little."

"A little? That's like being pregnant, honey; either you are, or you aren't. Now did he, or did he not, turn you on?"

"Not that it's any of your business, but yes, he did." Jackson made a low, guttural remark. "What did you say?" she asked.

"Nothing. Just forget it." He washed his hands in the sink, dried them, and flung the towel over the back of the sofa as he headed for the door.

"Where are you going?'

"I've got some eyewitnesses to talk to," he said, fishing around in the pocket of his tight jeans for his car keys. "Don't know how long I'll be gone, but see if you can't straighten up some of this mess"—he gestured to the boxes on the floor—"before I get back."

Long after Jackson had slammed out of the loft, Jillian sat on the sofa in deep thought. She stared at Moose, who had crawled up beside her and laid her massive head in Jillian's lap. No matter what the police thought, or could prove, she knew in her heart that Wyatt hadn't murdered his fiancée. And it was a stupid idea to think that he'd hired a look-alike. But maybe Northrop had.

"No!" Moose flinched at Jillian's sudden outburst. "No, Northrop wouldn't do that, either," she said to the Great Dane. "Jackson's right, don't you see? Northrop wouldn't want to kill Amanda; they had too good a thing going for them. But his wife had plenty of motive for wanting Amanda out of the way. Open marriage my foot. She may have admitted to knowing what was going on, but no woman's going to stand by and let her husband get away with sleeping around on her. Not unless she's sleeping around, too.

"Oh, heck! That doesn't hold water, either. Amanda's neighbors saw a man leaving her apartment, not a woman."

Jillian mulled it over for a moment, then mused aloud, "Now if Amanda was playing around on Wyatt with Northrop, chances are pretty good that at one time she played around with some other guy, too. Maybe she still was. Maybe she was juggling two or three at the same time. Ooo, kinky!"

Moose whined and thumped her tail on the sofa's arm.

"Yeah, it does make sense, doesn't it? But where would I go—no, where would Jackson go, and who would he talk to, to find out more about Amanda's love life?"

With a soft "woof," Moose lifted a paw and plopped it down on Jillian's leg. Sunlight gleamed off the bright-pink polish on the Great Dane's toes.

Jillian gave a shout of laughter and hugged the dog, kissing her right between her pointed ears. "You darling! Thank you! You're the smartest, the most wonderful dog in the whole wide world. Too bad Rusty and your master, old what'shisname, aren't more like you. Well, we girls will just have to take care of that, won't we?"

# CHAPTER 5

Jillian picked up the phone before it could ring a second time. Just as she'd done earlier, she caught herself before saying, "Accounting, Jillian Fletcher speaking." Old habits were hard to break; even habits that were just three months old. It might take a while, but in time she would get it straight.

"Fury Investigations," she said. "Jillian Fletcher speaking."

"Who the devil are you?" The voice at the other end of the line, obviously female, sounded vexed.

"I'm Mr. Fury's secretary," Jillian said, thinking, *Not another one!*

"His secretary! When did he get a secretary?"

"Quite recently." *Not that it's any of your business.* "Mr. Fury isn't in at the moment. May I take a message?"

"No, mess— Yes. Yes, as a matter of fact, you can take a message. Tell Jack that Monica called."

"Monica, at four-forty-five." As she spoke, Jillian wrote down the name and time on a pink while-you-were-out slip. "Will he know the name?"

"You bet your bleached hair and dark roots he will."

Suppressing the urge to set Monica straight as to the

shade of her hair, Jillian asked, in a businesslike voice, "Is there anything else you want me to tell him?"

"You can tell him that I said he could . . ."

Jillian listened to Monica's colorful, very descriptive suggestion, then pulled the phone away from her ear and blinked at the receiver. With eyebrows raised, she shook her head. "I don't think Mr. Fury is physically capable of doing such a thing, Miss, uh, Monica, but I'll be sure and tell him what you said."

"You do that."

The connection ended with a loud click, and Jillian put the phone back in its cradle. Smiling, she wrote down Monica's message, word for word, completing it on the back of the slip. She added it to the tray filled with other messages Jackson had received, then went back to scouring the *Yellow Pages*.

Somewhere in Dallas there had to be a hairdresser who had occasionally, if not regularly, done Amanda's hair. Jillian couldn't see a woman with Amanda's money sudsing up with a bottle of Prell. When you were rich, you pampered yourself with only the very best. Everyone knew that. But which hairdresser had Amanda gone to? And which one should she call first? At least a hundred were listed in the directory.

On a sudden whim, Jillian picked up the phone and called the one person she knew who might be able to help her. She waited through four rings and would have hung up on the fifth had Vinnie not answered it. In the background she could hear Vinnie Junior screaming above a loud metallic pounding.

"Did I call at a bad time?" she asked.

"Jill? Hang on a minute, would you? Let me shut this kid up so I can hear you." After a moment the baby stopped screaming, and Vinnie returned to the phone. "Hi, what's up?"

"Vinnie, you didn't do a half-gainer on that baby, did you?"

"Half-gainer? You mean half-Nelson. No, I just put him in his highchair and gave him a bowl of Spaghetti-O's. Gonna be hell changing his messy diapers, but that's my fault, right? What can I do for you?"

"I've got a problem, sort of, and I was wondering if you could help me."

"I'll try. Shoot."

"Don't you have a sister who works in a beauty shop? Or did work in one?"

"Yeah, Felicia. She don't do hair no more, though. She's like me now—stays home and takes care of kids. No, dummy, the spoon goes in your mouth, not your hair. Kid gets more like his mother every day. Why, what's up?"

"Look, I know this isn't going to make any sense, but I've got to find the one salon in town that a very wealthy, socially prominent woman would go to."

"That's easy. You should've been more specific in the first place. You want Coiffure d'Anglaise."

Jillian searched through the *Yellow Pages*, but couldn't find a Coiffure d'Anglaise. "Vinnie, the number's not in the phone book."

"That's because it's not listed. We're talking ultra-high-class joint here, Jill, not the neighborhood beauty parlor. You gotta know somebody who knows somebody else at Coiffure d'Anglaise, and even then you gotta give them references as long as your arm just to get in the front door. It's the only beauty shop in town that checks out your pedigree along with your credit rating."

"That exclusive, huh? How do you suppose someone like me would go about making an appointment?"

"That's easy, too. You call my cousin Angela."

"Vinnie, you've been holding out on me. I didn't know you had wealthy relatives."

"So who's wealthy? Angie's in charge of the manicure, pedicure, and facial department at Coiffure d'Anglaise; she don't own the joint. If she'd been a boy, she could've been a heavyweight. Girl had a right hook on her that would knock you out before you knew what hit you. Now she don't do nothing all day but rub on rich broads' bodies. Hey! Maybe that's why Aunt Gussie and Uncle Al worry about her not getting married."

Unable to believe her good luck, Jillian asked for and got Angela's phone number from Vinnie. When she called his cousin, who answered on the second ring, the high pitch of Angela's voice contradicted Vinnie's description. The woman sounded more like Betty Boop than Mohammed Ali.

"I hope you don't think I'm a crackpot, calling you out of the blue like this," Jillian said.

"Well, knowing my cousin Vinnie isn't the greatest recommendation in the world, I'll admit, but what can I do for you?"

Jillian went on to explain, in the vaguest manner possible, why she was calling, and asked if Amanda Strickland had ever been to Coiffure d'Anglaise.

"Sure," Angela said. "She's one—uh, she was one of our regulars. She came in, oh, two, sometimes three times a week. Why? You a reporter, or something?"

"No. Actually I'm an accountant. That is, I was an accountant, but now I'm a secretary. Look, I know what I'm saying doesn't make any sense, but I just can't be any more specific right now. All I can tell you is that I need to find out some things about Amanda's personal life. Do you think you could help me get an appointment? I understand they're awfully hard to make." An audience with the pope would be easier, Jillian thought. At least you knew where he lived.

After a lengthy pause, Angela said, "Oh, hell, why not? Not all of Vinnie's friends are weird. Let me check the appointment book first thing tomorrow morning, then I'll give you a call. Tomorrow's what, Thursday?"

"Yes."

"Good thing it's not Friday. Friday and Saturday are our busiest days. I'm almost certain I can set you up an appointment with Trevor. He's the guy you want to see."

"Just Trevor. No last name?"

"I'm sure he's got one, but you won't need it."

"Is there anybody else there I should talk to besides Trevor? I need to find out as much about Amanda as I can."

"Yeah, Bonita. She always did Amanda's manicures and pedicures. I'll make you an appointment with her, too."

Jillian looked down at her short, uneven nails and winced. "I'll be embarrassed for anyone to see my nails."

"Do you bite them?"

"No, they just don't grow. They get to a certain length, and then they break off."

"Don't worry, by the time Bonita gets through with them, they won't ever break again. You should have seen Amanda's when she first came in. They looked like the nails of a nervous teenager. She bit them down almost to the cuticles."

"Did you do her manicures?"

"Right at first, and then I got put in charge of facials. I'll make you an appointment for that, too. Might as well have the whole works done while you're in."

"Wait a minute. Just how much is all this going to cost me?"

"Well, it all depends on what Trevor decides to do to your hair."

"What Trevor decides? It's *my* hair."

"I know, but he's the stubborn, temperamental type. Very creative, too. Wait'll you meet him."

Jillian didn't want to think about what she would look

like when Trevor got through with her. She would probably end up with a spiked, magenta mohawk. "I can't wait."

Talking to Amanda's neighbors had been a big waste of time, Jackson mused later that night. Those who had bothered to talk to him told him almost verbatim what they'd told the police. They'd heard Wyatt threaten Amanda one night, and the next day they'd seen him leaving her apartment in bloody clothes. Jackson had asked one woman if she had ever seen other men going into or leaving Amanda's place, and the old biddy had given him a look like he'd just crawled out of a sewer, then slammed the door in his face. One thing about the upper class—they were a very close-mouthed bunch when it came to protecting one of their own. They would probably be shocked right out of their designer underwear to know they were no different from the blacks down in South Dallas, the Vietnamese in East Dallas, and the Chicanos in Little Mexico.

He adjusted the collar of his service overalls and pulled the Texas Rangers baseball cap farther down his forehead. The dead headphones he wore beneath the cap were plugged into a massive, portable stereo-radio/cassette-recorder now hooked to the utility cart. He had it tuned to a station that played mainly heavy-metal rock, but heard only silence. Arranging the mop and broom inside the big cart so that they partially hid his face, he moved off down the hall in a slouched shuffle toward the security guard's desk.

Tonight's foray into the world of crime would bring him some positive results, he hoped. In the past, he'd only resorted to breaking and entering—better known as "B and E" to the police and the burglars who made their living at it—when everything else failed. In this case, circumstances made it necessary for him to do his B-and-E*ing* up front. Wyatt was due to be arraigned tomorrow, and Jackson hoped to find some evidence, no matter how flimsy, against Northrop.

The guard, a big, florid-faced redhead, glanced up from his bank of closed-circuit monitors as Jackson started past the desk. "Say, where's Joe?"

Jackson unplugged the headphones. *"Que?"* he asked over the screeching guitars, pounding drums, and jarring saxophones that echoed off the marble floors and walls.

"Turn that damn thing down!"

Jackson pressed a button on the blaster and the music immediately softened. "What you say, man?"

"I asked where Joe was," the guard repeated.

"Beats me, man. I'm sitting at home, watching TV, when this old lady from the cleaning office calls. She tells me to come here and clean floors ten through fifteen tonight. She don't say nothing about no Joe, man. I clean six floors, you think they give me more than minimum wage?"

"Five."

*"Que?"*

"It's five floors, not six. Don't you know how to count?"

"Yeah." Jackson held up his hands, and ticked off his splayed fingers. "Ten, eleven, twelve, thirteen, fourteen, fifteen. That's six, man."

"No, five. We don't have a thirteenth floor."

Out of the corner of his eye, Jackson saw a second guard stepping out of the elevator. "Oh! So, do they give me more than minimum wage for five floors, or what?"

"Beats me," the first guard said. "Look, it's already past ten o'clock. You'd better get to work, if you wanna be through cleaning by the time the building opens up at seven."

"Yeah, okay." Jackson turned up the blaster, then plugged in his dead headphones and wheeled the cart toward the elevator. He passed the second guard on the way.

Inside the elevator, Jackson punched the button for the

fifteenth floor, then waited until the doors hissed closed
before he turned off the blaster and slid the headphones
slightly off his ears. He unzipped his coveralls, reached
inside his left breast pocket, and pulled out a set of lock
picks. Out of the right breast pocket he produced a slide
camera, and checked the number of exposures remaining on
the film.

No sooner had he gotten all his equipment ready than the
elevator reached the fifteenth floor. Keeping his head down,
he pushed his utility cart ahead of him into the corridor. A
quick look from beneath the brim of his baseball cap and he
located the two closed-circuit security cameras fixed high
on the walls, one at the end of the short hallway directly in
front of the elevator, and the other above Presidio Development's double-doored entrance.

As he headed toward the etched-glass doors, shuffling
past the humming cameras, Jackson conceded that it was at
times like this when the old saying, "It's not what you
know, but who you know that counts," really meant
something. A friend of his at City Hall had told him that
Presidio Development occupied the two top floors of the
building Wyatt and Northrop owned. Another guy who
owed him a long-overdue favor, and who just happened to
be in charge of personnel at the cleaning service embla-
zoned across the back of his jumpsuit, had given him the
location of all the offices, a set of keys with which to unlock
locked doors, and the specific order to "get rid of the damn
clothes as soon as you're out of that place, and for God's
sake don't mention my name to the cops if they catch you in
the act."

Jackson made his way through the reception area,
dumping ashtrays and trash cans into the garbage bag that
lined his utility cart, then headed down a long hallway. He
knew he was supposed to clean all the offices similarly, even
go so far as dust the furniture. But he didn't. There wasn't

enough time, so he ignored them. If he found what he was looking for, and had time afterward, he might get to them on his way out.

Passing framed sketches of past and current Presidio projects, he turned right at the end of the hall and found himself in yet another, much larger, reception area. This place was worse than a maze, he thought, pushing his cart toward one of the two six-paneled doors. He turned the knob, opened the door, and stepped inside a pitch-black room. A flick of the light switch at his elbow, a slight sputtering hesitation, and four recessed panels in the ceiling shed flourescent light onto the room.

"Well, it's about time," Jackson said, eyeing the large wall-hung portrait of Jonathan Northrop with his wife and two kids.

He headed for Northrop's massive desk, pulling his lock picks and camera out of his pocket. Now the fun part began.

# CHAPTER 6

Thursday, April 24

Eager to get some work done before she left for an early and hopefully long lunch, Jillian let herself into Jackson's loft with the set of keys he'd given her. Moose trotted across the room to greet her. When she bent over to give the dog a hug, Moose started sniffing at her tailored navy-blue skirt.

"That's just Rusty's scent, Moose," Jillian said. "He's my doggie, but I love you, too."

Moose gave a soft "woof," as if to say, "That's okay," then she turned and trotted back to the far sofa. Smiling, Jillian watched her crawl onto the cushions and lower her head to rest it on her front paws. Jillian's smile died when a bare, hairy leg suddenly flopped over the back of the sofa nearest her. Only then did she notice the clothes scattered across the floor.

"Oh, no, he wouldn't," she said quietly, and stepped closer to the sofa.

But he had. In fact, he still was. Sound asleep, with only a pair of blue-and-white-striped boxer shorts between him and total nudity, Jackson lay sprawled on the sofa, his arms and legs flung wide, his jaw lax as he emitted loud snores.

"This won't do," Jillian said. "This absolutely will not do. I won't put up with it. If he expects me to come in here and work every morning, we're going to have to set up and stick to some rules."

Moose's ears stood upright.

"Don't look at me like that. I know this is his home, and a man's home is his castle and all that garbage, but it's also a place of business."

A strangling noise made her jerk around in Jackson's direction. He didn't wake up, but turned onto his side, and curled his long, leanly muscular body into a ball. Despite the fact that he was thirty-four years old, and a stubborn, hard-headed sexist into the bargain, Jillian thought he looked positively adorable. She could imagine what he was like as a little boy, no older than two or three, curled up the way he was now, but sleeping with a thumb stuck in his mouth instead of snoring. He had probably even picked his mother's flowers, and then tracked mud through the house to give them to her.

"Shhh," Jillian said to Moose, pressing a finger to her lips. "Let's let him sleep."

Using the phone upstairs in Jackson's bedroom, Jillian called Angela, and was told that she did indeed have an appointment at Coiffure d'Anglaise at eleven o'clock that day. Jackson would be surprised when he found out what she was doing on her own, she thought as she quietly returned to the alcove. All those nights she'd spent watching private detectives at work on TV would finally pay off.

She spent the next few hours straightening the office and organizing Jackson's files. When ten o'clock rolled around, and Jackson showed no signs of waking up, she let herself out of the loft.

Twelve noon found her dressed in a pale-blue zippered caftan, freshly shampooed, and sitting in a plush chair. Trevor—a man of medium height, medium weight, medium coloring, and incredibly handsome looks—ran his fingers through her wet shoulder-length hair, pulling it first one way, and then another.

"Looks like you've come to the right place," he said, "and just in the nick of time."

"It's a mess, isn't it? You'd think I'd have the time to take care of it properly, but I don't."

"Well, it's not completely hopeless. A little trimming here, a bit more shaping there . . . You're not going to need a perm. You've got enough body to carry almost any style."

"I'll leave it to your capable hands. After all, Amanda trusted you," Jillian said with feigned somberness. Her curiosity about how much this little outing was going to cost her almost equaled her curiosity about the late socialite.

"Let's get started then, shall we?" Trevor pulled a pair of scissors out of his tight pants pocket. "By the time you hop that jet back to New York, you're going to look and feel like an entirely new woman."

"That's exactly what Amanda said when she first told me about Coiffure d'Anglaise." Jillian affected an emotional shudder. "You know, I still can't believe that she's dead." Maybe Jackson was right after all, she thought. Maybe she should have gone into acting instead of accounting. By the time she was finished here, she would have earned, at the very least, an Oscar nomination for her performance as one of Amanda's old college friends, currently in town for the funeral.

"So, you went to Vassar with Amanda, huh?" Trevor pulled on a section of Jillian's hair and snipped off a good two inches from the end.

"Mmm-hmm."

"Well, all I can say is—the Big Apple must have one heck of a fountain of youth in their water system."

"Excuse me?"

"You don't look as old as Amanda does—uh, did."

"Well, that's because she was a few years ahead of me at Vassar. Mandy was a friend of my sister's long before I ever met her. But Buffy couldn't come to the funeral, so I decided to come for both of us. Poor darling's going through a horrible divorce right now. The rat she married is giving her a rough time about the property settlement." Move over Meryl, Sally, and Sissy, Jillian thought. She didn't deserve just a nomination. She deserved the Oscar itself.

"Hold your head down," Trevor said. "Yes, that's good. You know, I always thought prenuptial agreements were for the birds until Amanda told me that she had insisted on having one, and why. In her case, though, I have to admit it was the right thing for her to do."

A prenuptial agreement between Amanda and Wyatt? Jillian wanted to remember that. It might be important. She would find out later, if and when she consulted with Jackson.

"If that maniac had waited to kill her until after they were married," said Trevor, "he still wouldn't have been able to touch her money."

Jillian shuddered. "It's hard to believe that Sterling would actually do such a thing."

"Did you know him?"

"Not as well as Mandy knew him obviously, but I'd met him. He seemed like such a nice guy."

"Believe me, he wasn't as nice as the other one."

A tingle of excitement surged through Jillian. *Play along with him*, she told herself. *Don't tip your hand too soon.* "You mean Jon Northrop?"

"Cherise's husband? No, he was just a pleasant convenience, according to Mandy. According to Cherise, too. She did her best to hide it, but I could tell she was really put out by their affair. No, I'm talking about the one that Amanda was going with before she got engaged to that bloodthirsty male Lizzy Borden. Surely she told you about him."

"She may have, but it's skipped my mind. What was his name?"

"I don't know. To tell you the truth, I don't think she ever mentioned his name. But I saw them together once at an art exhibit. That trendy little gallery on Routh Street."

"Describe him. I might recognize him."

"Well, he was tall. About as tall as Wyatt, I'd say. Big, too. You know, muscular, broad shoulders, but not fat. He had wonderful hair, too; I remember that. But it was a lighter shade of blond than Wyatt's."

Jillian forced a chuckle, then glanced at Trevor's mirrored reflection. "This may sound tacky, but Mandy had a—a thing for blond men. She knew quite a few of them. Did you happen to get a look at his face?"

"No, I was across the room from them. Come to think of it, I don't think he ever turned around. But they looked so happy together. Holding hands, standing with their arms around each other. She never did say or give any hints why she broke it off with him. If you ask me, it's because one of them did something unforgivable. It certainly wasn't because he was inattentive or unromantic."

"What do you mean?"

"The man sent her flowers all the time. He even had two dozen roses delivered to her here once while I was doing her hair. Magnificent lavender roses that smelled like heaven itself."

"It's a shame there aren't more men like him around these days," Jillian said.

"You're telling me!"

Although Jillian tried to keep the conversation centered on Amanda and Amanda's unknown lover, Trevor managed to channel it in a different direction. He finished cutting her hair and, telling her he was going to let her air-dry before he styled it, he handed her over to Angela for her facial.

"So, you're Cousin Vinnie's neighbor," Angela said,

gesturing for Jillian to have a seat in the long sheet-draped chair.

Jillian took note of the nearby worktable laden with jars and bottles, the goose-neck heatlamp, and the electrical devise on wheels that looked as if it might have come from a hospital's intensive-care unit. As she sat down, she took note of Angela, all four feet eleven inches, eighty-pounds of her, and smiled. "I'm really his tenant," she said, "considering he owns the duplex. I suppose I should apologize for staring at you—I know it's rude—but you're nothing like I imagined you'd be."

Angela laughed, twin dimples appearing in her plump cheeks. "Don't give it a second thought. I can just imagine what Vinnie's led you to believe. You thought I was some kind of hulking macho dyke, right?"

"Well . . ."

"Yeah, I thought so. You gotta understand my relationship with Vinnie. When we were kids I gave him a black eye, and to this day he still hasn't forgiven me. I didn't mean to do it; it was an accident, but you'll never convince him of that." Angela pushed a button and a motor began to whine, taking the sheet-draped chair with Jillian in it into a reclining position. "My mother and daddy are almost as bad. They can't understand why I don't want to settle down with one guy and start having babies. God, traditional families can be a pain in the ass at times, you know? How did it go with old magic-scissors Trevor? Did you learn anything?"

"Yes and no," said Jillian. "Is it safe for us to talk here?"

"For a while, until I get your mud pack on. Then, if you open your mouth, your face will crack."

"Look, do me a favor, will you? Don't go overboard on this. My budget already has stretch marks as it is."

"Don't worry, leave everything to me."

Jillian couldn't see where she had any choice when Angela began rubbing a white cream over her face and neck. "Did you and Amanda ever talk when she came to you for her facials?"

"Yeah, but never about anything specific. You know, nothing of a personal nature."

"Then she never said anything to you about who she was seeing."

"No, she didn't."

"Darn."

"Why, is it important?"

"I don't know. It could be. Trevor mentioned that she had been seeing a man before she became engaged to Sterling Wyatt. I was hoping you might know something about him."

"Are you talking about the guy who sent her the lavender-colored roses?"

"Yes! Did he—?"

"Look, I hate to disappoint you, but that's all I know. I was working back here with a client when the flowers were delivered up front. In fact, I never even saw them; I just heard about them."

Jillian groaned in frustration. "I need to find out if they came with a card attached to them and if somebody saw it."

"Bonita might have. Why don't you ask her when she does your nails?"

"I will."

"Even if she didn't see a card, she might have seen the florist's truck. Of course, this happened seven or eight months ago; knowing her, she may have forgotten it by now. Bonita's memory isn't the greatest in the world. Comes from sniffing all that nail-sculpting compound."

Bonita, however, did remember the roses. And she remembered the pink and blue stitching across the delivery man's jacket pocket saying that he was from Sasha's Florist.

And she remembered Amanda's reaction when she'd read the card that came attached to the arrangement.

"I mean it was like—'how nice.' No expression, no emotion, nothing. Geez, some guy ever sent me roses like that, I'd get a nosebleed doing cartwheels. Not that I'm speaking ill of the dead, you understand."

"No, of course not." Jillian sat on one side of a glass-topped table with both hands soaking in a cuticle-softening solution. Bonita sat on the other side, arranging her strange assortment of tools.

"It's just that some women take guys too much for granted. I don't think that's right. Like, I mean, guys shouldn't take us for granted either, even though they do. I once knew this guy—really bitchin' dude—like two or three years ago . . ."

As she carried on her incessant monologue, throwing in little tidbits of gossip about Coiffure d'Anglaise's clients, Bonita managed to transform Jillian's short, conservative nails into ten, perfectly matched talons. The longer Bonita talked, the more Jillian believed that the sculpting compound the girl used had affected her brain in some way; her speech center especially. The stuff smelled like a mixture of rancid chemicals. The awful odor aside, they did a terrific job.

Trevor did his magic on her, too, just as Angela had promised. Feeling elegant and sophisticated, Jillian left Coiffure d'Anglaise at four o'clock that afternoon, quite a few clues richer, but over three hundred dollars poorer.

# CHAPTER 7

With the late-afternoon sunlight streaming through the wall of windows, Jackson leaned a jean-clad hip against the kitchen counter and stared sleepily into a cup of strong, lukewarm coffee. He hated having to admit it, but he was getting old. If he didn't watch it, late nights like the one he'd just had would be the death of him. At seven that morning, he'd returned to the loft so exhausted he'd barely had the energy to strip off his clothes and collapse on the sofa.

Now if he could just wake up, he would go take a shower and shave. Maybe then he would feel like a human being again. At least on the outside. Breaking and entering was the one thing about his job that he hated most. Even when he hit paydirt, like last night, digging around in people's lives, in their private affairs, left him feeling dirty.

Jackson yawned, one hand scratching his bare, hairy chest. A second yawn soon followed the first and he let his hand descend to do some immodest exploratory scratching elsewhere. Before it reached its destination, the loft door opened and Jillian walked in.

Although his yawn had ended, his mouth remained open in awe at the sight of her transformation. From the neck down, she looked no different—a dark-blue shirt draping the rounded hips he lusted after; an open-collar blouse exposing a shadowy cleft between the firm breasts that drove him crazy; the creamy neck he would kill to nibble looking longer and more slender—but her face and that head full of jet-black hair . . . Dy-no-mite!

A brisk shake of his head rectified his temporary state of mute immobility. "That must have been some lunch," he said, glancing at his watch and noting the time. Where the hell had she gone, Paris?

"What do you think?" Smiling, Jillian did a graceful three-hundred-sixty-degree turn, giving Jackson the full benefit of her new hairdo and makeup job. Facing him again, she held out her hands and wiggled her fingers. "Well?"

Jackson swallowed convulsively at the sight of her long, apple-red nails. What did he think? No, he couldn't tell her what he was really thinking, that right now he'd give anything if she would scratch those nails across his back. Or his chest. Or the other place on him that was aching like hell, and that he was much better off not even thinking about. If he told her that, she'd slap his face and quit for sure.

"You, uh, you look real nice." Coffee splattered onto the counter as Jackson thrust his cup aside and headed for the stairs. "I think I'll just run upstairs and take a quick shower." Cold, he decided. An icy cold shower ought to do the trick. If it didn't, he was a dead man.

"Wait," Jillian said, "there's something I want to—"

"Save it for later, would you? I'll only be a minute," he called down from the top of the stairs. "There're some photographs on the desk. Look them over while I'm gone. Tell me what you think."

Once he was safe behind the glass-brick wall, Jackson staggered across the bedroom and into the bathroom. He stripped off his jeans, stepped into the sunken tub/shower, and turned on the tap. "Come on, cold water, do your stuff."

Twenty minutes later, soap and shampoo bubbles gurgled down the drain, taking most of Jackson's frustrations along with it. He moved to the sink with a towel wrapped around his hips, and shaved the overnight stubble off his face. It was amazing what a man could accomplish just by practicing a little self-control. Splashing aftershave on his face, he knew that he could face Jillian now and not worry about something embarrassing coming up.

He tossed the towel into the clothes hamper as he headed into his bedroom, intending to get clean underwear out of the dresser. One look at Jillian, however, who was sitting on his bed pouring over the proofs in her lap, had him back into the bathroom again.

"What the hell do you think you're doing?" he asked.

"I'm looking over these like you told me," she said. "How did you get hold of them anyway? Do you have any idea what all this means?"

"Yeah, it means I'm stuck in here because I can't get to my shorts."

"Your shorts?" Jillian glanced up in confusion and saw Jackson's nose and chin through the small crack in the bathroom door. Her eyes dropped, and she saw— "Oh, my gosh, you're na— Your shorts. Right. Yes, you do need your shorts, don't you? Okay, tell me where they are and I'll get them for you."

"Uh-uh. You go away and I'll get them myself."

"Oh, come on, Jackson. It's almost six o'clock. I've got to go home and feed Rusty."

Knowing she had him between a rock and a possibly embarrassing hard place, Jackson did the only thing left for him to do. He gave in. "All right. Look in my dresser, second drawer from the top," he said, closing the door.

"And be quick about it, would you? I'm starting to get goose bumps in here."

The sound of his drawer opening was soon followed by her soft chuckle. "Ooo, how sweet," she said.

"Oh, no," he groaned, his instincts telling him what she had found. Damn his sister Wanda and her warped sense of humor. If he could get his hands on her now, he'd gladly strangle her.

The bathroom door inched open and Jillian's long arm snaked inside. At the end of her fingers dangled a pair of boxer shorts covered with red cupids and hearts. Without a word of thanks, Jackson jerked them out of her hand, slammed the door shut, and pulled the shorts over his hips.

"Don't say it," he said a moment later as he stomped across the bedroom to his closet.

"Don't say what?" Jillian asked with an innocent grin. "Don't say how cute you look? Okay, I won't. And I wouldn't dream of telling you how, in my opinion, you don't look like the boxer-shorts type. Jockey shorts, yes, but never boxers." A pause, then, "Who gave them to you? A close, intimate friend?"

"Not hardly. They were a Christmas present from my mentally deranged sister." He kept his back to her as he zipped up his jeans, then he turned and saw the laughter in her eyes. Propelled by an unexplainable impulse, he slowly walked toward her.

Jillian saw the look in his eye. "Jackson?"

"You started it, sweetheart, but I'm gonna be the one to finish it."

"Now, Jackson—"

"So I don't look like the boxer-shorts type, do I?"

"No—no, you don't," Jillian said, feeling oddly breathless.

"Well, guess what? You sure as hell look like the raspberry see-through bra type to me." Slowly his eyes traveled down to the swell of her breasts. "Are you wearing it now under that prim little shirt?"

For some unexplainable reason, Jillian couldn't move, couldn't speak, couldn't breathe properly, and she couldn't evade Jackson's hands as they snaked out and pulled the collar of her blouse apart. He meant only to tease her, to give her back a little of what she had given him. Unfortunately, the stronger-than-intended jerk of his hands popped the top button off her shirt and it parted to expose the creamy expanse of her chest.

"Jesus," he said with a groan. His gaze locked on the twin mounds of flesh that were barely confined within the sheer, pale-pink nylon, the ache in his groin growing ten times worse than what it had been before.

The heady scent of his aftershave, combined with the close proximity of his broad, hairy chest, left Jillian's mouth dry. "Sexual harassment again, Fury?" she asked in a husky voice.

The slow, negative movement of his head preceded the reluctant ascension of his gaze. "Not harassment, Fletcher. This is a case of pure frustration. You got any idea what the sight of those, inside of that wispy little nothing you got on, do to me?"

Jillian's tongue flicked out to moisten her dry lips. "I took Biology one-oh-one. I've got a fairly good idea."

"Know what I'd like to do about it?"

The gradual return of her sanity thankfully washed away the glazed look in her eyes. "What you'd like to do, or what you're going to do?"

Jackson took a deep breath and, slowly exhaling it, dropped his hands and stepped away. "With just a little bit more cooperation from you, honey, we could be on that bed now, having ourselves one helluva picnic."

"With me as the main course? Sorry, Jackson, but I'm not in the mood." Jillian turned, breaking the electric contact between them, and gathered up the proofs scattered across his bed. "You'll be much better off if you keep your mind away from dangerous fantasies and concentrate only on the case. Do you know what these are?"

"I ought to; I'm the one who found them, photographed them, and did the developing. What do you think they are?"

"They look like copies of Northrop's letters, his canceled checks, deposits, and ledger entries."

"Notice who Northrop wrote the checks to," Jackson said.

"They're all made out to the same man."

"Guess who he is. Guess what he does."

"I don't have the foggiest idea."

"Well, then, I'll tell you. Not too long ago a guy hired me to be his bodyguard. He wanted me to make sure he stayed in one piece until he paid off a big debt he owed some gambler out in Las Vegas. The name of the gambler he owed the money to and the name on those checks are one and the same.

"Now take a good close look at the other proofs you're holding. See the dates? Northrop wrote company checks to Hammond Enterprises on the same day he deposited an equal amount of money into his personal account. Old sticky-fingers might have gotten away with his pilfering if I hadn't come across those same dates and amounts in his business ledger. Got any idea who owns Hammond Enterprises."

Jillian took a wild guess. "Northrop?"

"Smart lady," Jackson said with a wink. "Hammond happens to be his wife's maiden name."

"But I thought she was a Wyatt."

"No, her mother was a Wyatt. She changed her name to Hammond when she married Cherise's daddy."

Jillian studied the grainy proofs again more thoroughly. "Good gracious! Northrop's stolen thousands—no, hundreds of thousands from Presidio Development! Do you suppose Wyatt knows about this?"

"Your guess is as good as mine. One thing's for sure though, this is gonna take some of the heat off Wyatt."

"How will it do that?"

Jackson took the proofs from Jillian and sifted through them. "Well, we know by these letters that Northrop's up to his neck in debt to that gambler out in Vegas, and that he's been stealing small amounts to pay the guy off. Right?"

"Yes."

"Of course that in itself doesn't tie him in directly with the Strickland woman's murder, but—and this is just a hunch you understand, because I don't as yet have any concrete proof to back it up. But if Amanda Strickland knew that Northrop was stealing, and he knew that she knew, I'd say he had one helluva motive for him wanting her out of the way."

"I think I see what you're getting at."

"Do you?"

"Uh-huh."

"Remember now, it's only a hunch. The way I got it figured—Northrop was under a lot of pressure and, being no different from any other guy with a girlfriend on the side, he looked on Amanda sort of as a therapist. She was someone he could unload all his troubles on, someone who'd whisper sweet nothings in his ear and tell him everything was gonna be okay. Guy like that doesn't go home and unload it on his wife, 'cause chances are, she's the one who probably got him in debt in the first place.

"Northrop wouldn't necessarily have had to have told Amanda outright; he could have talked in his sleep, or let it slip out some other way. Who knows? Maybe Amanda knew about it all along. Maybe she was in on it with him from the beginning. Hell, we could go on speculating about it until doomsday, but without tangible evidence we can't prove a damn thing. The only thing we know for certain now is that someone other than Wyatt might have had a reason for wanting Amanda dead."

"Good heavens," Jillian said. If Jackson's theory was correct, then that meant Wyatt, Northrop, and the guy who had once sent Amanda flowers at Coiffure d'Anglaise were a . . . "A four-sided triangle."

Jackson frowned. "A what?"

"This is a four-sided triangle."

He shook his head. "Jill, honey, there's no such thing as a four-sided triangle."

"In this case there is."

"Sweetheart, triangles have three sides, and three sides only."

"I know that. I took geometry; I'm no dummy."

"Then don't make such dumb remarks."

"It's not dumb, Jackson. Do you have any idea where I've been all day?"

Cocking an eyebrow, he gave her a thorough once-over. "Yeah, at the beauty shop."

"That's right."

"Jill, I hope you don't take this the wrong way, because I think you look really terrific, but instead of sitting under a hair dryer all day, having your nails done, you should have been here working."

Jillian crossed her arms beneath her breasts in a pose of defiance. "I thought we agreed that you wouldn't hassle me about the length of my lunch hours."

"I know we did, and I'm not hassling you."

"You're not?"

"No."

"Well, what would you call it then?"

"How about employer–employee relationship adjustment."

Jillian stiffened and uncrossed her arms. "That's hassling." She turned on her heel and headed for the opening in the glass-brick wall.

"Hey, wait a minute." Jackson hurried down the spiral stairs after her. "Don't get mad and run off. If you'll just stop and think about it a minute you'll realize that I'm not asking for a lot. I am paying you to file, type, answer the phone, and whatever else it is you do. Or whatever it is you're supposed to do. The least you could do is do some of it."

"I did." Jillian stopped abruptly beside the desk and picked up her purse.

"You did?"

"Yes, I did!" She whirled around and the pouch of her shoulder bag struck his chest. "When I got here this morning, you were asleep on that couch, snoring so loudly that you rattled the windows. I didn't wake you up. It's obvious that your schedule's been so busy today, what with your nap and all, that you haven't had time to look at your desk."

Jackson angled his head and glanced at the desk behind Jillian. Mounds of loose paper no longer littered the surface. Pens, pencils, and paper clips that he'd never been able to find when he needed them before were now stored away in neat little containers. Stackable letter trays hugged one side of the desktop, while a desk calendar rested next to the phone on the other.

"Jill, I—"

"Oh, save it, Jackson. Here"—she thrust a fistful of checks at him—"endorse these and I'll drop them in the bank night depository on my way home."

"I'm sorry."

"I said, save it. I don't want your apology. I don't need it."

"Well, you're gonna get one just the same."

"Okay, you've apologized and"—she took a deep

breath—"and I suppose I'll do the polite thing and accept it. Everybody's entitled to be grouchy first thing in the morning. Or night, in your case. Now would you endorse those checks so I can get out of here? It's getting late."

"I'll be happy to," he said, smiling sheepishly, "on one condition."

"No, Jackson," she said, misinterpreting his smile. "I've already told you, I'm not interested in having any picnic with you upstairs."

"That's not what I had in mind."

Wary curiosity appeared in her eyes. "It wasn't?"

"Huh-uh. I was thinking that—well, I was kinda hoping that since I haven't had breakfast yet, and I know you haven't had dinner, I thought the two of us might go out and have something to eat together." He waited for a moment, then with a sigh, he shrugged and started to turn away. "But the way you're dressed and all, it's obvious you've already got a date tonight, so—"

"No, I don't!" The moment the words left her mouth, Jillian wanted to kick herself for sounding so eager. "I was just going to go home, feed Rusty, open up a can of soup or something, and eat it while I watched TV."

"You sure?"

"I'm positive."

"Well, then, I know this great little place out in Mesquite that makes the best chicken-fried steak in Dallas County. If you want, we can even get a couple of hamburgers to go, and you can feed them to Rusty later." He paused to give her time to decide, then added, "Coming with me will save you a trip home on the bus."


"You know, Jackson, there's a good chance they won't run out of steak before we get there."

Jillian gripped the edge of the frayed bucket seat, her knuckles turning white and her breath freezing in her throat,

as Jackson took a hard, quick left off Pearl Street and sped
down the ramp onto Thornton Freeway. Thank God they
weren't driving in heavy rush-hour traffic, she thought,
cringing as he slithered between two big diesel rigs. By now
they would have had a wreck for sure.

"I don't mean to sound picky or anything, but I'd feel a
whole lot safer if you would try and keep the car on all four
tires when you turn a corner."

"Am I driving too fast for you, Jill?"

"Just a tad, Jackson. Just a tad."

"You know something?" Jackson glanced into his rearview mirror, then stomped hard on the accelerator. "I never
figured you for a chicken."

Jillian's head snapped backward, thudding against the
high-backed headrest. "I'm a girl; I'm allowed to be
chicken if I want to be; there's no law against it."

At the Grand Avenue exit, Jackson swerved out of the far
right lane over to the left. He darted between a car with an
elderly, white-haired couple in the front seat and a big
Mayflower moving van. The speed of his maneuvers made
Jillian strain against her seat belt. Thinking he had finally
decided to drive in just one lane of the freeway instead of all
four, Jillian opened her eyes. Unfortunately, the sight of the
Pontiac's speedometer needle easing past eighty made her
want to close them again. With a groan, she slumped down
in her seat and turned her head in time to see the Texas State
Fair grounds zip by in the distance.

Jackson managed to keep one eye on the traffic behind
him and the other on the road ahead for a few more miles,
then without warning, he pulled out of the far left lane,
angled the Pontiac across the freeway, and took the
Ferguson Road exit.

Now driving at a slower speed—fifty instead of eighty in
the thirty-five residential zone—Jillian could think of
something other than instant death.

"My God," she said, suddenly realizing what had just happened, "someone's following us, aren't they?"

"Not anymore." A lazy grin tugged at one corner of Jackson's mouth as he slowed down to stop at a traffic light. "I just lost him."

"Who was it? Or is it safe to ask?"

"Ask, I don't care. Remember the day we met, some guy was tailing me?"

Although calmer now, Jillian was still badly shaken over their lightning-fast drive. She forced herself to think back to the Tuesday they had first met. "Vaguely," she said. "All I can remember is something about you having a client with an irate ex-husband."

"That's the one."

"He was chasing you?"

"Yep."

"But why? You weren't messing around with his wife, were you? I mean, ex-wife."

"No, Marsha was just my client, nothing else. You sure you want to hear this? Story's kinda long."

"Consider me a captive audience. I'm all ears."

"Marsha's husband—her ex-husband now—was a real penny-pinching scumbag. Like everybody else, Marsha thought he didn't have a dime to spare with all the deals he was involved in all the time. The creep was one of Dallas's biggest real-estate investors. On top of being a miser, he had a sweet young thing tucked away in some ritzy North Dallas condo. Everything was going along okay until he screwed up big by asking Marsha for a divorce. After fifteen years of living with the jerk, I guess she saw divorce as the only way of getting herself and her three girls out of a miserable, no-win situation. She jumped at the chance."

"That's all very interesting, Jackson, but just how do you fit into the picture?"

"I was coming to that. The lawyer she hired told her to

contact me. I'd worked for him once before, right after he got out of law school, but I hadn't heard from him in years. We're on much friendlier terms now. I started digging around, asking questions, and found out that the old man not only had this other woman but that he was worth a helluva lot more than everybody thought. I gave the evidence to Marsha and Burke—that's the lawyer—and as they say in the business, they took old Scrooge to the cleaners."

"So that's why he's after you," Jillian said.

"Yeah, that and the fact that when the divorce was final, Marsha signed over the old jerk's most valuable piece of property to me instead of paying my fee by check. None of us knew, of course, just how valuable the property was until I had it appraised. I offered to sign it back over to her, but she insisted that I keep it. She's one terrific lady in my book."

"What kind of property did you get? A house?"

"Sorta."

"Is it here in Dallas?"

"Yeah."

"Not that it's any of my business, but why don't you live in it instead of the West End loft?"

"Because it *is* the West End loft, Jill."

She turned slowly in her seat to look at him. "You own the loft?"

"More than that. I own the whole damn building."

"Good Lord!"

"Funny, that's what I said when I first saw it. Marsha's ex didn't know what a gold mine he had. He bought it years ago and was using it as a tax write-off. When the West End became Dallas's newest restoration area and all the young upwardly-mobiles moved in and started making changes, I guess he saw it as a way of making even more money. Before he messed up and lost it to Marsha in the divorce, he'd invested quite a bit in restoration and conversion costs."

"Then you made a killing, didn't you?"

"On that case, yeah. Some cases, though, I'm lucky to break even."

"But I thought all private investigators charged a set standard fee."

He nodded. "They do. My usual going rate's a hundred and a half a day plus expenses, but a lot of people in trouble don't have that kind of money. Marsha didn't. Old man Williamson didn't."

"Who's he?"

"Just a nice old duffer who owned an appliance store. Place was getting ripped off regularly until I installed his security system. He didn't have enough cash to pay my fee, so he gave me merchandise instead. You know that big-screen TV back at the loft? That was what I got instead of money. The big investigative firms might not do business the way I do, but then I don't think of myself as big league. Yet."

"You just like to help people in trouble, is that it?"

"Yeah, I suppose. Deep down, though, I'm not really all that noble. P.I. work is the one thing I'm really good at. The one thing I enjoy the hell out of doing. I'd go nuts if I had to put on a suit and tie every morning, then drive through bumper-to-bumper traffic just to sit at a desk and grow ulcers. I know, because I've done it."

"Really?" Jillian couldn't see him in a white-collar job. "What did you do before?"

"About the same thing I'm doing now, only from behind a desk and for somebody else. When I couldn't hack the headaches, or the hemorrhoids, or the smog down in Houston anymore, I quit and came back home to Dallas. Worked out of my apartment until I'd developed a reputation and the cases started getting bigger—still wasn't making much money, though. Then I met Burke, and you know the rest."

He nosed the Pontiac into the restaurant's parking lot, whipped into an empty slot near the entrance, and killed the engine. As he turned to face her, he rested an arm across the back of his bucket seat. "That's where I am today, sweetheart. You can tell me your life story over dinner."

# CHAPTER 8

Just as Jackson had promised, his "mom and pop" place made the best chicken-fried steak Jillian had ever eaten. The cook coated real steak, instead of thick hamburger patties, in heavy batter, then deep-fat-fried it until it formed a crunchy crust. Despite the method of cooking, it wasn't at all greasy. Even the gravy, always served with traditional Texas chicken-fried steak dinners, was out of this world.

"I can't understand," Jillian said, sitting back from her empty plate, "why something that tastes so good has to look like it's covered in kindergarten glue. You'd think someone would find a way to dress it up a little, change its color, or do something to make it look more appetizing."

"You kids want some more ice tea?" The waiter, a tall robust man in his mid-sixties, loomed up behind Jackson and clapped a hand on his shoulder as he grinned at Jillian. "Momma and the girls baked some pies this morning; how about I bring y'all a couple of great big old slices."

"None for me, thank you, Mr. Fury," Jillian said. "I couldn't eat another bite."

When Jackson had told her they were going to a "mom and pop" place, Jillian hadn't taken him literally. The waiter, Jackson's father, ran the restaurant with the help of two of his sons, while Jackson's mother and two of his sisters controlled the kitchen. On busy nights, usually Fridays and Saturdays, other members of the Fury clan came in to help out.

"Did they by any chance make lemon meringue?" Jackson asked.

"Sure did. This being Wednesday, they figured you'd be stopping by. I'll go get you a piece. Be right back." Mr. Fury turned to leave, but Jackson stopped him.

"Wait a minute, Dad. Who made it, Momma or Treeva Lynn?"

Mr. Fury chuckled and patted Jackson's back. "Don't worry, Son. Momma made this one. She knows better than to let your sister near the lemons." He turned to Jillian. "The first and only lemon meringue pie my daughter Treeva Lynn ever made was when she was about eleven years old. The dang thing was so sour, we all went around with our mouths puckered up for about a week."

"More than that, Dad. It killed my dog," Jackson said, deadpan.

"Naw, it didn't," said Mr. Fury. "Don't listen to him, Jill. Ring was so old, he was halfway to dog heaven anyway."

"I don't care what he says," Jackson said when his father had ambled off toward the kitchen. "If Treeva Lynn hadn't made that pie, Ring would have lived at least another two years."

"Ring? You named your dog Ring?"

"Yeah, short for Ring-tail Tooter." Staring at his glass of ice tea, Jackson slowly wiped away the condensation with a finger. "He didn't have a pedigree like Moose; he was just an old mutt my brothers and I found down by the creek when he was a puppy. Poor little thing was nothing but skin and bones. Had more fleas than he did hair." He shook his head with a wistful smile. "Ring sure was a good old dog."

Listening to Jackson talk about his childhood wasn't

unpleasant for Jillian, but it wasn't exactly a thrill either. She wanted him to change the subject so she could tell him what she'd learned at Coiffure d'Anglaise; that it looked as though a third man was connected with Amanda Strickland's murder.

So what was stopping her?

Cowardice, she decided. Plain and simple cowardice.

Jackson had said that he wanted her to help him solve this case, but he'd also let her know, in no uncertain terms that first day in his office, that he wanted her to keep her nose out of his business. He would probably have a fit if she told him she'd infringed on his professional turf. After all, he was her boss, the one with the know-how, the one with the investigator's license, while technically she was just the hired help. The worst thing he could do would be to fire her. Lord knows, it wasn't as though she'd never been without a job before. In this instance, however, an innocent man's future was a lot more important than her getting a paycheck.

"From what I've seen and heard so far," Jillian said at last, deciding to ease into the subject gracefully, "I know you're very close to your family."

"I try. Well, we all try, really, but it's not easy when a family's as big as ours. Everybody but Randy and Treeva Lynn have gotten married. The rest of us, if we're lucky, get to see each other when the holidays roll around."

"Is that the reason you work alone?" *That's it, Fletcher,* she thought with smug satisfaction. *Take it nice and slow, so he won't suspect what you're doing.*

"What do you mean?"

"Well, with as many brothers as you have, I'm surprised one of them isn't working with you. Your sisters, too; I shouldn't leave them out."

"It's like I told you before, I like working alone. See, I learned early on that in this business it's better that way. I guess I'm what you'd call a loner—always have been, in spite of having eleven brothers and sisters. I like doing things my way. If I don't have to answer to anybody, I don't ever have to depend on them, either. If I make a mistake and get hurt, it's my fault, and nobody else's."

*Terrific,* she thought gloomily. *Now I know he'll blow a fuse when I tell him what I've done.*

"But haven't you ever wished you had a partner?" she asked.

"A time or two, yeah. But usually I know ahead of time what I'm walking into. Spend a few years in this business, you develop instincts you never knew you had. Kind of like growing a second pair of eyes in the back of your head."

"I'm not talking about having help getting out of some sort of dangerous situation," Jillian said. "I mean having help with the easy, ordinary stuff. Like legwork. Isn't that what they call it?"

"Yeah, but legwork's no problem. That's how I get most of my leads. That old instinct again. Gets kinda frustrating at times when I keep running into dead ends, but that's all part of the business."

"Is it?" Keeping her voice bland, Jillian girded up her courage. *Here goes nothing,* she thought. "Now that you've brought it up, there's something I think you might want to know."

Unfortunately, Jackson's father arrived with Jackson's lemon meringue pie at that moment and Jillian lost what little ground she'd gained. As soon as his father walked away, Jackson immediately turned their conversation back to where it had been before.

"Okay, now it's your turn."

"My turn?"

"Yeah, I told you some of my life story, now you tell me a little about yours."

"I really don't have anything to tell," she said, holding back her frustration and disappointment.

"Everybody's got a story of some kind, Jill."

"Yes, I know they do, but mine's not half as interesting as yours."

Jackson gave her a long, measured look.

"Really," she said. "I mean, I'm only twenty-three; I haven't had time to have an interesting life yet."

"Where did you go to high school?"

"W. T. White, in North Dallas."

"Where did you go to college?"

"North Texas State, in Denton."

"Did you date?"

"Of course I dated. When I wasn't studying."

"The captain of the football team, right? Both in high school and college, I'll bet."

"No, neither one, as a matter of fact. Look, why the third degree all of a sudden?"

"This isn't a third degree, Jill. I just want to know a little bit about you. No, I take that back. I want to know a lot about you. Everything. What you did when you were a little girl. How many brothers and sisters you have . . ."

"No sisters. I have just one stepbrother, and Bobby's almost thirty."

"Your parents divorced?"

"No, Mother's still married to Robert, my stepfather."

"What about your real father? Did your mother divorce him, or did he die?"

Jillian eyed Jackson for a moment, then, with a slow expulsion of breath, lowered her eyes.

"Rough subject, huh?"

She nodded.

"Look, sweetheart, if you don't want to talk about it . . ."

"No, it's okay. After twenty years, you'd think it wouldn't bother me anymore, but it does. My real father walked out on us when I was three. I haven't seen or heard from him since, and Mother refuses to talk about him. The few times I have heard her refer to the past, I've gotten the feeling their marriage was anything but a picnic. I was five when she married Robert.''

"Are you and your stepbrother close?''

"No. We never have been, either. I think mainly because he didn't like the idea of his father marrying my mother. We weren't good enough. At least, that's the feeling I always got from him.''

"Y'all want some more ice tea?''

At the high-pitched query, Jillian looked up and saw a younger, more feminine version of Jackson standing beside their table, holding a brimming pitcher of ice tea.

Jackson grinned. "Jill, this little pest is my baby sister, Treeva Lynn. Treeva, my, uh, secretary, Jillian Fletcher.''

"Nice to meet you, Treeva,'' Jillian said, smiling.

"Nice to meet you, too . . . Jill?'' Jackson's sister smiled at her, and then giggled.

Puzzled, Jackson frowned at Jillian, then transferred the look to his sister. "What's so funny?''

"Oh, nothing.'' Treeva Lynn failed to stifle her amusement.

"Come on, kid, what is it?''

"Well . . .'' Treeva Lynn blushed as she looked at Jillian, and then at her brother. "I just think it's kind of cute, that's all.''

"What, that I brought my secretary here for supper?''

"Quit teasing, Jack. You know.''

"Know what? If I knew, Treeva, I wouldn't be asking.'' To Jillian, "You're a woman, do you know what she's talking about?''

Jillian shrugged and shook her head.

"Geez, Jack.'' Treeva Lynn sighed. "You're worse than Randy, and he's a nurd. Haven't you figured it out?''

"Figured what out, Treeva? You're not telling me anything."

"Jillian Fletcher and Jackson Fury," said Treeva Lynn.

Jackson silently mouthed his sister's words, frowning. "You think it's cute that we've both got the same initials?"

"No, stupid. Jack and Jill. Good grief, don't you remember? 'Jack and Jill went up the hill to fetch a pail of water . . .'"

"Nursery rhymes." Nodding with a deadpan expression, Jackson looked at Jillian. "They're teaching nursery rhymes to high-school seniors these days."

Jillian sat quietly, unable to look at either Jackson or his sister as she felt the heat slowly suffuse her neck and face.

"See, she knows," Treeva Lynn said with a broad grin. "I think it's cute. No, more than cute even. It's romantic."

"Jack and Jill," Jackson said when Treeva Lynn had walked away, his blank expression slowly giving way to a smile. "I'll be damned. Jack and Jill. You know, it never crossed my mind."

"I don't know what you're talking about," Jillian said, gathering up her purse as she prepared to leave.

Jackson snaked a hand across the table, stopping her before she could stand. "Think about it, sweetheart. Jack and Jill. Hell, with the same last initial, you won't even have to change the monogramming on the stuff in your hope chest. Face it, Jill. We were meant to be."

Jillian jerked her arm free and stood up. "It's getting late. I'd like to go home now, Jackson."

"Jack," he said. "From now on, I think you'd better make that Jack . . . Jill."

Thirty minutes later, Jackson turned off Greenville Avenue and nosed the Pontiac down a quiet, tree-lined street toward Jillian's apartment. Except for the final leg, when necessity had forced him to ask her for specific directions, they had made the trip in silence. For reasons he didn't yet understand, his and Treeva Lynn's teasing had touched a raw nerve in Jillian.

"Which one?" he asked.

"Second house on the left," Jillian said. "Just let me out in front."

Perverse as always, however, Jackson did more than just stop in front. He pulled into the driveway of the modest thirties-era "stacked" duplex and killed the engine. Jillian hopped out of the car and rummaged through her purse for her keys as she headed for the front door. Smiling, Jackson loped along behind her.

Knowing that he had followed her, Jillian gritted her teeth as she opened the iron gate. She climbed the outer stairs to the second floor, and started to insert her key into the duplex door when his outstretched hand intercepted hers.

"You're fighting a losing battle when you try to go against fate," he said. "You'd be better off just giving in."

"That's a lot of nonsense." Refusing to look at his eyes, Jillian watched his hands unlock and open the door. "It's just a coincidence that we both have the same initials. Nothing but a coincidence. And that Jack and Jill business is a silly fluke."

"Is it?"

"Yes." Jillian brushed past him and entered her apartment. Rusty ran toward her, barking and wagging his red flag of a tail, then skidded to a stop when Jackson entered. The Irish setter gave a small, pathetic whine, tucked his tail between his legs, and slunk into the bedroom.

"Come back here, you coward," Jillian said, throwing her purse onto a chair. "You're the poorest excuse for a watchdog I've ever—" She broke off abruptly as Jackson spun her around to face him.

Before she could protest, Jackson's head swooped down and his lips claimed hers in a hard, soul-searching kiss. Her initial outrage lasted no longer than half a heartbeat. Without warning, an alien warmth invaded her body, leaving her weak and pliant to his touch.

Touch her Jackson did. He held her in the tight circle of his arms until he felt her relax, then he slowly dropped his hands to mold her hips closer to his. His hungry, wayward tongue slipped past the soft barrier of her lips and tasted her inner sweetness. God, she felt good. She made him feel even better. Perhaps better than the first time he'd kissed her.

From her hips, his hands journeyed upward along the length of her spine, his arms forcing hers up to rest around his neck. His hands now free to explore at will, he grasped her rib cage, his thumbs settling beneath the full curves of her breasts. With a slight circular motion, they grazed her hardening tips.

The sudden surge of emotion that pulsed through Jillian made her gasp softly. And then her sanity returned.

"Don't." She stumbled out of his arms and turned her back to him.

"For God's sake, Jill." Her sudden absence only served to increase Jackson's need. He moved to stand behind her and wrapped his arms around her waist. Pressing himself full-length against her, he held her close and let his lips nuzzle the soft skin of her throat. I need you. Forget all that nonsense about our names, our initials. Forget everything, but us."

"I wish I could, Jack." The raspy feel of his stubbled jaw against her neck, coupled with the heat of his breath, played havoc with her senses. "I want to, but I can't."

"Yes, you can." He cupped one hand about the swell of her breast as the other slid down to the juncture of her thighs. His loins ground hard against her buttocks, giving her proof of the swollen extent of his arousal. "You feel so good, Jill. Give us a chance."

"Jack"—Jillian swallowed hard—"I can't. Not right now."

A moment of stark silence, almost rigid stillness, and Jackson slowly dropped his hands. "Oh, it's that time of the month?"

"No, that's not it." Feeling cool air replace his warmth on her back, she turned to face him. "It's just that I—I've never been with a man."

Jackson's disappointed expression evolved gradually into one of disbelief. "What did you say?"

"I said, I've never been with a man."

"Wait a minute. You're twenty-three years old and you're telling me that you've never . . ."

She nodded her head. "That's right. Never."

"My God! You're a vir—gin?"

Jillian nodded again.

"What the hell happened?"

"Nothing happened, that's why I'm still a virgin." She broke the eye contact between them by turning toward the kitchen. What they both needed now, she decided, was something to drink. Hot coffee for him; hot tea for her. More than likely, all that caffeine would keep them awake, but it looked like it was going to be a long night anyway.

"What was the matter with all those guys in high school and college?" Jackson asked, traipsing along behind her. "Were they sick or something?"

"No, they had nothing to do with it," Jillian said, filling the tea kettle with water. "The decision to remain, uh, intact was mine."

"But why?"

"Why not?" She placed the kettle on the stove, then took two cups and saucers out of the cabinet. "Honestly, Jack, there's nothing wrong with me. I'm not terminally ill, for heaven's sake. I'm just a virgin."

"But why?" he asked again, dropping into a kitchen chair.

"Well, I guess it has a lot to do with timing. That and not finding a man I really wanted to risk making love to."

"Risk?"

"Yes, risk. Remember that big herpes scare we had a few years back?"

"Oh, yeah. Uh, good thinking. Damn!"

"So you see? You shouldn't take it so personally; it has nothing to do with you. I mean, my gosh, we've only known each other for two days. Who knows, maybe after I get to know you a little better, I'll change my mind. Then again, maybe you might decide to change yours."

"Don't count on it." Jackson propped his elbows on the table and cradled his head in his hands. "Jesus! A virgin."

"We're not the dying breed everyone believes. There are still a lot of us out there. And we're not all ugly fourth graders, either. It's just that I'm the kind of person who doesn't like taking chances."

He angled his head to one side as he looked at her. "You being a virgin I can understand, but if you expect me to be—"

"No, I don't expect anything of the kind. Your sex life doesn't bother me. For a man, that sort of thing is almost preordained. But for a woman—for me, especially, I mean—it's different. I want it to be different. Special. Not just some casual, temporary fling that, with luck, might turn out to be permanent. More than that, though, I don't think I could handle an unwanted pregnancy, or worse, God forbid, a severe social disease."

"Well, hell, if that's all that's stopping you, I can take care of it with a quick trip to the drugstore."

"No, Jack. I'm sorry. Not tonight. It's too soon."

"When, then?"

"I don't know," she said with an uneasy chuckle as she

poured boiling water into their cups. "You don't schedule a thing like this like you do a dentist appointment. When it happens—if it happens—it'll just happen."

"If it does, will you tell me?"

"If you're the one, Jack, I won't have to tell you; you'll know."

As she reached for the jar of instant coffee, he stood up and turned her around. "I know now, Jill. I'm the one."

"Jack . . ."

"Don't worry, sweetheart, I'm not gonna rush you. You take all the time you need. But for my sake, don't let it be too long. I'll probably die of pneumonia from taking cold showers."

He dropped a gentle kiss on her upturned lips and stepped back. "I'll see you in the morning."

"Don't you want your coffee?"

"No thanks, I'll take a raincheck. You'd better skip your cup of tea, too. We've got a busy day ahead of us tomorrow. Wyatt's being arraigned, remember? Depending, of course, on what the judge sets his bail at, there's a good chance he'll be getting out of jail."

# CHAPTER 9

Friday, April 25

"Sasha's, may I help you?"

"Yes," Jillian said into the receiver. "At least, I certainly hope you can." *Come on, think of something,* she told herself. "You see, I'm with Unique Interior Designs Incorporated."

"Oh?" The voice on the other end of the line, a woman's, didn't sound impressed.

"Yes, we've decorated some of the finest homes in Dallas." *Lie! God's going to get you for lying, Fletcher!* "Well, the fact of the matter is, I was in Coiffure d'Anglaise a few months ago when you delivered some flowers to Mandy. Oh, I'm sorry, I mean, the late Miss Amanda Strickland."

"Did we?"

"Yes, a beautiful arrangement of lavender roses, as I recall."

"Miss, uh, what did you say your name was?"

"Fle—uh, Flemming. Two m's. Juliette Flemming."

"Well, Miss Flemming, if you know anything about Sasha's, you know that we specialize in roses and rare exotic blooms."

The woman's haughtiness grated on Jillian's nerves. Okay, if that's the way she wanted it, Jillian could dish it out, too. "I know, dear," she said condescendingly, "that's why I thought I'd call you first. I want only the best for Monsieur de Gaulle's newly decorated penthouse."

"Who?"

"De Gaulle. You know, France? Champagne? The Eiffel Tower? Surely you've heard the name before."

"Yes, but isn't he dead?" The woman's haughtiness was definitely slipping.

"This is another Monsieur de Gaulle. I wish I could explain further, but I've been sworn to secrecy. Needless to say, there is a slight family connection. As well as a close family resemblance." Jillian chuckled. "But off the subject of noses and back to the matter of roses. The flowers you delivered to poor Mandy—I mean, Miss Strickland—what were they?"

"I'd have to check my records. Can you hold a moment, please?"

"Of course. But please, don't be too long. Monsieur's private jet is due to land at DFW within the hour, so time is of the essence."

"I understand. I'll only be a moment."

"This private investigating business is more fun than I thought it would be," Jillian said to herself, holding her hand over the receiver.

Moments later, the woman returned. "Miss Flemming, are you still there?"

"Yes, I am."

"I found the receipt, and you were right, it is a lovely arrangement. Our loveliest, as a matter of fact. A dozen sterling silver roses, interspersed with an assortment of ferns and baby's breath, and delivered in a limited edition Waterford crystal vase. Two hundred and fifty dollars, plus tax and delivery fee."

Jillian didn't know that Waterford made limited editions,

but then who was she to question an expert. " 'Sterling silver,' you said?"

"Yes."

"Mmm, let me think a moment." *Okay, dummy, now that you've got the name of the rose out of her, get the name of the guy who sent the blasted things to Amanda.* "I'll need two arrangements just like the one you've described. Only you'd better make them with two dozen roses each instead of one."

"Two dozen?"

"Yes, that's what I said."

"Oh, two dozen, all right."

"And I suppose you can just charge them, like Mandy's."

"But Miss Strickland's weren't charged. The gentleman paid for them in cash."

Damn, no receipt! Jillian thought. "Well, naturally, leave it to"—*to whom, idiot? Think of something*—"to Jon to pay cash. He's never trusted plastic."

"Who?"

"Jon. Jon Northrop. Didn't he send them to Mandy?"

"No."

"You're kidding. That sly little fox. I mean, the poor darling. Who did send them to her then?"

"Well, really, Miss Flemming, I'm not at liberty to divulge that sort of—"

"Oh, come on. I was one of Mandy's closest friends, you can tell me."

"I wish I could, but we never require names with our cash purchases."

"Not even initials?"

"No, not even that."

"Curiouser and curiouser. My, my. Now you've really got me intrigued."

"He was very handsome, if that helps."

"Were you the one who waited on him?"

"Yes, I was."

Maybe, Jillian thought, she hadn't hit a dead end after all. "Tall? Blond hair?"

"Yes."

Then it hit her. Sterling silver roses. Sterling. Oh, no! It couldn't have been him. Not Sterling Wyatt. She took a deep breath and let it out slowly. "Was his photograph in the paper recently?"

"You mean, in connection with Miss Strickland's death?"

"Yes."

"No. At least, as far as I know, it wasn't."

Relief surged through Jillian. "Then it must have been someone else, but for the life of me, I can't think who. What did he look like? Other than being tall, blond, and handsome, of course."

"He was just very nice looking; that's all I remember. And polite. Yes, extremely polite, now that I recall. He smiled a lot. Beautiful smile. Lots of pretty white teeth."

A brief pause and then, "Well, I won't keep you any longer. Thank you for your help."

"Miss Flemming, what about the roses?"

"Just charge them to my American Express Gold Card. Thanks again. 'Bye."

Jillian quickly put the receiver down and breathed a sigh of relief. A three-hundred-dollar hairdo and makeup job was one thing, but two hundred and fifty dollars worth of roses that would wilt in a couple of days was something else entirely. She wasn't that stupid. Or that rich, for that matter.

The phone ringing made her jump.

"Good grief, Fletcher, cut it out," she told herself. "It's not her calling you back. You gave her the wrong name, remember?"

After the second ring, she picked it up. "Accoun—"

Making a face as she broke off, Jillian took a deep breath and began again. "Excuse me. I mean, Fury Investigations. Miss Fletcher speaking."

Jillian heard the soft, masculine groan through the receiver. Thinking it might be an obscene caller about to go into his act, she started to hang up, but stopped when the caller finally spoke.

"My God. It's really you, isn't it? The girl with the raspberry see-through bra." The caller issued a mirthless laugh that faded into a heavy sigh. "Now that I'm actually talking to you—it's funny, I—I don't know what to say."

Even without the embarrassing reminder of her underwear, Jillian recognized his voice. She shivered as a chill crawled up her spine. "Mr. Wyatt?"

"For heaven's sake, call me Sterling. After all the trouble you've gone to for me, the least we can do is call each other by our first names. I—I honestly don't know how to thank you, Jill."

"Then don't, please. I really haven't done anything to be thanked for."

Another mirthless snort. "You wouldn't say that if you'd spent the last two nights in jail like I've just done. I didn't know what hell was like until now." He paused, then said, "Listen, this may not be the right time to bring this up, and God knows it's not half what I'd like to do for you, what you deserve, but as soon as all this horrible mess is settled and behind me, I'd like to take you to dinner. Maybe get to know you better, if you don't mind. It's the least I can do."

Jillian swallowed the knot of emotion that had risen in her throat. "You don't need to do anything, Mr. Wy—uh, Sterling. But I'd be delighted to have dinner with you."

"If it was left up to me, Miss Fletcher, and I thought there was a chance you'd accept, I'd try to give you the world on a silver platter."

After a long, slightly uncomfortable pause, Jillian asked, "When did they release you?"

"About two hours ago. I promised Fury I'd call him the minute I got out. I would have, too, but I got tied up. Meetings with my legal advisors, urgent business with my department heads—that sort of thing. Two days in jail and the whole company all but grinds to a stop. Is he in?"

"Jack? I mean, Mr. Fury? No, not at the moment."

"Well, tell him that I'm at home now. He already knows the address. Tell him that I'll be here for the rest of the day and that he can come over anytime. I've given the staff the afternoon off, so we ought to be able to talk without interruption. After being in that cramped jail cell, I'll go crazy if I don't get some privacy."

"I'll tell him."

"Miss Fletcher?"

"Yes?"

"I know this is going to sound way out of line, but"— Sterling Wyatt took a deep breath—"right now, I'd give everything I own if I could kiss you. 'Bye."

Tears burned Jillian's eyes as she cradled the receiver. She reached for a tissue, blew her nose, and was wiping the moisture from her cheeks when the door opened and Moose pulled Jackson into the loft. They had gone out for an afternoon walk, but by the looks of the sweat that poured off of them, they had ended up having a hard run instead.

Panting for breath, tongue lolling out of the side of his mouth, Jackson sank to his haunches and wrestled the leash off the Great Dane's neck. "Too bad dogs can't enter the Olympics. Old Moose here would bring home the gold for sure. Wouldn't you, girl?" Patting the dog's neck, he looked up and saw Jillian's red eyes and nose. "Hey, what's the matter?"

"Sterling Wyatt just phoned," Jillian said, sniffling. "He's out of jail."

"Well, it's about time." Jackson stood up and moved toward the stairs.

"He sounded so grateful, Jack. So happy just to be out and free again. He thanked me. He told me how much he appreciated what I'd done, and—and I really didn't do anything to be thanked for. I'm crying, and—oh, heck, I don't even know why."

Jackson had grown up with six sisters who could shed tears at the drop of a hat, but the sight of a crying woman still made him uneasy. Mainly because he didn't know what to do or say to them. "Look, I'm gonna go shower and change. I'll be down again in a minute."

"Jack?"

Halfway up the stairs he stopped and looked down over the railing at her. "Yeah?"

"He said to tell you that he was at home, and that he'd be there for the rest of the day."

"Terrific." Jackson took off again, sprinting around the next spiral.

"Can I go with you?"

Jackson didn't answer. He had already disappeared behind the glass-brick wall and hadn't heard her.

"Well, I'm going," Jillian said to Moose, pausing to blow her nose. "Whether he likes it or not."

Fifteen minutes later, his wet hair slicked smooth against his skull, Jackson descended the stairs carrying his boots in one hand and tucking his shirt into his jeans with the other. "I've lost my car keys. I couldn't find them in the pockets of my other jeans."

He dropped onto one of the sofas and started pulling on his boots. As he struggled with the second boot, the Great Dane leaped up beside him and began licking his face. "Not now, Moose, I'm in a hurry. Jill, have you seen my damn keys? I might have left them in the kitchen."

He heard a familiar jingle behind him and glanced over

his shoulder. His misplaced keys were dangling between Jillian's fingers. "Thanks, sweetheart. I don't know what I'd do without you."

Jackson stood up and clipped the leather holster onto the back of his belted waist. He checked the cylinder of the snub-nose to make sure all the chambers were filled, then slipped the gun into its holster and fastened the safety strap. He took a step toward Jillian, intending to get his keys and kiss her before he left, but she pulled her arm behind her back and angled her head out of his way.

"Not so fast, Jack."

"Oh, come on, Jill. A little kiss on the cheek isn't sexual harassment."

"I know that."

"Then what's the matter?"

"Nothing's the matter." At least not yet, she thought. "I've just decided to go with you, that's all."

"Aw, now, Jill—"

"Don't 'Aw, now, Jill' me. I'm going with you, Jack, and that's final."

"Like hell it is! I make the decisions around here, 'cause I'm the boss, remember? I'm the one with the investigator's license too, not you. Damn it, Jill, I've got business to talk over with Wyatt."

"Well, so do I."

He stared at her for a moment, his indignation slowly changing to angry comprehension. "Business, my ass! Now I know why you were crying a while ago. Lover boy's finally out of jail, and you can't wait to go running to him. That's it, isn't it?"

"No, that's not it. I've told you before, Jackson Fury, that there is nothing like that between Sterling and me. Or have you already forgotten what happened between us last night?"

"Sterling? Since when did you start calling him Sterling?"

"Since about twenty minutes ago when he told me to, that's since when."

"Bastard hasn't been out an hour yet, and he's already trying to fuck around with you."

"Watch your mouth, buster!"

"Oh, come on, Jill. You've heard it before."

"Yes, I've heard it, but that doesn't mean I have to like it."

"Never thought you were that big a prude."

"Meaning that I am something of one, I suppose?"

"Look, I'm not gonna get into an argument with you now. I don't have time."

"That's right, we don't. We have an appointment to keep with Sterling."

"For God's sake, Jill, listen to reason, will you? I don't want you to get hurt."

"Now who's being unreasonable? Sterling wouldn't hurt me. He's not that kind of man."

"I'm not talking about Wyatt. I'm talking about somebody else."

"Who?"

"How the hell should I know? I haven't solved this case yet."

"So what's your problem?"

"You are!" Jackson took a deep breath, and added, calmly, "Look, honey, as it stands now, nobody knows that you're Wyatt's alibi. But if you show up at his place with me, and somebody's watching, chances are, they're gonna figure out your part in all this.

"Anyhow, you being there won't do any good; you'll probably just get in the way. I don't know how long this meeting's gonna take. And I sure as hell don't know how Wyatt's gonna react when I tell him that his partner's been stealing him blind for the past six months. So if you think my language was bad, you might not want to be around to hear his."

"I'll take my chances," Jillian said, folding her arms defiantly across her chest. "And that crack about me being in the way is a low blow, Jack. I'm a secretary, remember? I can take notes while the two of you talk. I've already got a steno pad, pens, and a tape recorder in my purse. No matter what you say, I'm going with you." A long pause, then, "Now, do we leave, or do we stand here and waste more time arguing?"

Sterling Wyatt's house looked like something straight out of *Architectural Digest*. An acre and a half of neatly clipped green lawn led up to the front of the sprawling two-story Colonial. Azalea bushes in full bloom graced both sides of the circular driveway while fifty-foot-tall shade trees guarded the sweeping veranda with its ten Doric columns. Jillian couldn't see what lay behind the house from the drive because the house, all ten thousand or so square feet of it, stood in the way.

According to what Sterling had vaguely told Jackson, and what Jackson had casually relayed to her, the house had been in the Wyatt family for over sixty years. It was the kind of house that any domestically inclined young woman would give her eyeteeth to live in. But not Jillian. Her attempts at domestic labor went no further than keeping her small one-bedroom apartment clean. The notion of coping with a house the size of this one boggled the mind.

"I'll bet he's got at least a dozen servants inside," she said quietly. "It would take that many just to keep the windows washed."

"Nope," Jackson said, parking the Pontiac in front of the wide marble steps. "No more than three."

"How do you— Oh, Sterling must have told you."

"No, your Sterling," he said with a sneer, "didn't tell me anything. The only time we talked, we had more important things to discuss than how many people he pays to keep his house clean."

"Then how do you know he's only got three?"

"Because in the past I've had clients who lived in houses this big. I've even been inside a couple that were bigger. You can't set up a security system long distance, Jill; you have to do it right on the premises.

"Slave labor went out with the Civil War, remember. Household help these days have to make a living just like the rest of us. People with a lot of money are lucky if they can keep one or two servants hired full-time. They hire outside professional cleaners to come in and do the big jobs."

"Oh." Feeling properly put in her place, Jillian got out of the car. Heck, what did she know about the rich anyway? Ordinary people like her worked nine to five, or some other eight-hour shift. They earned a little money, tried to pay their bills on time, and either saved or spent what was left over. In her case, unfortunately, she did more of the latter and precious little of the former.

As she followed Jackson up the wide front steps, a warm breeze ruffled the ends of her curly hair and teased the hem of her full skirt. Inhaling, she caught the faint scent of roses, honeysuckle, and newly mowed grass. If freedom had an odor, it probably smelled as fresh and sweet as this did. Lord knows, she had never been inside a jail, much less confined to a tiny cell, but considering what Sterling had recently endured, and why, she knew she would never again take her freedom for granted.

Jackson rang the doorbell and they waited silently for someone to answer it.

But no one did.

He rang it a second time, waited, then turned to her. "He did say that he was gonna be here, didn't he?"

"Yes, he did. Oh, I forgot. He also said he was giving the staff the afternoon off. Something about wanting to be by himself for a few minutes before you came. He may not have heard the bell ring; why don't you knock?"

Jackson did, and under the slight pressure of his fist the door creaked open.

"Jesus," he said, feeling the hair stand up on the back of his neck. He reached behind him and took his gun out of its holster as he nudged the door with his boot. "Get back in the car, Jill."

"What do you think you're doing? You're not going to need that gun. Not with Sterling."

"Just shut up and get back in the goddamn car. Move it!"

The idiot had been in the business so long he was getting paranoid, Jillian thought as she headed down the steps. Either that, or he was trying to pull a fast one on her so he could talk to Sterling alone.

At the car, she reached for the door handle, then stopped and turned around. Jackson, she noticed, had already slipped into the house.

Who the heck did he think he was, giving her orders? Who the heck was she, obeying them like an obedient child? Well, she wasn't a child; she was a woman. She had as much right to be inside that house as he did.

Goaded by a surge of stubborn determination, Jillian stomped back up the steps.

Jackson silently crept along the upper east-wing hallway. Fighting to control his nausea, he looked into each of the rooms as he came to them. They were all empty.

When he reached the end of the corridor, he stopped to listen for a sound, any sound that would tell him of the bastard's whereabouts. In less than two minutes, the time it had taken him to get Jillian out of his hair, discover the carnage in the study, and search through the house, the murdering son of a bitch had disappeared. Of course, he could have run off before they even arrived, but—

The ear-splitting scream that suddenly echoed up the stairwell shattered the silence as well as Jackson's calm. Instinct made him drop to his knees. He swung around and aimed his gun down the long, empty hallway behind him. The screaming stopped, there was a short pause, and another scream began.

"Jesus Christ!" Jackson said, finally realizing who the screamer was. "Jesus holy Christ!"

He raced back up the hallway, then down the winding stairs, taking them two at a time. Leaping over the last four to the first floor, he made a sharp right turn and headed toward the rear of the house. At the entrance to the study he skidded to a halt.

Jillian stood in the center of the room with her fists crammed into her gaping mouth, her face drained of all its natural color. Her attention, Jackson saw, was riveted on what he himself had found within seconds of entering the house.

He went up behind her and, grabbing hold of her stiff, unyielding body, spun her around hard. "It's gonna be okay, Jill," he said, wrapping her in his arms. "Hush now, honey, it's gonna be all right." Such useless, empty words, he conceded, considering the circumstances, but what else could he say to a woman who had been scared out of her wits?

Hours passed—or perhaps only minutes; Jackson didn't know—before Jillian's screams diminished into dry, hysterical sobs. Loosening his tight hold on her, he felt his stomach churn, his entire body shake at what he was about to do. He gritted his teeth and looked up.

It was still there, God help him. And God help poor,

hard-headed Jillian, who hadn't listened to him and stayed at the car, but who had come into the house and found this grisly scene.

Blood and gray matter were splattered on the wall. Across the desk in front of it lay what was left of Sterling Wyatt. His life, like the top of his once-handsome head of blond hair, had been blown away by a single bullet from the gun on the floor.

Jackson swallowed the sickening bile that rose in his throat and averted his gaze. "Come on, Jill, we've got to get out of here."

Her head fell back jerkily and she stared at Jackson through shock-glazed eyes. "We—we can't just leave him like that." Hoarse from her screams, she winced with each word.

"We have to, honey. We're gonna walk down that hall back to the living room, and then we're gonna phone the police." As Jackson spoke in soft, soothing tones that contradicted his own shocked state, he wound an arm around Jillian's waist and led her through the doorway. "We can't stay in this room, and we can't touch anything in the rest of the house, either. Do you understand?"

With all the vague innocence of a lost child, she shook her head. "No."

"Fingerprints. Remember fingerprints, Jill?"

A frown slowly creased her forehead. Jackson saw it and knew she was fighting hard to overcome her shock.

"Oh, fingerprints," she said at length, and blinked. "Yes, fingerprints. Fingerprints that—" With a sharp gasp, she stopped and grabbed Jackson shirt. "Jack, he didn't do it!"

"I know, baby, I know. Just don't talk about it now, okay? Don't even think about it."

"Sterling wouldn't kill himself!" Jillian's breathing grew labored, more agitated. "He couldn't."

"I know, honey. I know."

"He just got out of jail this morning. I talked to him myself on the phone, remember? He sounded so happy. Jack, happy people don't commit—"

A wave of uncontrollable fear took hold of Jillian and she wrenched herself out of Jackson's arms. Her eyes widened in horror at the gun he held in his hand. "Oh, my God!"

"No! Oh, Christ no, baby, I didn't do it!" Jackson quickly got rid of the gun by throwing it ahead of them into the living room. "Stop and think, Jill. For this one time only, think back and remember what you saw when you walked into that room and found Wyatt."

Though the horrified look in her eyes remained, he could see she was remembering. "There was a gun on the floor beside the desk, wasn't there?" he prompted.

She swallowed, blinked, then began to visibly relax. "Yes. Yes, there was a gun on the floor."

"That's the gun that killed him, Jill. My gun hasn't even been fired. Someone must have dropped the other one there to make it look like suicide."

"Oh, Jack!"

"It's all right, baby. Come on." He hugged her close to him again, thankful for the added warmth of her body, but even more thankful for the fact that she no longer feared him. A few steps toward the front of the house and they entered the living room.

"I thought you had—"

"I know what you thought." He pushed her gently onto a couch. "Finding Wyatt like that, you got scared. And when you saw my gun, you naturally thought that I had done it."

"But you didn't. You couldn't do a thing like that."

Jackson reached for the phone, but stopped before he made the one mistake that no seasoned P.I. would ever make. He whipped a handkerchief out of his hip pocket and wrapped it around the receiver. Using his own pen, he punched out the police's number.

"Could you?" Jillian asked as he heard the first ring.

A bodiless voice answered and Jackson gestured with his upraised index finger for Jillian to wait a minute. "Connect me with homicide," he said, and waited until a voice in homicide answered. "Hank McPherson, please . . . Oh, sorry, Hank, I didn't recognize your voice at first . . . Yeah, tell me about it. Look, uh, you'd better get over to the Wyatt place on Lawther Drive right away . . . Uh-huh, very big trouble." He took a deep breath. "I just found his body. Or what's left of it . . . Geez, that's right; her funeral is tomorrow . . . No, not with a knife. There's a forty-four Magnum on the floor beside his desk . . . I don't know, that's your department; I'll let you guys decide . . . Don't worry, we'll be here . . . My, uh, secretary, that's who."

"Could you?" Jillian asked again when Jackson sat down beside her.

"Could I what?"

"Could you kill a person?"

"I don't know. I guess it all depends."

"Have you ever?"

"Yeah," Jackson said reluctantly. "Once. My first and only tour of duty in Vietnam."

"That's different. That was a war."

"War's no different from peacetime, Jill. Killing is still killing, no matter how you look at it. You snuff out some slime-bag's life before he can snuff out yours, and then you try to go on with business as usual. It's not easy, though, let me tell you. Hell, it ain't easy at all."

In the long silence that followed, as they waited for the police to arrive, Jackson kept his arm wrapped around Jillian. She made no attempt to fight off his intimacy, but leaned against him, unaware that she gave him great comfort.

"Who killed him, Jack?" she asked. "What slime-bag came into this house and—and snuffed out Sterling's life?"

"I don't know," Jackson said.

But he had a good idea. Northrop.

Northrop had the most to gain with Wyatt's death, and the most to cover up. Not only would he get complete control of the company he was slowly bleeding dry, but his wife, as Wyatt's only living relative, would inherit her cousin's millions. With all that money at his disposal, Northrop could get himself off the hook with the guy in Vegas.

It made sense to Jackson. But while it gave Northrop a motive for killing Wyatt, it still didn't connect him with Amanda Strickland's murder.

Or did it?

A niggling thought took root in his mind. It would have grown, if the police hadn't decided to arrive at that moment.

# CHAPTER 10

"Oh, yeah," said Detective Wilkerson, Hank's gung-ho little hot-shot partner, as he strutted into the living room, "if that ain't a suicide, I'll eat my badge."

Where Jackson hid his amusement, Jillian was not so prudent. She opened her mouth to say something, but Jackson silenced her with a pointed look and a gentle squeeze of her hand. No need to embarrass the kid; it was obvious he wasn't long out of the police academy. Then he saw Hank, the stout, balding, nineteen-year Dallas Police Department veteran, roll his eyes in exasperation.

"Hey, Hank," Jackson said, "since when did y'all start taking guys with ESP into the department?"

"Lay off, will you, Fury?" Hank said, watching his young partner wander back out into the hall. The kid tried to strike up a conversation with the two uniformed policemen who'd questioned Jackson and Jillian earlier, but he didn't succeed.

Shaking his head, Hank leaned close to Jackson. "Just between you and me," he said, "my three kids make that little jerk-off look like a mental retard. And we both know what assholes my kids are. Take some free advice from one who knows, Fury; don't ever have teenagers."

"I don't plan on it," Jackson said. "At least, not right

away. Say, you think maybe your young Sherlock there knows anything about standard police procedure in cases like this? Or is he like the rest of the department's trainees, ad-libbing as he goes along?"

"Why don't you just ignore him? I do. He's easier to take that way." Hank checked the time on his wristwatch. "Wonder what's holding up the crime-science boys? They should've been here by now."

Pausing, Hank scratched his chin as he looked at Jillian, then Jackson. "Uh, hate like hell to hafta put you two through this again, but I gotta ask y'all some more questions. For my report, you know?"

"Yeah, we know," Jackson said. "Go ahead."

Notebook in hand and Bic pen poised, Hank asked, "Which one of you found him first?"

"I did," said Jackson.

"And where was . . ."

"Jillian Fletcher. Miss Jillian Fletcher," Jackson said, looking over Hank's shoulder as the detective scribbled Jillian's name in his notebook. "No, she spells it with two *L*s and an *A* instead of an *E*. Yeah, that's right. Anyway, Jill was gonna come in with me until I knocked on the front door and it opened by itself. Suspected something might be wrong, so I told her to go back to the car and wait for me."

"Suspected?" Hank asked.

"Yeah, suspected. You've been on the force for twenty years, you know the feeling I'm talking about. Kinda light-headed, hands break out in a cold sweat, hairs standing up on the back of your neck?"

"Yeah, that feeling." Hank shuddered. "Go on. What happened then?"

"Well, I came on in the house and found Wyatt back there in the study. Couldn't find a pulse, but I knew he hadn't been dead long; he was still warm. I didn't know if he was alone here in the house, or if someone else was with him, so I searched it before I called you guys."

"You run across anybody?"

"No."

"Did you disturb anything?"

"Come on, Hank, you know me better than that. If you find my prints on anything, they may be on a couple of doorknobs upstairs, but that's all."

"What about you, Miss Fletcher?"

"No." Jillian shook her head and wrapped her arms tightly across her waist as if she were cold. "No, I'm sure I didn't touch anything either."

"Look, it's gonna be all right, Miss," Hank said comfortingly. "I know this hasn't been easy for you, finding a dead man the way you did, but try and relax, okay? What was your relation to the deceased?"

"Relation? We aren't—I mean, we weren't related at all."

"No, what I meant was, why are you here?"

"Oh. We came to see him," Jillian said, "to talk to him. He just got out of jail a few hours ago."

"Wyatt was my client," Jackson said.

"No kidding," said Hank. "Since when did you start working for Collins?"

"Never. This was what you might call a one-time-only deal. I had some infor—something I thought Wyatt and Collins—I thought the two of them might be interested in something I knew." Jackson realized he was doing a lousy job of being evasive."

"With regards to what?" Hank asked.

"With regards to the Amanda Strickland murder."

"Information, I think you started to say." Hank nodded slowly. "Withholding evidence in a murder case is a criminal offense. You know that, don't you, Fury?"

"Evidence, yeah, but speculation, no way, Hank."

"Speculation!" Jillian said, unaware that Hank's partner had reentered the room.

"Hey, you know something you're keeping from us, lady?"

"Wilkerson, if you don't mind, I'll ask the questions here. You just keep your mouth shut, okay?" Under his breath he muttered, "Never know, you just might learn something."

"But, Lieutenant—"

"Look, I got an idea. Why don't you go outside on the porch and wait for the crime-science boys to get here? Or better still, go stand watch over the corpse. You never know, somebody just might try and run off with some evidence."

"Yeah, they might. Okay, Lieutenant."

"See what I mean?" Hank said as soon as Wilkerson had gone. "Kid's a grade-A asshole. Probably work his way up to captain, if he's not careful. Now, where were we?" Hank peered through his half-moon bifocals for a time, studying his notes.

"Hey, Lieutenant!" Wilkerson called out.

"Dammit!" Hank mumbled, then yelled over his shoulder, "What do you want?"

"Come here a sec!"

"Jesus. If that stiff's got up and walked off, I'm retiring from the force right now. And to hell with my twenty-year pension."

Hank's departure coincided with the arrival of the county medical examiner's investigator, a dapper little man sporting a bow tie, wire-framed glasses, and a vague what-am-I-doing-here? expression. Jackson thought the man looked like a confused Wallace Shawn.

The patrolman stationed at the front door aimed Wally in

the direction of the study. No sooner had the policeman closed the door than he had to open it again. Two plainclothesmen entered, each carrying a heavy-looking case. They, like Wally, ambled down the hall toward the study.

"What was all that 'speculation' nonsense about?" Jillian asked tersely. They were alone in the living room, but she had the sense to keep her voice down. "We weren't speculating. We had positive proof that Sterling didn't kill Amanda. Me!"

"Yeah, but remember what the man just said, sweetheart. Withholding evidence in a murder case is a criminal offense."

"If you're so afraid of going to jail, why didn't you let me go to the police like I wanted to in the first place?"

"Because, it would've been the dumbest thing you could've done! Look, I didn't tell you before, because I didn't think you needed to know, but the day I met with Collins and Wyatt, Collins suggested, and I agreed, that we'd be better off keeping you, as Wyatt's alibi, to ourselves. That way, the D.A. wouldn't know anything about you until the trial."

"The trial?"

"Yeah, the trial. There would've been one, believe me. At that point, Collins was gonna spring you as the defense's surprise witness."

"Jack, there wouldn't have had to be a trial if I'd been allowed to go to the police."

"Right. I agree. You're one hundred percent on the money. With this maniac on the loose, running around killing people, there's a good chance you would've ended up dead like Wyatt."

"What?"

"Fod God's sake, Jill, wake up. The guy's not kidding

around. He means business. He's already killed twice; first Amanda, and now Wyatt. We don't know what the hell he's gonna do next. But if he should decide to kill again, I'm not gonna let you be victim number three.''

"Will wonders never cease," Hank said as he came back into the living room. Guiltily, both Jackson and Jillian swung around to face him. "My personal little pain in the ass? He might be of some use to the department after all."

"What'd he do?" Jackson asked.

"You won't believe it."

"Try me," Jackson said.

"He found something both of us overlooked."

"What's that?"

"The deceased has a faint red mark on the back of his neck."

Jackson narrowed his eyes thoughtfully. "You figuring he took a direct hit on his cranial nerves?"

"That's what it looks like. 'Course, we won't know for sure until the medical examiner does the autopsy. Could be the chair he's sitting in caused it. It's got kind of a high back."

"But you don't think that's what did it" said Jackson.

"Nope, I sure don't," said Hank. "Listen, you two knew Wyatt. Do you know if he had any enemies?"

"I didn't know him at all," Jackson said. "The first and only time I ever met him, he was with his attorney, and Collins did most of the talking. What does Wal—I mean, the medical examiner think? Is it suicide? Or is he saying yet?"

"Who knows with that guy?" Hank said. "You never can get anything out of him. The other investigators are pretty straightforward. But this turkey's right out of the Twilight Zone. Every murder case he's assigned to, he stumbles around like he's spaced out on ozone or something, but the minute you get him on the stand at a coroner's inquest, he becomes an entirely different person. Man can spit out facts faster than a computer. And the weird thing is that he's never wrong. Every case he's ever investigated, we've always nailed the right guy.

"Whoa! Hold the phone," Hank said suddenly. "I just thought of something."

"What?" asked Jackson.

"Now that Wyatt's dead and out of the picture, the D.A.'s got no one to prosecute. With no one to prosecute, he's gonna have to shut down the Strickland investigation. Whatcha wanna bet it winds up in the unsolved file by the end of the day?"

"They can't do that!" Jillian said. "They can't just forget about it."

"Not much else they can do, Miss" Hank said. "Wyatt was the D.A.'s prime suspect. His only suspect, as a matter of fact. The D.A.'s good, one of the best, but ain't no way he can prosecute a corpse."

"He might not be able to prosecute a corpse," Jillian said later as she and Jackson drove through late-afternoon traffic to the West End, "but he could at least try to clear him."

"And make a lot of the taxpayers mad by wasting their money? Come on, Jill. If the D.A. did that, he wouldn't be able to get himself elected dogcatcher."

"But it's not fair, Jack. They've charged an innocent man with a crime that he didn't commit. Now that he's dead, the least they can do is—is uncharge him."

"Acquit."

"What?"

"They don't uncharge him, Jill, they acquit him. Either that, or they drop the charges altogether if they find evidence pointing to somebody else. Haven't you ever watched *Perry Mason*?"

"No, it comes on too late at night, and stop trying to change the subject. Can't you see the point I'm trying to make?"

"Yeah, I can see," he said, and thought, Kind of. I think.

"I don't know who's the worst," Jillian said, "the judicial system or the newspapers. They say something wrong or harmful about a person on the front page, and if they ever have to print a retraction, they take the coward's way out and stick it in next to the classifieds. How many times have you seen a judge, or a district attorney, or somebody important like that come on TV and admit that he's made a mistake and then apologize to the person he's harmed? Never, I'll bet."

"No, there was one," Jackson said. "Remember not too long ago, that young black guy who was found guilty for— was it armed robbery and murder, or just armed robbery? I forget which exactly. Anyway, he served time in prison before they found out he was innocent. When he was released, they came out and made a public apology to him."

"That's right. I'd forgotten about— No, wait a minute! He was released, all right, but only after one of those TV in-depth news shows did an exposé on what had happened to him. The idiots who put him in prison in the first place never did apologize. And that's precisely the thing I'm talking about, Jack. When the D.A., or whoever, finds out that Wyatt is innocent, they'll be so closemouthed about it that the rest of the country will still believe he's guilty."

"What do you want me to do, Jill? Say it's unfair? Okay, it is. It's very unfair. But then so are a lot of other little injustices in life. Not much we can do about it, except maybe learn to live with it."

A terrific philosophy to share with someone so young and idealistic, Jackson thought. The pacifists of the world really ought to be proud of him. Too bad it was mostly bullshit. If he told Jillian what he really thought, what he intended doing to set the matter straight, she might get so worked up that he never would be able to calm her down.

Deep in his gut, he had the feeling that Northrop was the link between Amanda and Wyatt. Come hell or high water, he was going to prove it, too.

# CHAPTER 11

Saturday, April 26

"This is the finest vault we carry," said the assistant
funeral director in a soft, somber voice. In his late twenties,
he stood a couple of inches shorter than Jackson, but his
dark hair, beaklike nose, and gray eyes bore the distinct
Fury trademark. "It's guaranteed to protect your loved one
against moisture and vermin invasion for the generations he
or she is interred."

"You mean worms and termites, don't you, Frank?"

"Come on, Jack, cool it, will ya?" His somber voice,
like his consoling attitude, disappeared. "If the old man
hears us, he'll have my ass. I'm supposed to be giving you,
the bereaved, my best sales pitch. God knows this job ain't
much to brag about, but it's the only one I got."

"But an undertaker. Why, Frank?"

"I gotta eat, don't I? And it's mortician, not undertaker.
Undertakers went out with the horse and buggy. It's not so
bad. Once you get used to the smell. And the cold skin."

"Jesus, Frank, you're making my skin crawl. Momma
always said Aunt Lou-Lou married into a weird family, but
working with stiffs is downright creepy."

"They don't talk back to you. And you wouldn't believe
the turnover we get. Haven't had a dissatisfied customer
yet."

"Look, I gotta get out of here before I get sick and throw up," Jackson said. "How long you get before you can take a coffee break?"

" 'Bout fifteen minutes. We're kinda busy this morning, what with the Cranshaw funeral at ten, and the Strickland one at two-thirty. Word is, both of them's gonna be packed. You want me to meet you someplace later, or have something delivered here?"

"Are you kidding? Y'all actually eat in this place?"

"Yeah, we got a little kitchen upstairs right next to the embalming room where—"

"Never mind," Jackson said with a shudder, "I don't want to hear about it. I'll meet you across the— No, down the street. Way down the street at the Down-Home Cookin' place."

"Okay."

Jackson was never so glad to get outside in his life. Breathing diesel fumes was a helluva lot better on the lungs than formaldehyde, or whatever they used these days. An undertaker, for crissakes. The kid used to be normal, and now he was an undertaker.

He nosed the Pontiac out of the funeral-home parking lot and into the heavy traffic along Hillcrest Boulevard. Two red lights later, he saw the restaurant sign.

What the hell had happened to all the zoning laws? Jackson wondered. Right in the backyard of North Dallas's most exclusive neighborhoods they go and stick a damn funeral home. The homeowners nearby probably had nightmares regularly of mass resurrections. God knows, he would. The rich died just like the poor did, he decided as he parked the car in a slot next to the restaurant. Only thing was, the rich got sent off in a little better style.

"What's up?" Frank asked sometime later when he joined Jackson in a secluded back booth. "I figure something's gotta be wrong, or you wouldn't come see me at work."

"I need you to do me a favor."

"You're kidding."

"No, I'm dead serious. Pardon the pun."

"You want *me* to do you a favor?"

"Mmm-hmm."

A waitress hurried over to their booth. She smiled at Jackson as she placed a cup and saucer in front of Frank, filled it with coffee, and refilled Jackson's cup. "Would y'all like something to eat, or are you just having coffee this morning?"

"I could do with a couple of cinnamon rolls, if they're fresh," Jackson said.

"They're better than fresh," said the waitress. "We took them right out of the oven just a minute ago." Her sunny disposition faded as she turned to Frank. "And how about you?"

"Yeah, cinnamon rolls sound good," he said, not noticing how she wrinkled her nose. "I'll have two. Better bring us some more cream when you come back."

As the waitress hurried off, Frank turned to Jackson. "What kind of favor you got in mind, Cousin?"

"You said you were having Strickland's funeral today, right?"

"Yeah. Let me tell you something—that's one corpse I'll be happy to see the last of. You wouldn't believe all the work they had to do on her."

"I don't need to know all the gory details."

"What's someone like Strickland got to do with you?"

"I'd rather not answer that, if you don't mind. Client confidentiality."

"Whoa! Strickland was your client? Geez, you sure have come up in the world, Jack."

"No, she wasn't my client. Somebody else was. Somebody very close to Amanda Strickland."

Frank's eyes took on a speculative look. "His name wouldn't by any chance be Wyatt, would it?"

"How the hell did you know that?"

"Didn't. Just a good guess. We got a call from some woman by the name of Northrop this morning. Said she was his cousin. Said she wanted us to pick up his body and prepare it for burial."

"No kidding?"

"No, no kidding. I had to tell her we couldn't touch her cousin 'til the county medical examiner had released his remains. That won't be for another day or two, when he's through doing the autopsy."

"Talk about luck of the Irish," Jackson muttered.

"Irish? I thought Momma once said she and Uncle T. J. were part French."

"They are, but all that's beside the point. Look, the favor I need from you . . ."

"Yeah?"

"Don't you guys supply guest books, or something like that, at your funerals? You know, something kinda like the book everybody signed at Grandma's funeral."

"Yeah."

"Is the Strickland woman getting one?"

"You bet. Top of the line. Leather bound, parchment pages edged in fourteen-karat gold leaf. I helped her great aunt pick it out. You wouldn't believe that old woman, Jack. Ninety, if she's a day. Over eighty degrees outside and she pulls up in this shiny black stretch limo and steps out, blue hair and all, wearing a full-length mink coat. Had diamond rings on her fingers the size of hen's eggs. Only the best for her little Mandy, she says, and writes us out a check for twenty-five thousand dollars."

"The cost of dying these days is expensive, huh?" said Jackson.

"Yeah, but the boss is making money a killing." Frank snickered, then sobered at Jackson's bland expression. "Sorry. Just a little inside joke."

"Little's right."

"Look, the work sure beats the shit out of digging ditches."

Their conversation lagged again as the waitress arrived, all smiles for Jackson, with their orders. The two enormous cinnamon rolls, covered in a thick sugar glaze and topped with melting butter, overflowed both plates she placed in front of them. She refilled their coffee cups, placed a fresh pitcher of cream on the table, then wandered off again.

"Back to the book," Jackson said, after he had consumed one of the rolls in three bites. "I need to see who signs it."

"Is that the favor?"

"Yeah. You think you can do it?"

Frank shrugged. "I dunno. Guess I could try. You gotta understand something up front, though—I can't let you have the original. That's gotta go to the family. Best I can do is maybe Xerox some of the pages."

"Not just some, Frank. I gotta have all the pages. All those that are filled, or even partially filled."

"Mind if I ask why?"

"No. Don't mind at all."

A long pause, then Frank said, "I get it. You're not saying."

"Yeah, sorry. To tell you the truth, at this point I don't even know if I'm barking up the right tree. It's just a hunch I got, and a slim one at that. I don't even know if it's gonna pan out. But while we're on the subject—seeing as how you're handling Wyatt's funeral . . ."

"Don't tell me, let me guess. You want me to Xerox his book too, right?"

"Yeah, it sure would be a big help."

Frank thought about it for a moment, then released a long breath. "What the hell. The worst that can happen is the boss'll catch me and fire me. Don't want to, but I guess I could always go back to digging ditches. Okay."

"Thanks, Frank. I owe you one. If there's ever—"

"There is, now that you mention it," Frank said, a sly look darting across his eyes.

"What? Just name it, it's yours."

"Your big-screen TV."

"My TV? Hell, Frank. I know we used to share a lot of stuff when we were kids, but that's kinda steep, isn't it? A four-thousand-dollar piece of high-tech equipment just for Xeroxing some pages out of a couple of books?"

"No, Jack. I don't want the damn set to keep. I just want to watch it."

"Oh! Why didn't you say so in the first place?"

"For every single one of the N.B.A. playoff games," Frank added. "And you furnish the beer and sandwiches."

Jackson laughed. "Hell, Cousin, you got yourself a deal."


"Gosh, Gran, I don't know. I'm kind of busy this weekend. Don't you have a bridge-club meeting or something?" With the receiver wedged between her shoulder and chin, Jillian pulled her black pantyhose over each leg and then up to her hips.

"We're not talking about me, Jill; we're talking about you. It's been over two months since they last saw you."

"I know."

"Your mother and Robert worry about you."

"I know, Gran."

"I worry about you too, for that matter. In my opinion, you're too young to be living alone in that apartment—even if that neighborhood is supposed to be one of the safest in Dallas."

"It is, Gran, really. We've never even had a hint of a break-in. I guess one look at Vinnie gives all the would-be burglars and rapists second thoughts. Besides, it's nice and quiet here, and close to work."

"Well, I still think you'd be better off living at home with your mother and Robert."

"Gran, how many times have we been through all this before? You know darn good and well that if I lived with them, it would take me over an hour to drive to work. Going home in the afternoon would be a lot worse. Geez, I'd have to battle all that traffic on Central Expressway, and then fight for a parking place near the courthouse."

"The courthouse? But that's at the west end of town. I thought you worked at the east end."

Jillian grimaced, realizing too late that she hadn't yet told her grandmother or mother that she'd changed jobs. "I did," she said.

"Did? Jillian, are you telling me you got fired again?"

"Well . . . sort of. But there's nothing for you to get upset about. I found another job the very next day. And I like this one a lot better. Believe me, Gran, it's terrific."

"Mmm-hmm."

"No, really, it is! The next time you or Mother are in town, you'll have to stop by and see me at the off—uh, that is, if you call me first, I'll meet y'all somewhere for lunch."

"Jillian, just what is it you're doing now anyway?"

"I—I'm getting dressed to go out."

"That's not what I mean, and you know it. What kind of job do you have now?"

"I'm doing a little of this, a little of that. I'm sort of a, uh, Jill of all trades," she said with a half-hearted giggle.

"What, exactly, does that mean?"

"All right, Gran. If you must know, I'm a secretary-bookkeeper for a one-man business."

"And just who is this one man you're working for?"

"His name is Jackson Fury."

"What does he do?"

"He sort of handles private security matters."

"Which means?"

Jillian couldn't see any way out of it; she would have to tell her grandmother the truth. "He's a private investigator."

The silence at the other end of the line had Jillian reaching for a chair. What had she done now? Sent Gran into a state of shock? Caused the poor old dear to have a heart attack?

"Gran?" she asked cautiously. "Are you still there?"

"Yes, Jill, I'm still here. Did you say a private investigator?"

"Yes."

"Like *Cannon* and *Barnaby Jones*?"

"No, more like *Magnum* and *Moonlighting*."

"Oh! Well, that's nice. Tell me, dear, is he nice-looking and single?"

"Yes, he is."

"Just how old is your—what did you say his name was again?"

"Fury. Jackson Fury."

"Jackson Fury." Her grandmother made the slow pronunciation sound like a sensual caress. Her grandmother read a lot of romance novels. Tons of them, in fact. Her mother and Robert often complained about how Gran had transformed her house into one of the biggest fire hazards they had ever seen. If spontaneous combustion ever occurred, the insurance company would be out a small fortune just in paperback replacement alone.

"Jackson Fury," her grandmother said again. "You

know, the more I think about it, the more I like the sound of that name, Jill. I get this very clear image of someone who's tall, dark, very good-looking, with lots of rippling muscles, and, mmm-mmm, broad shoulders."

"Gran, are Mother and Robert where they can hear you now?"

"No, dear. I may be over sixty, and on my way to senility, but I'm not stupid. Whenever I daydream, I make sure I'm alone. So, tell me—what day next week do you want me to meet you for lunch? Your mother's tied up all day Monday, thank God, but I'm free. I can be there at eight, or seven-thirty even."

"Gran, that's not lunch, that's breakfast. Since when have you become such a dirty old woman?"

"Well, why not? You haven't made me a great-grand-mother yet. And from the looks of it, you're not going to make me a grandmother-in-law anytime soon, either. I have to do something to occupy my idle time."

If her grandmother was so desperate for something to do, she should concentrate on nagging Bobby, Jillian thought. Her stepbrother was no closer to the altar than she was, but that obviously didn't worry Gran.

"I'm afraid next week is out, Gran. We're sort of involved with a very important case."

"We?"

"Yes, we! I'm helping."

Her grandmother's laughter made Jillian bare her teeth in an angry grimace. "Jillian, you don't know the first thing about private investigating."

"You wanna bet?"

A slight pause, and then, "Jillian?"

"Oh, my gosh, look at the time. I hate to be rude, Gran, but I've got to go now."

"Don't you dare hang up on me, Jillian Kathleen

Fletcher! I'm your grandmother, remember?" Another pause. "Jillian?"

"Yes, Gran?"

"What did you mean by that 'we' business? Just exactly what are you and this Jackson Fury person doing?"

Jillian exhaled on a long sigh. "Well, if you must know, we're working on a murder case together."

"Oh, my God."

"Now, don't get upset. Remember your blood pressure. I'm not in any danger."

"My blood pressure be damned!"

"Gran, listen to me. I said I'm not in any danger. They don't know I'm involved. Heck, they don't even know I exist. If anyone's risking his neck, it's Jack."

"Jack? You call him Jack, not Mister Fury?"

"Well, I sort of fell into the habit when his sister pointed out the fact that we were Jack and Jill the night I met his family."

"Let me see if I've got this straight," her grandmother said in a terse, clipped tone. "You've actually gone so far as to meet his family? This man—this oversexed hunk of a private eye you just started working for—has taken you to meet his family, and you haven't had the decency to even introduce him to me and your mother and Robert first?"

"It wasn't like that, Gran. His parents own a nice little restaurant out in Mesquite, and we decided to eat dinner there one night. I didn't even know where we were going until we got there, for Pete's sake. I probably said about a dozen words to his father, and I never did get to meet his mother because she was busy working in the kitchen with his brothers and sisters. Jack did not take me there to get his family's approval, I swear he didn't."

"Oh, no?"

"No! Gran, you know I wouldn't do a thing like that to you and Mother and Robert."

"Well, damn! I was working up a good mad for nothing then, wasn't I?"

"Yes, you sure were. Now aren't you ashamed of—" The time on the bedside alarm clock caught her eye, and she gasped. "Oh, my gosh! It's almost one-thirty, the funeral starts at two, and I'm not even dressed yet. I really do have to go now, Gran."

"Funeral? Did you say funeral? What funeral, Jillian? Who died?"

"I haven't got time to tell you right now. We'll talk again later, okay? Kiss Mother and Robert for me. 'Bye, Gran." Jillian slammed the receiver down before her grandmother could say another word.

She didn't know which was worse, parents or grand-parents. Stepping into her black satin and lace teddy, then reaching for her pencil-slim black skirt, she realized that both could make you feel guiltier than sin when there was absolutely nothing to feel guilty about. It probably had something to do with hormones. Hormones, that was it. They lay dormant until the birth process triggered them off, then they went haywire on you as you got older. That sounded logical. But she didn't have time to think about hormones now; she had to finish getting dressed.

Thirty minutes later, Jillian sat behind the wheel of her pride and joy, a bright red Mustang GT, as she zipped in and out of the heavy traffic that clogged North Central Express-way. Even on Saturdays it was bumper-to-bumper. She hoped that one of these days the powers-that-be at city hall, or wherever, would get their act together and finally do something about this mess. So far, their great plans to solve the traffic problem along Central had only made the traffic worse.

Seeing the Walnut Hill Lane exit sign loom up ahead, she whipped the Mustang into the right-hand lane, her bumper coming within inches of a big diesel rig. The rig's driver

sent her a long, angry blast from his horn a split second
before she heard him slam on the brakes. Glancing up at her
rearview mirror, she saw the diesel jump onto the curb and
bounce back down in the lane again. Then a familiar-
looking beat-up burgundy Pontiac whipped into sight and
the diesel was forced to swerve again.

"Damn," Jillian said, speeding down the exit ramp and
slowing to a stop behind the line of cars that were waiting
for the light to change. She glanced up into the mirror and
saw that Jackson was three cars behind her. "Damn!" He
was either following her or going to Amanda's funeral too.

No, he couldn't be following her, she decided. He didn't
know that she owned a car. He couldn't have recognized
her, either, because all of the Mustang's windows were
covered with a dark transparent film to keep out the hot
Texas sun.

The light changed, and following the cars ahead of her,
she turned left onto Walnut Hill. Two red lights later, and
over a dozen glances up at the mirror, she pulled into the
church parking lot. An attendant waved her in the direction
of another attendant who, in turn, directed her down a row
of expensive, late-model cars. She pulled into an empty
space next to a sleek Lamborghini and, not wanting to wait
around and see who parked next to her, grabbed her clutch
purse and got out of the car. Just as she closed her door, the
Pontiac's loud dual exhausts announced Jackson's arrival.

Might as well stay here and face the music now, Jillian
thought. With so many strangers around, he wouldn't dare
lose his temper and yell at her. She flattened herself against
the Mustang's door as he pulled into the space beside her.

"What the hell are you doing here?" Jackson asked,
getting out of the Pontiac and slamming the door. "And
where the hell did you get that?"

"Where did I . . . get what?" Jillian's voice faltered at
the sight of Jackson, who was dressed like a G. Q. fashion

layout in a three-piece black suit, striped tie, and—black boots? The man was at a funeral, for heaven's sake, not a cattle auction. Didn't he have any other kind of shoes to wear besides joggers or boots?

"That," Jackson said, pointing at the Mustang. "Where'd you get it?"

"My car? At a Ford dealership over on—"

"Wait a minute. This is your car? I thought you told me you didn't drive."

"I did. And I don't. At least, not to work. Do you know what this car would look like if I let a bunch of sick-o parking attendants get their hands on it? In a month it would look as bad as your car does now."

"Hey, don't go bad-mouthing my car. There's nothing wrong with it. It gets where I want to go."

"So does a bus. That's why I ride one to work every day. They're cheaper and a lot more convenient. Everywhere else I go, I drive."

"Is that what you call it? Driving? Honey, whoever taught you must have been a World War Two kamikaze pilot. That's the worst example of driving I've ever seen." Jackson took hold of her arm and propelled her gently toward the church. "You damn near made that eighteen-wheeler turn over back there on Central."

"Did I?" she asked innocently. "Gosh, it must have slipped my mind during the excitement of watching *you* almost make him turn over. Look, Jack, let's not argue, okay? We're at a funeral. Why don't we try and conduct ourselves like mourners, and not bicker like—like . . ."

"A couple of old married folks?"

"That's not exactly the analogy I had in mind, but I suppose it'll do."

"Fits better'n anything I can think of. You know, it's funny."

"What is, the funeral?"

"No, us. We've been striking sparks ever since we first met."

"So I've noticed," Jillian said quietly. "But that doesn't mean I have to like it."

"Nothing there to like, Jill. You just gotta learn to accept it."

As they approached the steps to the church, weaving through other mourners headed in the same direction, Jackson leaned his head close to Jillian's. "I guess it's too late to get you to back out now and not go through with this," he whispered.

"Yes, it certainly is. I've got as much right to be here as you do."

"Okay, have it your way. But do me a small favor, would you?"

"It all depends on what the favor is."

"Once we get inside, keep your mouth shut and your eyes open."

"Believe me, I'd planned to."

"And your ears."

"My ears?"

"Yeah. I don't know how many funerals you've been to, but at times like this, people are under a lot of stress. Once the tears start, they tend to lose all control. Things they've kept bottled up inside them for years just come spilling out without them knowing it. So keep your pretty little ears open and try to remember everything you hear, okay?"

"All right, I'll try."

Upon entering the crowded vestibule, Jillian noted the two doorways that led into the sanctuary. She began to gravitate toward the one on the right, but stopped when she sensed Jackson's absence. A look over her shoulder told her that he was gravitating to the doorway on the left.

"Psst, Jack!" she called. "Where are you going?"

Turning, Jackson faced an affluent, middle-aged couple

who, by the looks on their faces, had obviously heard Jillian. "Gotta be real careful which stranger you talk to in parking lots these days," he said with a solemn, apologetic smile. "One hello, and now she thinks she owns me."

As the couple exchanged slightly apprehensive glances and hurried on past him, Jackson moved to Jillian's side.

"Look, would you try and keep your voice down? This is a high-class funeral, not some East Texas hog-calling contest."

"It's not a drag race, either. But then I don't suppose you realize that that car of yours looks like a teenager's dream of heaven on wheels. Honestly, Jack, you should have seen the way people stared at you and your souped-up hot rod. It was . . . embarrassing. Nobody in this part of town drives a car like that."

"Yeah, well, I was kinda tied up this morning. I didn't have time to go back to the warehouse for my Rolls."

His deadpan expression, coupled with the bland tone of his voice, made Jillian wonder if he really did own a Rolls. No, she decided with a brisk shake of her head. Now was neither the time nor the place to ask him. "Just where were you going anyway? I thought we were going to sit together."

"Nope. This is where you and I part company for a while, sweetheart." Jackson saw the uncertainty appear in hr blue eyes, and had to resist the urge to touch her cheek. One touch, he knew, wouldn't be enough. "You're the one who wanted to come, remember."

"I know, but—"

"Don't worry; I won't be far away."

"But why couldn't we—"

"Because we can cover twice as much territory sitting apart, that's why. I'll meet you back at the cars after the service is over. If you happen to get there first, wait for me."

"Jack? Are we going to the cemetery, too?"

"Yeah, 'fraid we have to, honey. We gotta see this thing through to the very end. And that won't be till after they've planted poor old Amanda."

A cold finger of dread crawled up Jillian's spine as she watched Jackson walk away. "Planted poor old Amanda" was a terribly crude way of putting it, she thought as she entered the sanctuary. Crude, but accurate.

Two pews from the back, she sat down next to an elderly white-haired lady. Following Jackson's instructions, she furtively began to observe the other mourners around her. What good this would do, she didn't know. From what she could see, not one person looked even remotely suspicious or out of place, and no one was talking either.

The somber organ music began to play; an old Protestant favorite that reminded Jillian of her grandfather's funeral. Why did they always have to play such sad music at these affairs? It certainly didn't help ease the pain of loss. If anything, it only made matters worse. For everyone, she conceded, feeling tears sting her eyes.

She sniffed and tried to hold back the knot of emotion rising in her throat. It didn't work; the melancholy music was definitely getting to her. Realizing that if she didn't do something, she would soon disgrace herself over a total stranger, she opened her purse and dug around inside it for a tissue. None were there. Damn, she must have forgotten her Kleenexes when she changed purses that morning.

Not wanting anyone to witness her silly weakness, Jillian kept her watery gaze focused on her lap. A movement beside her, a glance out the corner of her eye, and she watched a pair of dark-suited legs settle down next to her. Oh, no. Now sandwiched between an old woman and a man, she couldn't get up and leave. This funeral business was turning out to be the absolute pits, she decided with another sniffle.

She tried harder to get a grip on herself, but the somber music made it impossible. More tears threatened and after a few more sniffles she knew she was going to lose the battle with her control. She started to wipe her cheeks again, but instead of touching her face, she encountered a large masculine hand holding a handkerchief.

Glancing up at the man, Jillian accepted his handkerchief with a grateful "Thank you." In an instant, the shock of recognition slammed through her, obliterating her tears. Good Lord! Garner Taggart, the president of the company she'd worked for and been fired from just five days ago, was sitting right next to her.

Aware of Taggart's slow double take, Jillian turned her attention on the pulpit. The last person she ever expected to see, let alone sit beside, at this funeral was Mr. Taggart. From the look she'd seen on his face, it was obvious that he was just as surprised to see her, one of his ex-employees. With over six hundred people on his payroll, maybe he didn't yet know she'd been fired.

Suddenly it hit her. Garner Taggart was here at Amanda Strickland's funeral. Why? What the heck for? Surely he hadn't been one of Amanda's lovers.

*Get serious, Fletcher,* Jillian told herself as she drove home from the cemetery hours later. Yes, Amanda had been promiscuous, but that didn't mean she had slept with every man who had attended the funeral. Good gracious, she would have had to be superwoman to do that. No, chances were, Taggart had been there for no other reason than to pay his last respects to a socially prominent young woman. Perhaps even to gain some extra brownie points with Dallas's upper crust. After all, hadn't she seen city council members, a couple of congressmen, and even the mayor among the attendees? What better place to make future business contacts?

The thought of her close call with emotional disaster

made her shudder with embarrassment. The way she'd carried on, Mr. Taggart probably thought she was one of Amanda's oldest and dearest friends. Heaven knows, she hadn't intended to lose control, but being an emotional person to begin with, she just hadn't been able to stop herself.

"Lord!" Jillian groaned. "If I was that bad at Amanda's funeral, I'll probably be a nervous wreck at Sterling's."

# CHAPTER 12

Monday, April 28

Jackson followed the uniformed maid down the hall of the Northrop's stately Willow Bend home. Nice place, he thought. Nice neighborhood, too. No cars parked on the street. No kids running around, screaming at each other. Real convenient to shopping centers, schools, and the Willow Bend Polo Club. Too bad he wasn't into horses or houses with eight-million-dollar price tags.

The maid stopped at an opened door and gestured for him to enter the room. He did, and saw Cherise Northrop standing before a wall of windows, gazing out at the pool and tennis court in the distance. Sizing her up, he decided she was in the mid- to late-thirties range and looked like a fashion model who'd just stepped out of an advertisement for a jewelry store specializing in big diamonds and eighteen-karat gold. Her outfit hadn't come from J. C. Penney's either. Not bad-looking, though. Not bad-looking at all. Nice blond hair, a health-club-firm body, but if he wasn't mistaken, she had slightly bowed legs. Well, hell, living here at Willow Bend, she probably owned and trained her own string of polo ponies.

Cherise turned to face him just as a ray of morning sunlight streamed through the window behind her. He saw the tiny wrinkles form at the outer corners of her eyes and knew she wasn't overjoyed to have him here in her house. She managed to look down her nose at him, even though he towered over her by a good twelve inches.

Time to break the silence, he thought, and stepped toward her, extending his right hand. "I'm Jackson Fury, Mrs. Northrop."

Cherise looked down at Jackson's hand, then up at him. She gave him a disdainful blink, then drifted past him toward the wet bar that ran the full length of the opposite wall. "I don't know why I agreed to let you come here this morning. I can assure you that if Walter hadn't phoned me you wouldn't have made it past the front door."

"Nice to meet you too, ma'am."

"Please don't, Mr. Fury. I'm in no mood for any form of humorous sarcasm. Just what is it you want from me? I've already spoken with the police and told them all I know."

"I'm aware of that, Mrs. Northrop. Believe me, I wouldn't be bothering you at a time like this if I didn't think it was necessary. I was working for your cousin before he died."

"You worked for Sterling," she repeated with boredom.

"Yes, ma'am."

"That in itself doesn't tell me a thing," she said, splashing Perrier into a glass of ice. "A lot of people worked for him."

Jackson frowned. "Just what did Walter Collins tell you when he phoned?"

"I really couldn't say, to tell you the truth. I've learned over the years that most lawyers, Walter included, have the art of double-talking down to a science. Now would you please tell me what you want? I've got an important appointment in about an hour."

Jackson thought he could understand why her husband slept around. Cherise Northrop might look like a woman on the surface, but beneath her designer underwear, he suspected she was better hung than a seed bull.

"Okay," he said, "if it's business you want, it's business you'll get. I'm here to ask you to help me clear Sterling of Amanda Strickland's murder."

A ghost of a smile tugged at one corner of Cherise's red lips. "Me, help clear Sterling?"

"Yeah. You were his cousin, the only living family he had, weren't you?" And his only heir, Jackson reminded himself.

"Yes, that much is true, but it's obvious that you don't know very much about the Wyatts, or you wouldn't be making such a ridiculous request."

"Nothing ridiculous about it, Mrs. Northrop. Wyatt was innocent."

"Cherise," she said, and took a deep breath. Her full breasts almost popped out of her neckline as she floated toward him. "You may as well call me Cherise. By the time we're through sifting through all the family skeletons, I have a feeling we'll be on a first-name basis. Do sit down. Would you like something to drink?"

"No thanks."

Jackson sat down on one of the three small, matching couches, and Cherise settled herself beside him. Her nearness didn't make his heart go pitty-pat, but the sight of her boobs did elevate his blood pressure more than just a tad.

"All right, where should I begin, Jackson? You don't mind if I call you Jackson, do you?"

"No, ma'am, not at all."

"Good. To begin—I know you may find this hard to believe, but although Sterling and I were cousins, and Jonathan, my husband, was his business partner, the two of us went out of our way to avoid each other."

"Any particular reason for the animosity?"

"Animosity is much too mild a word to describe our relationship, Jackson. Hate, I think, would be more appropriate. And yes, there was a very good reason for it. This may sound like a badly written soap opera, but I can assure you it's all quite true.

"I suppose you could say it started when our grandfather disowned my mother for marrying my father. Grandpapa didn't think Daddy was good enough—he was only marrying Mother for her money, that sort of thing. When Grandpapa died, Sterling's father naturally inherited every penny of the Wyatt fortune. Mother got nothing. Poor darling wasn't even mentioned in the will, but that's beside the point.

"Anyway, Grandpapa had a great deal of influence over Uncle Gordon—Sterling's father. So much so that Uncle Gordon was positively paranoid about Daddy. I can only suppose that Sterling inherited his paranoia. Daddy, of course, wasn't the leach they both thought. He may have started out penniless, but he died a multimillionaire."

"And that was the reason for the mutual dislike?" Jackson asked.

"Hatred, remember? No, it started sometime after that. Before I married Jon—before I even knew he existed, actually—Sterling and I had an affair in Paris. At the time, we had no idea we were related. How could we when Sterling had lived here in Dallas all his life, and I was born and raised in Chicago. As I was growing up, my parents never spoke of the Wyatts—it was too painful for them, I suppose. And Uncle Gordon obviously never told Sterling about me. We Hammonds were outcasts, you see. The untouchables.

"Well, the worst thing imaginable happened in Paris. Sterling and I met, we fell in love, and he asked me to marry him. Foolish child that I was then, I said yes. We phoned our parents to tell them the good news, and that's when we discovered we were first cousins."

The amused look that slowly crossed Cherise's face told Jackson that his expression must have mirrored his disbelief.

"I told you this would sound like a badly written soap opera, didn't I? But it happened just this way."

"You must've been upset."

"Upset? No, as a matter of fact, I was shocked to find out that I was in love with my own cousin. Although not as shocked as I was when he left me without a word. It was a mutual friend who told me he'd caught the first available plane back to Dallas. At that point, I came very close to having a nervous breakdown. I suppose, if I'd been able, I would have followed him, but I was studying art and couldn't leave Paris. By the time I was able to leave, I'd discovered I was pregnant.

"Needless to say, I didn't have the baby. With Sterling as its father, it would have been born an idiot. As far as I know, he never suspected anything, either.

"I didn't have an easy time of it, recovering from the abortion and all that. A few weeks later, Jonathan entered my life. You know the old saying about lightning never striking twice in the same place? Well, don't believe it. It does. That is, it did with me. I knew next to nothing about Jon, especially not about his being Sterling's partner and co-owner of Presidio Development."

Cherise inhaled a deep breath and slowly released it. "I could make a lot of excuses—I was too young and didn't realize what I was doing; I was confused and hurt by what Sterling had done to me—but I won't. I wanted Jon. More than that, I needed him to sweep me off my feet, and he did. I married him because he made me forget about Sterling, not because I loved him.

"Well, after we honeymooned in Greece, we came home

to Dallas, and that's when I discovered that Jon was
Sterling's business partner. To make matters worse, after I'd
had my second baby, I found out that Jon was into other
diversions and had been for quite some time."

"Women?" Jackson asked hesitantly.

"Oh, you know about them, do you? Well, of course you
do; you're a private investigator. How many women did Jon
have before Amanda, do you know? I lost count at fifteen."

"I only know about your husband's alleged association
with Miss Strickland."

Cherise chuckled. "It was a lot more than just alleged,
Jackson. Jon and Mandy were having a rip-roaring love
affair, in full glorious technicolor. For heaven's sake, don't
look so surprised; I don't mind. Not now. Jon's affairs may
have upset me at one time, but they don't any longer. No, he
can do what he pleases, with whom he pleases, as often as
he pleases . . . as long as he leaves me alone. Does that
sound cold to you?"

At a loss for words, Jackson merely shrugged.

"Of course it does. Don't feel you have to be polite.
Contrary to the way things seem, however—the way I may
seem—I'm not a frigid woman. Far from it. Jon and I aren't
in love. I seriously doubt we ever were. Over the years
we've managed to develop a comfortable respect for each
other. I suppose you could say that we're friends who just
happen to be married.

"But to get back to my helping you find proof that
Sterling didn't murder Mandy . . . I'm just sorry that he
took the coward's way out by committing suicide. I'd love
to have seen him rot in prison for the rest of his life."

"Then you believe he was guilty of murdering Miss
Strickland."

"Oh, I didn't say that. Sterling was many things, but a
murderer wasn't one of them. He lacked the necessary
backbone for that sort of thing. However, if a jury of his

peers were to have found him guilty, who would I be to disagree with them?" She ran a long finger slowly around the rim of her glass, making it ring. "I suppose Walter told you that Mandy and I were friends."

Jackson, unable to look directly at Cherise, stared at a painting on the far side of the room. Its subject matter wasn't half as confusing as its owner. "He mentioned something along those lines, yes."

"And you're not the kind of man who approves of a wife sharing her husband with her friends, are you?"

Jackson felt the blood rush to his face and lowered his head.

"That's all right." Smiling, Cherise reached out and patted his knee, letting her hand drift lightly down to his thigh. "You don't have to answer that, I can read it in your face."

The lull in their conversation served only to increase Jackson's uneasiness. He could feel her eyes rake over him.

"Jackson," Cherise said, her voice smooth as a provocative piece of silk, "has anyone ever told you that you have very intriguing looks?"

"No, ma'am, can't say they have."

"Well, you do. In fact, they fascinate the hell out of me. I'm an artist."

"No kidding."

"I know nothing about you or your background, but if I were to guess, I'd say you're a mixture of ancient Celt and American Indian. Your face is decidedly Celtic—long, lean, and angular—but those prominent cheekbones are pure Indian. Turn around and let me see your eyes."

Jackson hesitated, trying to figure out a way to get out of the house and away from Cherise. She took the matter out of his hands by taking hold of his chin and turning his face toward her.

"My God, they're gray! Blue or brown, I could understand, but gray . . . Fury. That's what, French?"

"Yeah."

"Is your father French?"

"No, he's a Texan, born and bred. But his daddy came from Louisiana."

"Ah, Creole."

"No, Cajun."

"Well, I was close. They're almost the same."

Cherise leaned forward and the front of her blouse fell away from her chest. Jackson cast a quick glance down at her cleavage and felt his blood pressure accelerate dramatically. The most dangerous animal alive, he decided at that moment, was the horny female.

"I'd love to paint you," Cherise said softly, her hand inching closer to his groin. "Have you ever posed in the nude before?"

"No, ma'am!" Jackson said, all but leaping to his feet. "And no offense, Mrs. Northrop, but I probably never will, either. Ji—that is, my lady wouldn't like it."

"Your lady, not your girlfriend. I like the way you put that, Jackson. It's so mature, so masculine. I suppose that means you're taken?"

"Same as." Jackson began moving toward the door and freedom.

"You're not going to leave now, are you? We're just getting to know one another."

"Yeah, I got to. You got that appointment, remember? And I really need to be running along. Listen, I appreciate all your help."

"But I didn't do anything. Did I?"

More than you'll ever know, lady, Jackson thought, and turned to leave.

• • •

"Why the hell didn't you warn me about her, Collins?" Jackson asked as he entered the lawyer's office.

"Who, Cherise Northrop?" Collins asked.

"Well, we're not talking about Mother Theresa, are we?" Jackson dismissed the scenic view of Turtle Creek Boulevard behind Collins as he dropped into a high-backed leather chair near the lawyer's desk. "Hell, I was expecting to find some pathetic little wife with a tomcat for a husband. Woman's the closest thing to a man-hungry she-wolf I've ever met. No wonder Northrop sleeps around. It's safer for him that way."

Collins blinked. "What happened? Did she make a pass at you?"

"You could say that, yeah."

"Oh," Collins said, and fell silent for a moment. "Well, I suppose I owe you an apology for the way she behaved. It's obvious that she got to you."

"Not quite," Jackson said. "I managed to get out of the house, intact, before that happened."

Collins cleared his throat. "Well, aside from her straight-forwardness, did she tell you anything helpful?"

"Did she ever. I got an earful of her side of the story."

"What story would that be?"

"The one about her affair with Wyatt."

Collins's eyes widened. "She and Sterling had an affair?"

"Yeah, that's what she said."

"When was this?"

"Years ago, right before she married Northrop. You mean you didn't know?"

"No, I didn't," said Collins, watching his thumb rub the arm of his chair. "To be perfectly honest, Fury, I don't know all that much about her and Jon. But, my God, an affair with Sterling."

"Yep. And in Paris, of all places."

"Paris, France?"

"They sure don't give painting lessons in Paris, Texas, do they?"

"Cherise studied art in Paris."

"That's what she told me," Jackson said. "You should've seen some of the weird shit hanging on her walls. I may not know diddly-squat about art, but I know one thing—if she painted the pictures I saw today, she's either got serious mental problems or she's in bad need of more lessons. Got little nieces and nephews who can draw better than—" he broke off, seeing the amused skepticism on Collins's face.

"Are you certain Cherise wasn't just trying to sell you a bill of goods? I mean, the idea of her and Sterling . . . No." Collins shook his head. "No, Sterling has too much sense to get involved with his own cousin."

"Well, according to what she told me, at the time it happened, they didn't know they were related."

Collins thought for a moment. "Now that I might buy. Sterling's father was a strange old bird. Worse than his grandfather from what I've heard. Get on Gordon Wyatt's bad side once, and you'd be there forever."

"Fits what she said. She told me that her mother had been disowned, written completely out of the family will, when she married Hammond."

"You know, now that I think about it, she could very well have met Sterling in Paris. About twelve or thirteen years ago, Presidio did a job over there. I remember that Sterling started the project, but he came back home for some reason, and then Jon went over and finished it."

"Then it's possible she could've been telling the truth about her pregnancy and abortion."

"Abor—" Collins shot Jackson a cautious look. "Whose . . ."

"Wyatt's, she said."

With a groan, Collins shook his head. "I knew something had to be behind it, but I never thought it was that. You know, it's strange, but after all these years, it's finally starting to make sense."

"What is?"

"Their—feud, I suppose, for want of a better word. No, actually, it was her feud more than it was Sterling's, because it was all so one-sided. To my knowledge, he never said one word against Cherise, though Lord knows, the way she behaved, the way she often treated him, he had plenty of reasons. Jesus. He even left her everything in his will."

"You figure he did it out of guilt?"

"What other reason could there be?"

"Because he abandoned her in Paris after their affair? Or because she killed their baby?"

"I don't know. Could be both. And it's not killed in legalese. It's terminated."

"Not in my book, Collins. It's murder."

Leaving Collins's office sometime later, Jackson took the elevator down to the underground garage where he'd parked his car. The way things were beginning to look, he had another name to add to his mental list of suspects. First Northrop's, and now Cherise's.

Could be that the family who killed together stayed together, Jackson thought as he stepped out of the elevator and headed for his Pontiac. No, not exactly together. Northrop and Cherise might have both had a hand in planning the murders, but only one of them had held the knife and pulled the trigger. And Jackson felt sure that that hand belonged to Northrop.

"Fury, you son of a bitch!"

Jackson reached instinctively for his gun as he whirled around. Unfortunately, he never got the gun out of its holster. The small, muscular man behind him clipped him with a solid left hook, making his head snap backward. A swift hard right to his stomach sent him sprawling onto the garage floor.

Jillian was straightening up the desk, getting ready to leave for the day, when she heard the loft door open. She turned just as Jackson stumbled into the room.

"Oh, my gosh!" Dropping the things in her hand, she ran to him and threw a shoulder under his arm for support. "What happened?"

Grateful just to have her near in his time of need, Jackson leaned on her as she led him to the couch. His own angel of mercy, he thought, regarding her worried expression through swollen eyes. Feeling her arm tighten about his waist, he winced, and the movement made his split lip begin to bleed again. "Damn, Jill, take it easy, will you? Don't hold me so tight."

"Oh, I'm sorry. Who in the world did this to you?"

"Well, it wasn't Marsha's ex-husband, if that's what you're thinking."

"Marsha's ex? You mean, the guy who was chasing us on Thornton Freeway that night we had dinner at your parents' place?"

"Yeah, it wasn't him. Must've been somebody else's ex-husband. Look, honey, let me sit down before I fall down. I don't feel good at all."

"I'll bet you don't. You know, you might be hurt somewhere internally and not even know it. You really ought to go see a doctor."

"No! Don't want or need no goddamn doctor. Just leave me alone, I'll be all right."

Finally reaching the couch, the simple effort of sitting down made Jackson gasp sharply. In turn, the sharp gasp caused him to feel as though someone were sticking a knife in his ribs.

"Well, darn it, if you won't go see a doctor, I'll just call one and have him come here."

"You go near that phone, Jill Fletcher, and so help me God, I'll break your arm."

"Honestly, Jack, you're in no condition to break my arm, or anyone else's for that matter, so why don't you shut up!"

"I'm not gonna go see a doctor."

"You are without a doubt the most stubborn—" Jillian broke off and inhaled a deep, calming breath. "All right, we'll do it your way. This time. God knows, I'm no nurse, but I'll see what I can do. Where do you keep the alcohol?"

"Alcohol? Jesus Christ! I'm in enough pain as it is and you want to make it worse by giving me an alcohol rub?"

"Not a rubdown, stupid. Those cuts on your face have got to be cleaned so they won't get infected."

"With alcohol?"

"Yes, with alcohol. Have you got any better suggestions?"

"Yeah. Water. Nice, cool water. No soap, either, you hear? Jesus, alcohol."

Jillian disappeared into the kitchen where he heard her muttering to herself as she opened and closed the cabinet doors.

"That beating you took could have damaged something inside your head, Jack. No, I take that back. Your skull's too blasted thick."

"Come on, have a little pity, Jill. I'm a wounded man. Look, I'm gonna be okay. I haven't coughed up or peed any blood yet. Couple of ribs might be busted, but they'll heal. At least, they always did in the past. Why don't you just go home and let me lay here and rest awhile."

Jillian reappeared, carrying a bowl and some clean cloths. She knelt down on the floor beside him. As she placed her things on the coffee table, some of the liquid splashed out of the bowl. Jackson watched closely as she

soaked the cloth and then wrung it out. "You didn't put anything in there, did you?" he asked.

Gently, taking care not to press down too hard, she
covered his face with the cloth. "What do you think?"

The cool dampness felt good, very good, at first. And
then the alcohol seeped into the cuts and made them burn
like a son of a bitch.

"Oh, for Pete's sake, stop being such a baby," Jillian said
over Jackson's loud yelps. "If you're stupid enough to get
into a fight, you'll just have to learn to accept the
consequences."

"Goddammit, it hurts! Oh, shit, my ribs!"

"Do you always swear so much?"

"Only when someone's trying to kill me."

"Jack, a little diluted vodka won't kill you."

"Vodka!" He slapped her hand aside and glared at her.
"You're washing my face with my vodka?"

"What else could I use? I couldn't find any isopropyl."

"That stuff cost me twelve bucks a bottle!"

"Well, think of it this way—it's better for your cuts than
it is for your liver."

Jackson curled his upper lip in a snarl. "Anyone ever tell
you you're a mean, heartless woman?"

"No, but then I've never played Florence Nightingale to
a big baby before, either." Jillian wrung the cloth out,
folded it, and placed it across his swollen eyes. "What can I
use to bandage your ribs with?"

Jackson jerked the cloth aside. "Nothing! Not a damn
thing. You just keep your grubby hands away from my
ribs!"

"But, Jack—"

"They don't bandage ribs anymore, Jill. If you don't
believe me, call a doctor and ask him yourself."

"You've got to be kidding."

"No, I'm not. I'm serious. Hell, the last thing I need now is for pneumonia to set in."

"Pneumonia?".

"Yeah. It's got something to do with not enough air getting into the lungs 'cause the chest's not moving. Fluid builds up, and the next thing you know you're under an oxygen tent with tubes sticking out of your nose. I sure as hell don't want that."

Jillian frowned for a thoughtful moment; then, with a shrug of acceptance, she stood up and carried her things back into the kitchen.

"Jack?" she called to him.

"Yeah?"

"What did you do to the guy?"

"What do you mean, what did I do to him?"

Jillian moved back into view, drying her hands on a towel. "Well, when someone comes in looking as bad as you do, don't they usually say, 'Yeah, but you oughta see the other guy?'"

"Oh."

"They do say that, don't they, Jack?"

"Yeah, I guess."

She sat down on the couch across from Jackson. "So what did you do to him?"

He gave her a quick, sullen look, then turned his face into the back of the couch. "Not now, Jill. I'm really in no condition to give you a play-by-play description of what happened between me and that good-for-nothing little fart."

A brief pause, and then her low twitter of laughter had him turning over to look at her again.

"You didn't touch him, did you?"

"Now, Jill—"

"That's what happened, isn't it, Jack? What did he do, jump you from behind?"

"No!"

"Yes, he did. He jumped you, and I'll bet you didn't even lay a finger on him."

"Well . . ."

"It's all right, Jack. It doesn't bother me that you're not the big macho hunk who can win every fight. Losing once in a while only shows how human you are."

"Maybe, but it's still depressing as hell," he groaned sourly. "Little fart knocked me flat on my back before I even knew what hit me. Got one look at his bald head, white chest, and gold chains, then everything just sorta went black. Next thing I knew, I was waking up on the floor of the parking garage."

Jillian blinked. "What?"

"That's where he got me. In the basement garage of Collins's—"

"No, I don't mean that. I mean the part about the gold chains you saw before you blacked out."

"Oh, that. Yeah, I did."

"You know something? I'll bet it was Harry."

"Who?"

"Harry. You remember, don't you? Evelyn's husband."

"Who the hell is Evelyn?"

"Evelyn, for heaven's sake. She was here one day last week with Richard, the delivery man from the office-supply store."

"That dumpy blond with diarrhea of the mouth?"

"Yes. She said her husband's name was Harry. At least, I think that's what she said."

"But I didn't— I mean, she didn't— She walked out of here before—"

"Yes, I know. That's what's so— Wait a minute! I'll bet she went straight home and told Harry that she'd come to see you. Trying to put the fear of God in him, I bet. It's possible she even stretched the truth a little so he would think she'd actually hired a private investigator. You."

Jillian clicked her tongue. "You're in a very dangerous business, Jack."

"Yeah, tell me about it."

"Getting chased on the freeway by an angry ex-husband who has a right to hate you isn't half as scary as nearly getting beaten to a pulp by a total stranger with no cause at all."

"You don't have to rub it in."

After a pause, Jillian asked, "Are you going to file charges against him?"

"Who, Harry? Or whatever his name is? Are you kidding? What would I tell the police?"

"Well, for openers, you could tell them what happened."

"Sure. I go in looking like two hundred and ten pounds of freshly ground hamburger and tell them that a short, bald-headed guy wearing gold chains sucker-punched me."

"It's the truth, isn't it?"

"Truth sometimes don't mean a whole lot in this business, Jill. Getting beat up and shot at are some of the risks a P.I. has to take. But, okay, say I did go to the cops. You know the first thing they'd do? Remember, I'm sort of their competition. They'd laugh at me; that's what they'd do. And then when they stopped rolling around on the floor, they'd dust themselves off, maybe fill out a few forms—just to make it look like they're doing their job—then they'd start talking. To anybody and everybody who'd listen. It's taken me ten years to build up the reputation I got, sweetheart. Filing charges against some middle-aged pipsqueak who thinks he's got a grudge ain't no way to keep it."

"So just for the sake of your untarnished reputation, you're going to let it slide, not do anything at all, is that it?"

"You got it."

Jillian stood up slowly. "That's the dumbest thing I've ever heard, Jack. Really the dumbest."

"Maybe, but it goes with the territory."

Somberness replaced her anger. "I suppose that finding one of your clients murdered goes with the territory, too?"

"No, Jill, that's just one of the more unfortunate hazards."

"Do you know the first thing that popped into my mind when you walked in here tonight?"

"No."

"I thought that Sterling's murderer had . . ." Her voice trailed off and she turned her head with a shudder.

Despite his pain, Jackson got to his feet and went to her. He wrapped his arms carefully around her from behind and held her close. "It's all right, honey. Nothing like that happened. It didn't even come close."

"But it could have happened, Jack. Don't you see? What if it hadn't been Evelyn's husband in that basement garage today; what if it had been the maniac who killed Sterling and Amanda? You'd be dead right now, just like them."

Jillian's logic sank in too deeply and much too quickly for comfort. Jackson wished he could contradict her, but he knew he couldn't. What she said made more sense than he cared to admit.

# CHAPTER 13

Tuesday, April 29

The two men seated on stools at the counter kept their attention focused on the cups in front of them when Jackson entered the coffee shop. The waitress, filling a dozen or more sugar dispensers behind the counter, merely gave him a cursory glance, then yawned, exposing a couple of missing molars. Well, at five-thirty in the morning, and looking almost as bad as his old beat-up Pontiac, Jackson could understand why no one gave him a standing ovation.

Letting his eyes scan the single narrow aisle, he saw Hank sitting in a back booth. Like everyone else, the detective looked half-asleep.

Carefully Jackson made his way toward the booth and eased his bruised body onto the seat across from Hank. "This mine?" he asked, nodding at the cup of coffee on his side of the table.

"Yeah, I thought—" Hank broke off as he looked up, his face contorting at the sight of Jackson's black eye and swollen jaw. "Jesus! What happened to you?"

"It's a long story, and I ain't in no mood right now to tell it."

"That's a humdinger of a shiner," Hank said, a lascivious grin appearing slowly at one corner of his mouth. "Why, you horny old devil, you. Bet I can guess how you got it.

Your secretary with the big lungs—what's her name—Jill Fletcher? Girl looks like she could really pack a solid punch if she put half a mind to it."

Jackson stared unsmiling at the detective. "I thought you wanted to see me this morning to give me the latest on Wyatt, not pump me about Jill."

"I did, but—"

"No buts, okay? I don't ask what goes on between you and your wife, do I?"

Hank snorted. "That'd be easy to answer if you did. Nothing goes on between us. Hasn't for years."

"Well, there's nothing between me and Jill either." At least, not yet, Jackson amended thoughtfully. "Just for the record, though, she didn't have anything to do with my getting this black eye."

"If you say so."

"I do. Now what's the latest on Wyatt?"

"Got a copy of the county medical examiner's report late yesterday afternoon."

"It sure as hell took them long enough."

"Yeah, and you know why, too. It's because they're overworked and underpaid, just like the rest of us. You wouldn't believe the backlog of paperwork we've got. We're all at least a week behind."

"The report, Hank," Jackson prompted. "What did the M.E. find?"

"Well, he's calling Wyatt's death a homicide, not suicide."

"I could've told them that the day we found him."

"Then why the hell didn't you?"

" 'Cause at the time, I wasn't one hundred percent sure. Not knowing Wyatt all that well, there was a slim chance he could've pulled the trigger."

"Still, I've told you how many times before, Fury, that withholding evidence—"

"Wasn't no evidence to withhold. Nothing concrete, at least. All I had was a hunch, and we both know how far a hunch will get you in a court of law these days. The D.A. wouldn't have touched it with a ten-foot pole, not without the evidence behind it so he could get a solid conviction."

"All right, all right. So, what's this hunch of yours?"

Jackson took a sip of his coffee and sat the mug down on the table. "I think I might know who killed Wyatt and Amanda Strickland. Think, mind you. Just think. Until I know for certain, I'm gonna keep my mouth shut. And don't give me any more of that bullshit about withholding evidence. I'll be more than happy to let you have the collar, if and when I know I'm right."

"You better be playing straight with me, Fury."

"I am. Trust me."

"Got less than two years to go 'til I retire. I can't afford to let you or anybody else screw things up for me."

"Come on, Hank. You know me better than that. Name one time when I screwed things up intentionally?"

"All right. Remember Thornquist and that rapist he was—"

"That was a coincidence and you know it. I didn't set out to get the guy demoted to desk sergeant; he did that all by himself."

"You won't ever convince him of that."

"Too bad. Look, about the M.E.'s report. What else did it say?"

Hank paused to drink the last of his coffee. "Well, it looks like whoever murdered Wyatt blew the back of his head off after he killed him."

"Wait a minute," Jackson said, confused. "I always thought dead was dead, no matter how you looked at it."

"It is."

"Then what you're saying don't make a whole lot of sense."

"Yeah, it does, too. Remember that red mark Wilkerson found on the back of Wyatt's neck?"

Jackson did. "Yeah! So you were right. Wyatt did take a direct hit on his cranial nerves."

Hank nodded. "The M.E. said that the blow to the back of Wyatt's neck caused instant paralysis. His heart and lungs stopped functioning at the moment of impact, so he died of suffocation."

"Then whoever hit him from behind put the gun in his mouth and squeezed the trigger."

"That's the way I figure it happened. Hell, it's the only way it could've happened. Bastard must've had a black belt in karate. Either that, or he lucked out with the first blow. One thing's for certain, to do what he did, he's bound to have a cast-iron stomach."

"And no conscience," Jackson said. "We're dealing with a sick mind here, Hank."

"Yeah, a sick, thorough mind. Betcha he's a perfectionist."

"How you figure that?"

"Well, for one thing, he didn't run off after he killed Wyatt. He took the time to make it look like a real suicide. I mean, he blew the guy's brains out, draped him across the desk, and let the gun drop to the floor beneath Wyatt's hand. You gotta give him this much, Fury: He's one smart amateur. He almost committed the perfect murder."

"So when are you gonna arrest this amateur genius?" Jackson asked, goading the detective good-naturedly.

"When do you think? As soon as we know who he is, that's when. Anybody ever tell you you're getting to be an awful pain in the ass in your old age?"

"My momma. Every chance she gets."

"Smart lady, your momma." Anger replaced the humor in Hank's eyes. "You know, not many people I'd admit this to, Fury, but I'm stumped. Not just me, either. The whole damn department's been running around with their heads up their asses. This jerk's got us by the balls. We don't know who he is, what motive he had for killing Wyatt and the Strickland woman—shit, at this point, we don't even know if he's responsible for both murders; we're just supposing he is.

"To hell with you and your professional ethics," Hank said, leaning forward as he dropped his voice to just above a whisper. "You've been on this case as long as we have, you got a good idea who Wyatt's enemies were—better'n we do, leastways. I gotta know the name of that hunch of yours."

It would be so simple, Jackson thought, so easy to do. Just tell Hank that he suspected Northrop and let the police worry about it from here out. But what if he was wrong? What if Northrop wasn't connected with either Amanda Strickland's or Wyatt's murder? Jackson would end up with egg on his face and another innocent man would be charged with a murder he didn't commit.

Aside from his own uncertainties, Jackson realized that he owed Hank. Owed him a great deal. The guy had saved his ass more times than he cared to think about. Now that he had a chance to help him, it was only fitting that he at least try. God knows, getting credit for solving two big-society murders could very well be the crowning point of Hank's twenty-year career.

"Okay," Jackson said. "It's Northrop. Jonathan Northrop."

"Wyatt's partner?"

"Yeah."

Hank considered his disclosure for a moment with a thoughtful frown. "Well, I can see how getting rid of Wyatt would give Northrop total control of the company, but why? I mean, from what I hear, the guy's got money coming out his ears. What's he need more for?"

Jackson relayed to Hank what he'd discovered—leaving

out, of course, the illegal means by which he'd acquired the information—that Northrop was heavily in debt to the gambler in Vegas, that he'd stolen from the company to pay off those debts, that he was having an affair with Amanda Strickland. "If that's not bad enough," Jackson concluded, "Northrop's wife, Cherise, is Wyatt's only heir. Woman's due to inherit millions when the will finally clears probate."

"Makes sense, now that I think about it," Hank said. "Northrop needs money, so he gets rid of the Strickland woman first, lets Wyatt take the blame, then he kills Wyatt so that it looks like suicide. Yeah, makes a lot of sense. Except for one hitch. Northrop's got an iron-clad alibi for both murders."

"He could've hired someone."

"Yeah, there's that possibility. So why didn't you tell me all this sooner?"

"Because, like I told you before, it's still nothing but a hunch. Only thing I know for certain is that Northrop stole money from Presidio Development. He's got it in an account under a bogus name and uses it to pay off the guy in Vegas. It's not much, is it?"

"Nope. But it's better than nothing."

"Think you can use any of it?"

"Who knows?" With a shrug, Hank glanced toward the front of the coffee shop and saw the wall clock behind the cash register. "Shit!" he said, jumping to his feet. "I got less than five minutes to make it to the station for roll call. Look, if you come across anything else, phone me."

"I will," Jackson said and grabbed hold of the detective's hand before he could thrust it inside his pants pocket. "Hey, keep your money. Coffee's on me this morning."

"You sure?"

"Yeah, I'm sure. I'm just feeding Moose; you got a house full of teenagers."

"Moose," Hank said, chuckling. "Ain't a whole lot of difference between the two, is there?"

"No, come to think of it, there ain't."

"Look, I gotta run, Fury. You gonna be in your office the rest of the day? I'd like to know just in case I need you for something."

"No, couple of things I gotta do this morning, then I'm going to Wyatt's funeral this afternoon."

"Helluva day for one," Hank said, looking out the window at the overcast sky.

"All things considered, sweetheart, I think you held up pretty well," Jackson said, eyeing Jillian at the other end of the couch they shared. He took a sip from one of the six long-neck bottles of beer he had picked up on the way home from the cemetery as she stirred artificial sweetener into her glass of ice tea.

"You're just saying that, Jack. I was never so embarrassed in my whole life."

"No, I'm not. I know it hasn't been easy for you lately, what with finding Wyatt's body the way we did, but you're snapping out of it."

"Still, if you hadn't been there to catch me today, I'd have fallen flat on my face. Honestly, that's the first time I've even come close to fainting."

"You gotta remember, honey—it was hotter'n hell out there today. Last night's thunderstorm made the humidity worse than ever. Fact is, I felt kind of light-headed myself."

Jillian shuddered. "I get goose bumps just thinking about what almost happened."

"Then don't. Don't think about it at all. Just forget it. You didn't faint, that's the main thing."

"I'm not talking about that. I'm talking about how different Amanda's and Sterling's funerals were. The same people were there—I recognized a few of them, but they all behaved so—so weird."

In Jackson's opinion, considering all the mourners who had been inside the church, and the gawking spectators who had lurked outside the cemetery gates, Wyatt's funeral had been more like a New Year's Day Cotton Bowl Parade than a solemn religious ceremony. "Yeah, looks even posthumously, poor old Wyatt's *persona non grata.*"

"And he'll stay that way unless we can clear him. I swear, Jack, people can be such hypocrites at times. You'd think with the kind of life Amanda led, especially the number of men she must have slept with, she'd have made a few enemies. Women enemies. But everyone at her funeral carried on as if butter wouldn't melt in their mouth. And then today everyone acted as though Sterling was Jack the Ripper. I halfway expected to see someone walk up to his coffin and spit on it."

"Well, as Hemingway once said, 'The rich are different from you and I.' Or something like that."

"No, Jack, you got it wrong."

"Got what wrong?"

"It wasn't Hemingway who said it; it was F. Scott Fitzgerald. He was talking to Hemingway at the time, and supposedly Hemingway came back with, 'Yes, they have more money.'"

"Okay, so I got it wrong. What difference does it make? They gonna rise up out of the grave and sue me?"

"No, but if you're going to quote someone, you should at least quote them correctly."

Jackson gave her a perplexed look. "I'm trying to reassure you, comfort you a little, and you're correcting some dumb quote? Let's just forget it, okay? I'm sorry I even said anything." He stopped, thought for a moment, frowned, and then asked, "What the hell were we talking about anyway?"

"The rich being different."

"Yeah, that. The point I was trying to make is that rich folks live by a set of standards that we middle-class folks just can't afford."

"It doesn't take a lot of money to swap wives and husbands, or mistresses and lovers, as often as they change cars, Jack. But I agree with you; their standards are different from ours. In my opinion, they're a lot lower."

Jackson shrugged. "I guess you ought to know."

"Just what do you mean by that?" Jillian asked, giving him a long, cold look.

"Obviously not what you think. I only meant that since you were raised in white-collar North Dallas and not good ol' red-neck South Pleasant Grove where I grew up, you ought to know better than I do what goes on there."

"Then you weren't implying that my parents—"

"No! Good God, Jill, I don't even know your folks. Even if I did, I sure wouldn't say a thing like that."

"Yes, well, you're right about my knowing what goes on among the upper class. A lot of my friends' parents made a habit of forgetting their marriage vows. But I can assure you that mine never did." At least her mother hadn't, Jillian amended silently. Her stepfather Robert, on the other hand, was a different matter entirely. "It's strange."

"What is?"

"Amanda. And the women at her funeral. Why were they all crying? I can tell you this much—if I'd known or even suspected that she was sleeping with my husband, I would have been celebrating, not crying *my* heart out. But then, maybe the wives of the husbands she slept with didn't go."

"The Northrops did."

"You're kidding."

Jackson shook his head.

"The Northrops were at her funeral last week? Both of them? Together?"

"Yep. They sat two rows ahead of me. They were at Wyatt's funeral together, too. For a while today, Cherise, uh, I mean, Mrs. Northrop, was crying so hard that I thought he was gonna have to take her away. Woman looked like she was about to come apart at the seams."

"How did he behave?"

"No different from a lot of the other men at Amanda Strickland's funeral. When that damned organ music got heavy, I saw him wipe his eyes and blow his nose a time or two. Other than that, though, he was solid as a rock."

"The jerk," Jillian said quietly. "What about today?"

"From where I was sitting, he looked pretty shook up. Not heartbroken like he was burying his best friend or something, but scared. That's what's confusing. With all that money he's stolen, looks to me like he should've been relieved, not scared."

"He's not only a jerk, he's a two-timing hypocrite."

"Maybe he is, maybe he isn't. We don't know."

"He was cheating on his wife. We know that, Jack. And she knew about it!"

Rusty whined at the rising inflection of Jillian's voice. With his tail tucked between his legs, he crawled out of the room and into the kitchen.

"Honey, does that dog of yours have a problem?"

"No, he just acts that way sometimes around strangers. He's been like that since he was a puppy," Jillian said, then lapsed into a pensive silence.

"What's the matter?"

"Nothing really. I was just thinking."

"About what?"

"Life. And death. It's frightening. You can die at any time, without any warning. Look at Amanda and Sterling. They had so much going for them, so much to live for, Sterling especially, and it was all taken away from them."

"Yeah, well, that's how it happens sometimes." Jackson

didn't like the direction their conversation was taking; it reminded him of his own mortality. In his line of business, he was much better off not thinking about such things.

He swung his feet off the coffee table and sat up, arching his back and extending his arms in a wide stretch. As he slowly relaxed, his hand dropped to Jillian's upraised knee. He let it rest there for a moment, then gave the back of her calf a friendly pat and stood up. "Hate to leave you alone like this, but it's getting late, and I gotta get going."

"Heavy date tonight?"

Towering over her, Jackson gave a mirthless snort. "Yeah, real heavy. With my washer, dryer, and vacuum cleaner."

"Jackson Fury. Are you telling me that you do your own housecleaning?"

"Somebody's got to do it. Why not me?"

"I don't know." Angling her head to one side, Jillian gave him a slow once-over. "I guess it's because you don't exactly fit the image of the domestic type."

Jackson leaned over and braced his hands on the back of the couch, his face lowering until it stopped mere inches from hers. "You'd be amazed at what I can do around the house, honey. I'm an absolute whiz in the bedroom."

The soft huskiness of his voice ignited strange tremors within Jillian. For some strange reason, she couldn't tear her eyes away from his mouth. "I bet," she said quietly.

"You wanna come back to the loft with me and help straighten out a couple of things?"

Slowly her eyes traveled up the groove in his upper lip, over the bumpy ridge of his beakish nose, and settled on his deep, gray eyes. "Gee, I don't know if I could stand the excitement."

"You don't know what excitement is, sweetheart, until you've put clean sheets on my bed"—lightly his fingers trailed down her bare arm—"fluffed up my king-size pillows"—they curled around her flesh, catching part of her T-shirt, his thumb grazing the lower curve of her breast—"then messed them up again." A gentle tug on the thin fabric presented him with a clear outline of her hardening nipple.

Jillian noted the rising flush in his cheeks, the darkening in his eyes. Something clicked inside her and the room suddenly went fuzzy. "Jack?" she said hoarsely, her arms floating up and winding around his neck.

The dewy glitter in her eyes, the feel of her arms holding him, and that same something clicked inside Jackson. "Jill?"

"Jack, I—I think it's time."

"Time?" Although he sounded confused, Jackson knew exactly what she meant. "Now? No kidding?"

"Uh-huh." Jillian nodded, amazed.

"Jesus!" There was no figuring women, he thought. If he lived to be a hundred, he'd never understand their sense of reason or timing. But then who the hell was he to question it at a time like this? With a husky groan, he dropped his head and took possession of her mouth.

The brief kisses they had shared in the past paled in comparison to the one they shared now. Before either knew what was happening, emotions and sensations overtook and surpassed all rational thought. In moments, merely kissing wasn't satisfying enough. A deeper, hungrier need led to hands that groped, pushed aside, pulled off, and discarded unnecessary clothing that got in the way.

"Go easy on the shirt, honey," Jackson murmured into the curve of Jillian's throat. He wedged one knee between her hip and the couch as he straightened the other leg and dug his toes into the rug for support. "I'm lousy at sewing buttons back on."

Jillian flung his ripped shirt aside and gazed through half-closed eyes at the dark hair on his chest. "I'll sew them back on for you."

More kisses, more groping, a lot of heavy breathing, and then, "Lift up a little, Jill. Lemme get your T-shirt off . . . Atta girl . . . My God! Is this the—"

"Uh-huh."

"Jesus! I think I just fell in love with raspberry. On you the color is terrific." A ravenous impulse made Jackson move his head down her chest.

Jillian inhaled on a sharp gasp. "Wh-what are you doing?"

"Eatin' raspberries. Great big juicy ones."

"But you're getting me all wet."

"Yeah. Geez, Jill, you're delicious."

"Aren't you supposed to take my bra off first?"

"Want me to?"

"Uh-huh."

Jackson slowly did a modified pushup and looked at her. "Really?"

Jillian gave her head a jerky, affirmative nod.

"Jill, honey, do you know what'll happen when—"

Her fingers covered his lips. "I know, Jack. I want it to happen. Now. With you. It's time."

Jackson swallowed, then willed his shaking fingers to unfasten the single front hook of her raspberry bra. The two semitransparent halves fell apart, and her pale, full breasts with deep-pink crests spilled out. "Jill— Oh, Christ!"

Suddenly embarrassed, Jillian tried to cover herself, but Jackson intercepted her hand. He lifted it to his mouth and kissed the palm. "Don't, honey. Don't ever feel you have to hide yourself from me. You're beautiful, don't you know that?"

Her eyes riveted on Jackson's face, Jillian gently pulled her hand from his. Although she had no actual firsthand knowledge of the act of lovemaking, years of reading her grandmother's paperback romances, largely the good parts, gave her a fairly good idea of what to do next. She raked her long, sculpted nails through the silky hair on Jackson's chest, her fingers drifting lower and lower until they slid beneath the waistband of his black-suit trousers.

When she encountered something hard and unfamiliar, and saw Jackson begin to tremble, she abruptly ceased her explorations. "Did I do something wrong?"

"No! No, you did something right. Go on. Don't stop now."

Clumsily she unfastened his fastener and unzipped his zipper. Watching the slow descent of his pants down his hips, her eyes grew almost as big as the thing that pushed through the funny little hole in the front of his boxer shorts. Good Lord! No wonder they never told you about this sort of thing in high-school health classes, or college Biology 101. Not even those long, uncomfortable chats she'd had with her mother would have prepared her for a shock of this magnitude. Whatever else, though, she had an entirely new definition for the term *phallic symbolism*.

Jackson stopped trembling and stared down at her. "You okay, sweetheart?"

Her eyes flew up to his. "Yes. I think so. It's just that I've never seen . . ."

"Aw, Jill, I'm sorry. I forgot this is your first time." Levering himself off of the couch and her, he stood up and refastened his pants.

"Jack?"

Words weren't necessary; his expression promised that it was far from being over. Bending over, he scooped her up in his arms and headed for the open bedroom door he spied at the front of the apartment.

"Jack, what're you— You're gonna hurt your back. I'm not all that little, you know."

"So? You're just the right size for me."

"Oh, Jack." Jillian wound her arms tightly around his neck and buried her face against his chest. "I wish I weren't so stupid."

"Stupid?" he asked, hesitating beside the multipaned window. "Who said you were stupid?"

"I did, because I am. I don't know the first thing to do in bed. Or the first thing to say."

"Don't worry, sweetheart. You just do or say whatever comes naturally."

"But I want to be good for you. Very good."

"You will be," he said, heading once again toward the bedroom. "You already are."

Jillian, unfortunately, never heard the last of his declaration. A car backfired in the street outside, causing one of the windowpanes to burst from its wooden frame. Surprise held Jackson frozen for half a heartbeat, but when the car backfired a second time, his instincts took over and he dove to the floor with Jillian.

The backfiring seemed to continue incessantly, each explosion shattering more windowpanes and sending glass hurtling into the room. Jackson cringed at the deafening noise, but made sure that his body covered every inch of Jillian's bare flesh. He lay there until his curiosity got the better of him. Using his arm as a protective shield, he looked up and immediately felt sickness churn in his stomach. Bullets were ripping into the wall he'd leaned against seconds earlier, leaving holes the size of hens' eggs in the sheetrock. Stuffing exploded out of a chair and showered like snow about the room. Jillian's arrangement of framed prints and photographs fell victim just before the bullets reached the apartment door and turned it into splinters. Then the lamp disintegrated into a thousand pieces, throwing the room into darkness.

Suddenly, silence.

Hours passed. Or perhaps merely seconds. With his ears still ringing, Jackson couldn't be sure.

Reality returned along with the sound of heavy feet running up the stairs. Jackson blinked and inhaled his first deep breath when he saw the silhouette of a large, muscle-bound man appear through the splintered door.

"*Jesus Christ*, what happened? Jill, are you in there?"

Jackson heard a tiny whimper and felt something move beneath him. Slowly he pushed himself off Jillian, the shattered glass on his back tinkling to the floor as he stood up on shaky legs.

"Who the hell are you?" Vinnie asked. "What the hell have you done with Jill?"

"Nothing. She's right here," Jackson said. "She's okay. I think."

A savage kick of Vinnie's foot against what remained of the door made it fall from its hinges. He stalked into the apartment, flexing his hands into fists as he headed straight for Jackson. "So answer me, buster. Who the hell are you?"

"V—Vinnie?" Jillian said in a thready voice.

Jackson reached down and pulled her up into his arms. He held her close to him, needing her comforting nearness more than he needed to hide her nakedness.

His movements, however, were far too slow. Vinnie had seen Jillian's breasts, as well as Jackson's bare chest and unzipped pants. "You two, uh, know each other?"

"Yeah, I'm Jackson Fury, Jill's—"

"Jill's boss," Vinnie said, nodding. "The pervert."

"The what?" Jackson asked.

"Vincent?"

Dim light from the outside porch silhouetted the petite blond standing in the doorway. Jackson watched her hoist the big, squalling toddler higher on her hip as she entered the room.

"Vincent, is Jill okay?"

"For God's sake, Jan! I told you to stay downstairs."

Seeing Jillian in the arms of a stranger, Janine ignored her husband and headed for her friend. "Jill, are you all right? What happened?"

"Jan, is it?" Jackson asked, running his hands over Jillian's shivering body.

"Yes."

"Look, Jill's pretty shaken up right now, but I think she's gonna be okay."

"You sure?"

"Yeah. We've both been cut a little by all this glass, but that's all. None of the bullets hit us."

"Bullets!" Vinnie and Janine said in unison.

"I thought it was a gas explosion," Janine said. Then she turned and gasped when she saw the mangled wall.

Jackson knew he had to get rid of Jan before she fell apart. One woman scared out of her wits was all he could handle at a time. The muscle-bound husband, however, was another matter. "Jan?"

"Huh?"

"I tell you what," Jackson said. "Somebody's got to go phone the police. I don't think I should leave Jill right now, so would you mind phoning them for me? They're probably on their way, but go call 'em anyhow. Okay?"

"Yeah, all right." Dazedly Janine carried herself and Vinnie Junior, still screaming, out of the apartment.

"Okay, pervert," Vinnie said, "start talking. And if you don't want to look like a part of this place, you'll make it good."

"In a minute," Jackson said.

"No, not in a minute. Right now."

"Listen to me, Vinnie. All I'm gonna do is take Jill into the bedroom there and put some clothes on her. When she's dressed, I promise I'll come back out and answer all your questions.''

"You're not gonna try nothing with her, are you?"

Jackson peered down at Jillian, feeling her face press deeper into his shoulder. ''No,'' he said, squeezing her tightly, ''I won't try anything. You have my word on it.''

"Would you please stop doing that and listen to me, Jack?'' Jillian watched him continue to throw her clothes into suitcases, grocery bags, boxes, and anything else he could find. ''Staying on the case now is much too dangerous. I don't care about it anymore. I just want you to drop it and forget about it.''

The police had come and gone. Vinnie, dissatisfied with the answers Jackson gave him, had been dragged downstairs by Janine, leaving Jackson alone with Jillian in what was left of her apartment. He hadn't asked; he'd told her he was taking her back to the loft with him, and when she hadn't objected, he'd started packing her things. Now that some of the shock was wearing off, her mouth was working nonstop.

"Worrying about me, honey, is a big waste of time. I know how to take care of myself.''

"No, you don't. Have you forgotten what Harry did to you? My God, Jack, someone tried to kill us tonight.''

"Me,'' Jackson said, slicing her a hard, no-nonsense look. ''Someone was gunning for me, sweetheart, not you. He doesn't even know you exist, remember? No one knows about you. Not even Collins.''

"You're wrong, Jack. You've got to be wrong. Somehow, they figured out that I'm part of all this.''

Jackson threw a handful of silky underwear into a grocery sack and sat down beside her on the bed. ''Honey, unless the guy's psychic, there's no way in hell he can know about you.''

"Psychic! No psychic turned my apartment into a battle zone; a maniac did. For heaven's sake, Jack, how can you say a thing like that?"

"Easy. I've got it all figured out. He must have followed me here from the funeral. Shit, for all I know, he's been on my tail from the very beginning, and I just haven't noticed."

"Well, isn't that reason enough to quit? Isn't this?" She encompassed the room with a wide sweep of her arm.

"No, sweetheart, it sure as hell isn't." Now more than before, Jackson was doubly determined to get Northrop.

"Darn it!" Jillian punched his arm hard with her fist. "Do I have to spell it out to you, you stupid idiot? You mean something to me and I don't want anything to happen to you. But if you're stupid enough to stay on this case, Jackson Fury, and that maniac out there kills you, so help me God, I'll never speak to you again."

A slow grin tugged at one corner of Jackson's mouth. "No kidding?"

"Yes. No kidding."

"I really mean something to you?"

"Oh . . . *damnation!* You didn't hear a word I said. You never do."

"I listen, Jill. Sometimes, if I try real hard, I can even understand."

"But not this time, right?"

"Right, so stop getting all worked up over nothing."

"Nothing!"

"Yeah, nothing. I know, the son of a bitch showed off tonight and it scared you, but trust me, I know how to take care of myself. That incident with Harry was just a weird fluke. Hell, I haven't been in this business for almost ten years without learning something."

"Maybe so, but I still don't like the idea of you staying on this case."

"Like I've said before, Jill, there's nothing to like. That's the way things are, and they're not gonna change."

"So just learn to live with it, is that what you're saying?"

Jackson lifted a shoulder in a you-got-a-better-idea? shrug.

"Okay, Jack, you win. This time. But I still think you're an idiot."

"That's better'n nothing, I guess," he said with a crooked grin.

# CHAPTER 14

Thursday, May 1

After two days of living with Jillian, Jackson knew he was on his way to developing a split personality. When he was around her, he tried to act as if nothing had happened, as if the attack on them was an ordinary, everyday event. He didn't want her to worry or be frightened. Alone, however, he was constantly on alert. He knew it was just a matter of time before Northrop, or the gun Northrop had hired, if there was one, tried to get to him again. Or maybe living with Jillian was just making him feel paranoid.

Northrop wasn't helping matters either, especially when it came to keeping track of him. The morning after Wyatt's funeral, just hours after Jillian's apartment had been shot to hell, Northrop hopped a jet to Vegas—to pay off some of his gambling debts, Jackson assumed—and hadn't as yet returned.

Jackson's frustration over Northrop's prolonged absence, however, took a backseat to the havoc Jillian's presence created in his life. Living with someone as beautiful and vulnerable as Jillian wasn't as easy as he'd thought it would be. They hadn't come close to finishing what they'd started that night in her apartment, and the sexual tension alone was about to drive him nuts.

179

The matter of his horniness aside, there were other things just as bad. Like her furniture for instance.

Jillian had insisted on moving what was left of her furniture into his loft, and being the concerned gentleman his mother had raised him to be, he hadn't objected. After all, it wasn't as though he was cramped for space. Since then, he'd lost track of the times he had reached for something of his and grabbed something of hers instead. He could never seem to find his clothes in the loft's one and only closet. Somehow Jillian had pushed all of his things to one end of the closet and hung her dresses, skirts, blouses, jeans, and heaven knows what else in their place. The woman had more shoes, purses, belts, and jewelry than did his mother and six sisters put together. What was worse, nearly every day she went out and brought in more. He hadn't known she had this thing about shopping.

In the past, when seven o'clock rolled around and he was at home, not working on a case, Jackson hadn't given a thought to stripping down to his underwear and relaxing in front of the TV. Now that Jillian was around, he had to stay dressed until she decided to go to bed. Which, of late, hadn't been before eleven o'clock.

She would spend the evening either rearranging their eclectic combination of furniture, which didn't look half-bad in Jackson's opinion; tending her two dozen or more houseplants that had transformed his sparse loft into an urban mini-Amazon; or puttering around in the kitchen. While some of her culinary efforts left a lot to be desired, he had to admit that she had Toll-House cookie making down to a science. He'd probably gained five pounds since she'd moved in and taken over the kitchen duties.

Last, but not least, there was her neurotic dog. A miracle occurred the moment Jillian had dragged the poor animal into the loft. Rusty had taken one look at Moose and let out the ungodliest howl Jackson had ever heard. In just two days, the once-shy and withdrawn setter had become one of the major nuisances in his life. Despite the fact that Rusty was always getting in his way, but never Jillian's, the dog had a nasty habit of chewing on his boots. Not five minutes ago, Jillian had torn one from the dog's destructive jaws, after she had stopped it from leaping back and forth over the sofa that Moose was trying to take a nap on. Like Jackson, Moose looked as though she didn't know what the hell to think.

"He'll settle down," Jillian said, scratching Rusty's belly and making him whine like a puppy, "just about the time I find a new apartment and have to move him again."

Jackson decided to let that one slide by without a comment. In spite of his constant sexual frustration, her plants, her clothes, and her stupid dog, he really liked having her around. The thought of her leaving unnerved him.

"Jill," he said, "I know it's none of my business, but have you ever considered taking him to an animal therapist?"

"Funny, that's what Gran said when I first got him."

"Who?"

"My grandmother. There's nothing wrong with Rusty; he's just going through a confused faze. Give him some time, and a lot of love and attention, and he'll be okay. Isn't that right, Rusty?"

As the setter whined, Moose looked up at Jackson and whoofed.

"Naw, I don't buy it either, girl."

The phone rang and Rusty began barking.

"Hush," Jillian said, wrapping her hands around his muzzle. "Here, Jack, let me get that."

"No, you stay put. I'll get it," Jackson said, picking up the receiver. "Hello?"

"Fury?"

"Hey!" Jackson recognized Hank's voice but, suspecting he knew the reason behind the call, decided to keep Jillian in the dark. "How you doin'?"

A pause, and then cautiously, "Uh, okay, I guess."

"No kidding! How long you gonna be in town?"

"How long— Wait a minute. I live here, remember?"

"Sure, no problem. I'll be glad to come and meet you. What hotel you staying at?"

"Oh! I get it," Hank said. "Somebody's there and you can't talk, right?"

"Uh-huh."

"Okay. How about we meet at that coffee shop west of Neiman-Marcus where we had coffee the other morning?"

"Thirty minutes? Yeah, I can be there," Jackson said.

"Good, I'll see what I can do. If you get there first, wait for me."

"Will do. See you soon. 'Bye."

"Who was that?" Jillian asked, smiling at Jackson as he headed for the door.

"Oh, just Ha—Harrellson. Bubba Harrellson. A friend I haven't seen since high school. He's in town for a—a convention, I think he said. Can you handle the fort for a while?"

"Of course. Jack, is something wrong?"

"No, not a thing."

"You're acting kind of strange."

"Nah, that's just your imagination. Look, I don't know how long I'll be gone."

"Well, then, take your time."

"All right, I will. Hey, be sure and lock the door behind me."

"Why? For heaven's sake, Jack, it's broad daylight outside."

"Well, it never hurts to be cautious. Especially in this part of town."

"This part of town?" Jillian said as Jackson closed the door behind him. The West End was just a few blocks from the county courthouse; police or the mounted horse unit patrolled the area at all hours of the day or night.

"Either he got a mild case of shell shock from all that gunfire the other night," Jillian said to the two dogs, "or he's keeping something from me. That's it, isn't it? He's keeping something from me. No, he just thinks he is. But we know I'm smarter than that, don't we?"

"I'll be damned," Hank said, grinning. "Never thought I'd see the day that you got hooked, Fury. Shacking up with your own secretary. Somebody else's I could maybe—"

"We are not shacking up," Jackson said firmly. "It's like I told you before, we're just living together for a while."

"Same thing, isn't it?"

"Not quite."

"Hey, come on, this is me you're talking to. You expect me to believe that two normal, healthy people haven't—"

"That's right, we haven't," Jackson said. And by the looks of things, they weren't going to, either. "She's got the bedroom all to herself, and I sleep on the sofa downstairs."

Slowly Hank shook his head. "Living with a lady as good-looking as she is, it must be kinda rough."

"It's not easy, I'll admit," Jackson said, and decided that it was time to change the subject. "Look, what did you want me for anyway? After the other night, I don't think I ought to stay away from Jill too long."

"That's why I called this morning. To bring you up to date on the investigation."

"You guys got any leads on who did it?"

"No, not yet. We questioned some people in the neighborhood—those who were home. Only two would admit to even seeing anything, and each of them told us a different story."

"How different?"

"Well, one lady said she thought she saw a dark pickup truck turning off La Vista onto Greenville, but she couldn't remember if she saw it before or after y'all had been shot at. The man we talked to said he was certain it was before the firing started but that it was a foreign sports car."

"Damn!" Jackson said. "Dallas is full of pickups and foreign jobs. Especially along Greenville Avenue. What about Northrop? You check him out yet?"

"Yeah, but he turned out to be clean as a whistle." Hank, clearly frustrated, scratched the back of his head. "I hate to say this, but I got a feeling we're barking up the wrong tree with that guy."

"Come on, Hank, he had the perfect motive."

"Yeah, for stealing, but not murder. We've run him through the computer I don't know how many times, and the only thing we came up with was a speeding ticket he got seven years ago. And you know that theory of yours—that he might've hired a hit man?—it don't check out either. No known paid guns were in town when the Strickland woman and Wyatt bought it."

"Not even a rookie?" Jackson asked, and watched the look of uncertainty flash across Hank's face. "Hell, we both know that Wyatt wasn't wasted by a pro. No pro would've gone to all the trouble of making it look like suicide."

"Unless that's what he was hired to do. But say you're right. Say it was a rookie who killed Wyatt. That don't help us any. If anything, it puts us in a bigger fix than we are now. You know how many unsolved murders we got on file?"

"No."

"That makes two of us then, 'cause I don't either. All I know is that there's a lot of them. Over half of 'em won't ever be solved, either. Some guy goes out and wastes another guy, for one reason or other, and takes it with him to the grave. Shit, for all we know Strickland and Wyatt may have been killed by two different people for two entirely different reasons."

"Maybe," Jackson said. "But I don't think so."

"Gut feeling, huh?"

"Yeah."

"Well, I'd be a fool to laugh at a gut feeling," Hank said. "Gut feelings mean a helluva lot in this business. But unless you can come up with something more solid on Northrop, I gotta lay off him. I got a little over eighteen more months to go till I retire, Fury. I can't afford to get myself charged with harassment now. Especially from a guy with Northrop's clout."

"I know. I wouldn't expect you to go that far, anyway, Hank. But do me a favor, would you? Don't file Northrop away yet. Hang in there with him, just for a little while longer. Then, if I can't come up with something on him in the next couple of days, I guess we'll both forget him."

"Okay. What's a couple of days more or less? But I'm warning you, Fury, you'd better keep it legal."

"I will, don't worry. I've decided it's about time I stopped pussy-footing around."

"Which means?"

"Which means," Jackson said, "I'm gonna go see the man. The minute he gets back to Dallas."

# CHAPTER 15

Monday, May 5

Jackson made a face as he leaned closer to the pay phone and cupped one hand over his ear to shut out the nearby street noises.

"Presidio Development," he heard a woman's voice say.

"Jonathan Northrop, please."

"Is Mr. Northrop expecting your call, sir?"

"No."

"Oh. Well, I'm afraid Mr. Northrop is unavailable at the moment. May I take a message and have him return your call?"

"No, I'd prefer to speak to him now. I don't have much time."

"All right. Hold a moment, please. I'll connect you with Mrs. Winters, his secretary."

Bland elevator music came through the receiver and Jackson turned to watch the bumper-to-bumper traffic crawl by the rain-slicked street barricades along nearby Preston Road. The constant construction here in far North Dallas never failed to amaze him. When they weren't widening the streets, they were building new skyscrapers. Nine times out of ten, when the skyscrapers were finished, they had to widen the streets again to handle the additional traffic.

"Mr. Northrop's office, Mrs. Winters speaking, may I help you?"

Jackson jerked his attention back to the phone. "Yes, I want to speak to Jonathan Northrop."

"Who may I say is calling?"

"Jack Fournier." Jackson hoped he correctly pronounced the name he'd read in a rare book long ago. The book wasn't rare—it was just a paperback—but reading one was.

"Do you spell that J-A-C-Q-U-E-S, or J-A-C-K, sir?"

"J-A-C-Q-U-E-S," Jackson said.

"And how is your last name spelled, Mr. Fournier?" To the best of his ability, Jackson told her.

"French?"

"No, Canadian." Then, remembering his Texas accent, "South Canada."

"Mmm. Well, I'm very sorry, Mr. Fournier, but I'm afraid Mr. Northrop is tied up with another call at the moment. Would it be possible for him to return— Oh, excuse me. His other call just ended. Hold on a moment, please. I'll see if I can connect you."

Again Jackson held, feeling no anxiety, no apprehension, just cool calm.

"Mr. Fournier." Despite the noise of squealing brakes that drowned out some of the sound, the masculine voice came over the line loudly and clearly. "This is Jon Northrop. What can I do for you?"

Jackson dropped all pretenses. "You can talk to me; that's what."

A pause, and then Northrop said, "Beg your pardon?"

The apprehension in Northrop's voice satisfied Jackson. "My name's not Fournier, Northrop. It's Fury. Jackson Fury. Ring any bells?"

"N-no. Should it?"

"Don't know. Guess that all depends."

Another pause, and then, nervously, "What the hell do you want with me?"

"To talk. That's all."

"Look, I've told him—"

"Just shut up and listen to me a minute, Northrop. I know all about Vegas—your trips there, the money you owe. Which means I know about Hammond Enterprises and what you've been using it for."

"If you think you're going to extort money—"

"I don't want your goddamn money."

"Then what do you want?"

"Like I told you before, to talk. That's all I want. For now."

"Who are you, anyway?"

"Jackson Fury. I'm a private investigator."

Another pause, and then, "So? What's that got to do with me?"

"A lot, seeing as how Wyatt hired me before he was murdered. I'm still working for him, too. He didn't kill Amanda Strickland; he was framed. But then, you already know that, don't you?"

"Not about him being framed, no. Sterling could never— Oh, my God, you think I did it? You think I killed Mandy? No. No, you're wrong. I didn't do it. I wasn't even near her place when she—"

"Who was then?"

"What?"

"You heard me. If you didn't do it, then who did?" Jackson let the silence stretch, let the implied threat sink in deeper in Northrop's head. "Was it your wife? Did she do it?"

"Cherise? I—I don't . . ."

"Jesus, it just now dawned on you that she could've done it? What'd you think, Northrop, that your wife was different from all the others? That it didn't piss her off, knowing you were sleeping with Amanda?"

"It didn't. I know it didn't. She was all for it. God knows, she even encouraged us. You want to know why? Because she couldn't stand me touching her, that's why. I haven't been allowed near her for over seven fucking years. What was I supposed to do, become a monk?"

That old argument again, Jackson thought, shaking his head.

"Maybe things'll change now that she's filed for divorce," Northrop said, the hopeful tone of his voice surprising Jackson. "But you're wrong about Cherise; you've got to be. She couldn't have killed Mandy. Or Sterling. Cherise may be a—a lot of things, but a murderer's not one of them."

"Then who did kill them?"

Another long pause.

"Northrop?"

"Yes, I'm here."

Jackson was getting tired of bending over talking into the phone, tired of straining to listen, tired of the rain and the mud and the noisy traffic. He wanted to talk to Northrop's face, not just his voice, to know for certain whether the guy was putting on an act, or telling him the truth.

"Look," Jackson said, "let's cut out this bullshit and get right to the point. You're halfway to being charged with a double murder and I think you know it."

"Are you saying the police suspect—"

"I didn't say nothing about the police. Forget them. They don't figure into any of this. Yet. But that doesn't mean they won't. Way I see it, one way or another, you need help. Meet me someplace. Let's get this thing straightened out once and for all."

"Yes," Northrop said with a more positive note in his voice. "Yes, that's a very good idea."

"You name the time and place and I'll be there."

Northrop hesitated, then gave Jackson the name of a restaurant across town.

"When?" Jackson asked.

"Give me a couple of hours. I've got to see— I've got to see somebody first."

Jackson hung up the pay phone and climbed back into his car. Northrop was up to something; he could feel it in his bones. Although what that something was, God only knew.

Five hours later, Jackson stalked out of the freight elevator, hot, tired, and madder than hell.

"That son of a bitch," he snarled. "Last time I'll ever trust a suspect."

Instead of driving straight to the restaurant and waiting four and a half hours in the parking lot for Northrop to show, Jackson realized he should have hung around and tailed the bastard. Hell, he'd been right across the street from Presidio Development when he'd made the call.

He shoved his key into the lock, wrenched open the door, then slammed it behind him as he entered the loft. Jillian jumped, startled by his obtrusive arrival.

"Jack? What's the matter?"

"Northrop's the matter. That son of a bitch." He headed for the kitchen, wanting a cold beer.

"You mean, you've heard?"

"Heard what?" Jillian said something, but he didn't pay any attention. He looked inside the refrigerator and saw nothing but empty shelves. "Goddammit! You'd think as often as I drink the stuff I'd remember to buy it. Or were you the last one to go to the store? Yeah, that's right; it was your turn. Shit, don't tell me I forgot to tell you to put beer down on the grocery—" He stopped abruptly and went very still. "What did you just say?"

"I said, Northrop's dead. He plowed his car into an oncoming lane of traffic on LBJ Freeway and it exploded, with him in it, about three hours ago."

# CHAPTER 16

Friday, May 9

"I can't get a straight answer out of anybody," Jackson said. "Nobody seems to know if Northrop's car crashed through that railing because his brakes failed, because the car had faulty steering, or because he felt guilty and trapped and just suddenly took a notion to end it all."

As soon as his shock had worn off, Jackson had called Hank, but Hank had told him it was too soon to give out any information. The county coroner hadn't gotten around to doing Northrop's autopsy yet, Hank said, and considering the backlog of work the department had, it didn't look as though they'd be getting around to it anytime soon, either. Jackson took "backlog" to mean bodies. Dead bodies. All stacked up in the hall. Just take a number and wait your turn—the sum total of modern civilization.

"So you came here," said Walter Collins, studying Jackson over the rim of his reading glasses, "thinking you could get an answer from me."

"Yeah. You were his attorney."

"Wrong. I was Sterling's attorney, not Jon's. The only contact I had with him was on the one or two occasions when Presidio's legal staff called me in as a consultant; they were involved in a couple of iffy liability cases. But that's minor to what you're talking about.

"Hate to say this, Fury, but you're wasting both my time and yours asking me what happened. I know as much about it as you do. Which is next to nothing, apparently."

"Then you don't have any idea who Northrop was gonna meet, who he met before he died."

"He was meeting somebody?" Intrigued, Collins leaned forward, resting his elbows on the desk. "How did you find this out?"

"I called him."

"When?"

"Just before he died. Hell, the way things are beginning to look, I was the last one outside his office to even talk to him."

"What did you call him for?"

"To see if I could set up a meeting with him. I wanted to talk to him face-to-face. Maybe get a confession out of him."

"Confession? Out of Jon?"

"Yeah. I know it's dumb, but I had this screw-ball notion that he killed Amanda Strickland and Wyatt. The guy had more of a motive than anyone else to want to get rid of them. And he sure as hell had the means, with his contact in Vegas."

Collins leaned back again. "Would I be correct in assuming that, other than the one telephone conversation with him, you didn't talk to him?"

Jackson nodded. "He agreed to see me, but he never showed up." Then, thoughtfully, "You know, something about this whole thing doesn't make sense. When I accused Northrop over the phone, he sounded—shocked. Like it really surprised him that someone would think he could have murdered them. All this time, I believed he was the one. Now I don't think he was.

"He knew who did kill them, though. Deep down in my

gut, I'm sure he knew. It's the way he talked; nothing he said, but the way he said it. I heard it, and dammit, at the time, it just didn't register. Now that he's dead, I don't suppose I'll ever know for sure."

"So, in essence, you're back to square one."

"Yeah." Jackson slouched in the chair with his legs crossed and chewed worriedly on his thumbnail.

"You're not going to like me saying this, Fury, but you're a lot better off than the rest of us are."

"I am?" Jackson snorted skeptically. "How you figure that?"

"I'm executor of Sterling's estate, but then, I don't suppose you knew that, did you?"

"No, can't say that I did." Jackson wondered what Collins's position as executor could possibly have to do with Northrop dying. Or with himself, for that matter.

"Well, I am. And because I am, I know a lot of what goes on inside Presidio Development, mainly because most of Sterling's estate is tied up in the company. Last contact I had with the board of directors was shortly after his funeral. Poor bastards were running around in circles; nobody knew what to do. Now that Jon's dead—" Collins shook his head. "Needless to say, the company's on pretty shaky ground. They've got three projects in the works and two still in the planning stage, and quite a number of employees with families to feed. If they don't get their act together soon, Presidio might go right down the tubes.

"There's no need for you to worry," the lawyer added. "When all of this is over, you'll still be paid. Sterling made certain of that before he was released from jail."

"Whoa, back up there a minute." Jackson uncrossed his legs and leaned forward. "Wyatt doesn't owe me anything."

"On the contrary, he felt he owed you quite a lot. In this instance, I have to agree with him, too."

"But he didn't hire me. Ji—Wyatt's alibi did."

"That doesn't matter. Sterling wanted you to be reimbursed for your time and effort, and you will be. He was—" Collins broke off to clear the emotion from his throat. "He was an unusual man. Honorable, when it's so easy, so fashionable, these days to be dishonorable. I for one am going to miss him.

"Enough of that," Collins said. "Let's get back to the matter at hand. Namely Jon's death."

"Yeah," Jackson said, feeling a twinge of uneasiness when it came to discussing Wyatt. "So what you're saying is that the company's up the creek now that Northrop's gone."

"That's the way it looks, yes."

"They can't hire somebody else to come in and take over?"

"Of course they could, but who? Sterling and Jon ran that company like a well-oiled piece of machinery. It'll take the board months, maybe even years, to find someone who can run Presidio as well as they did."

"What about Northrop's wife, uh, widow?" Jackson's suggestion came as a surprise, even to himself.

"Cherise?"

"Yeah, why not? I know she'd filed for divorce— Northrop let it slip when we were talking over the phone— but I'll bet she knows a little about what her husband did. Most wives do, don't they? Why not put her in the hot seat until you can find someone permanent to take over."

"No, I don't think Cherise would— Then again, who knows? Maybe she would."

"Won't hurt anything to give her a shot," Jackson said, thinking how really terrific his idea sounded. Making Cherise temporary head of the company would tie her down so that she couldn't leave town. It would also give him enough time to check her out.

Later, as he left Collins's office, Jackson realized that he wasn't back to square one yet. He still had one suspect high on his list. Good old, horny Cherise.

# CHAPTER 17

Saturday, May 10

"This is dumb, Jill. I mean really dumb." Jackson tried to keep his voice low, not wanting any of the elegantly dressed art patrons mingling nearby to hear him.

All trussed up in the monkey-suit Jillian had made him rent, he felt like a Thanksgiving turkey right before the big event. Why he had let her talk him into coming tonight, he didn't know. Art galleries weren't his scene. Football games, basketball games, or wrestling matches, where you could cuss, burp, and scratch if you felt like it, but not this. He'd never been to a "showing," as Jillian called it, before, but he already knew he wouldn't like it.

Running a finger inside the tight collar of his shirt, he pulled it away from his neck. Hell, they probably didn't even serve beer at a prissy, high-brow to-do like this. No beer, a suffocating room full of overdressed stuffed shirts, and the weirdest pictures he'd ever laid eyes on—some terrific way to spend an evening. The best thing he'd seen so far was Jillian herself. Dressed in a strapless black dress that defied gravity, and with one of her long legs showing through the thigh-high slit in her skirt, she looked good enough to eat. Which he might be tempted to do before the night was over; if he could get lucky and talk her into it, that is.

"What do I need pictures for?" he asked.

"Well for one thing, these paintings, not pictures, would be a very good investment," she said. "And for another, your loft is in desperate need of some color. I have no idea how long you've been there—it's none of my business, really—but in my opinion, it still looks like a warehouse."

"Hey, don't be bad-mouthing my home. Our home, I mean."

"That's another thing—I'm glad you brought it up—but we'll get into that later. Right now we're talking about paintings. These paintings. They're originals, Jack, done by up-and-coming artists. The best kind of investment you could make."

Jackson studied the huge, unframed canvas on the wall near his shoulder for all of three seconds. Any longer and the bold slashes of red and black on a stark white background would have given him a headache.

"I wouldn't invest my money in this kind of junk if you paid me, Jill. It's not worth two cents, let alone"—seeing the price tag—"Jesus! Fifteen hundred bucks?"

"Look at it this way, Jack—in ten or twenty years from now, it might be worth fifteen thousand. And it's not junk. It's impressionistic. The subject matter goes hand in hand with the artist's interpretation of rage unrestrained. Look in the catalog they handed to us when we came in the door; it'll tell you all the names of the paintings being shown tonight, and who the artists are."

Jackson didn't follow Jillian's suggestion. Just behind her, he'd caught sight of a group of men who were huddled together on the far side of the room. Each was holding a drink in his hand. Hot damn, he thought, maybe this place had a watering hole after all.

"Impressionistic, huh?" he said, wondering how long it would take him to maneuver her away from the pictures and to the bar. "I thought impressionist stuff had a bunch of goofy-looking women with blue boobs. Say, I'm getting thirsty. You want something to drink?"

"No, not right now, thank you. You've got impressionistic confused with cubist. Probably because you're thinking of some of Picasso's work. This is definitely an impressionistic painting by"—consulting her program—"Fullerton."

Realizing that his ploy had failed, Jackson reluctantly tore his gaze from the bar and let it return to the canvas. The damn thing still didn't look any better. Whoever Fullerton was, he or she was badly screwed up. Rage unrestrained, huh? It didn't look like rage unrestrained to him. What someone would flush down the toilet after throwing up, maybe, but not rage.

"Don't they have any pictures in this place with real 'subject matter' I'd recognize?"

"By real, do you mean something like little kids with big soulful eyes?"

"Yeah."

"No, Jack, this art gallery deals only in one-of-a-kind originals, not in mass-produced prints. You might be able to find that kind of picture at, oh, K-Mart maybe."

"Okay, you don't have to rub it in. I get the message. I may not be cultured, but I'll tell you one thing—K-Mart's a lot more my speed than this place is. Hell, even if I did have artistic taste, this junk still wouldn't match my furniture."

"People don't invest in art because it matches their furniture."

"Yeah, well, people who sink their hard-earned money into stuff like this are either crazy, or they're really hard-up to impress somebody. And I ain't neither one."

Jillian averted her head and suppressed a smile. It didn't take a genius to know that Jackson was a basic red-neck at heart. Truth to tell, that in itself wasn't so very bad. She liked him just the way he was, and would not want him to change.

"Come on," she said, looping her arm through his, "let's look around and see if they have something here more to your liking."

They had gone but a few feet when Jillian heard her name being called. Instantly recognizing the voice, she went cold inside. Oh, no, she thought. Why here, of all places? And tonight of all nights, when she had something important to do?

Unlike Jillian, who stood stock still, Jackson turned and saw a tall, elegant woman gliding toward them. At first, he thought she was around forty years of age, but as she drew closer, he realized she was closer to forty-five. Fifty tops, and a damn good-looking fifty at that. Wide streaks of silver highlighted the black hair that swept softly away from her unlined face, accentuating her high cheekbones and flawless skin. Vaguely familiar eyes, as blue as the dress she wore, assessed him in much the same way he assessed her. He caught a whiff of her light, but very provocative, perfume when she moved past him and embraced Jillian, who, he was surprised to see, hugged and kissed her in return.

"Why didn't you tell me you were going to be here tonight?" the woman asked.

"Because I didn't know we were," Jillian said. "Coming here was sort of a last-minute decision."

"Yeah," Jackson said, running his finger inside his tight collar again, "I wanted to go to the drive-in and see a Sylvester Stallone movie, but Jill wanted to come here. We flipped a coin for it and she won."

The woman looked at him, smiled, and Jackson fell head over heels in love.

"Don't tell me," she said. "You've got to be Jackson Fury."

"Yes, ma'am." Jackson clasped her extended hand, noting the number of diamonds she wore. The strength and self-assurance of her grip made him wish he were a few years older. Or she was a few years younger.

"Jack," Jillian said, "this is my grandmother, Mrs. Mercedes Underwood."

Jackson blinked in disbelief at Jillian, then turned to stare at the woman. "She's kidding, right? You're not really her grandmother, are you, Mrs. Underwood?"

"But I am. And please, don't call me Mrs. Underwood. Call me Mercy. Or better yet"—a sly glance at Jillian—"call me Gran."

"Naw, you can't be her grandmother. You're not old enough."

"Jill, I think I'm gonna like this boy." Gran's eyes twinkled as she slid her hand around Jackson's arm. "This time, honey, I do believe you've picked yourself a winner."

When they turned and started to walk away, Jillian called out, "Gran, wait . . ."

"Now, Jill," Gran said over her shoulder, "Jack and I are just gonna take ourselves off somewhere and get to know one another a little better, that's all. You can entertain yourself for a while, can't you? That's a good girl."

Jackson didn't say a word as Gran led him through the crowded gallery. Whoever had given this woman the name of Mercy knew exactly what they were doing, he thought. She was truly an angel of deliverance, because she was taking him straight to the bar.

The bartender beamed at Gran. "Good evening, Mrs. Underwood."

"Good evening, Chuck. Nice crowd tonight."

"Sure is. Would you folks care for something to drink?"

"Yes, we would," Gran said. "I believe my young friend here could do with a cold draft beer right about now."

"And what'll you have, Mrs. Underwood?"

"Oh, a Wild Turkey with either a splash of branch water or on the rocks. Whatever's easiest for you."

"How did you know I wanted a beer?" Jackson asked when the bartender turned away.

"Because you remind me of my husbands."

"Husbands?" Jackson repeated, stressing the plural.

"Yes. Better make that late husbands. I'm a widow, Jack, not a bigamist. All three of them were honest-to-God men, too, just like you. Not a thing, I'm happy to say, like that questionable little priss who's heading our way now."

Her "questionable little priss" was an effete-looking character with a silk scarf around his neck. As he floated past them, limp wrist and all, both suppressed a chuckle.

Jackson knew then that Gran was a woman after his own heart. He couldn't believe she was really Jill's grandmother.

"So," Gran said, "as I understand it from Jill, you're a private investigator."

"Yes, ma'am, that's right."

"Sounds exciting."

"Oh, it is. Sometimes," Jackson said. "Most of the time, though, it's no different from any other job. After a while, it can get to be routine and boring."

They accepted their drinks from the bartender, then wandered toward a quiet corner behind a large, potted palm.

"Jill seems to really like her work," Gran said. "At least, that's the impression I got."

"Well, your granddaughter's very good at what she does. Fact is, I don't know what I'd've done if she hadn't come to work for me." Probably still been knee-deep in paperwork, he decided. Definitely at home in his underwear watching TV instead of being stuck here in this place.

"Jack, I hope you won't think I'm a meddlesome old woman . . ."

"Oh, no, ma'am, not at all."

"If I were you, I wouldn't be so quick to answer. You'd better hear me out first."

"All right," Jackson said, wondering what she was leading to.

"You see, Jill's my only granddaughter."

"Yes, ma'am."

"And because my daughter, Jill's mother, doesn't know what she's up to, I think I should find out exactly what all's going on."

What Jillian was up to? Jackson wondered uneasily. Oh, damn! Surely she hadn't told her grandmother that she was living with him. He quickly perused Gran's matronly curves. Detecting no bulging signs of a pistol, he realized he was safe on that score. Okay, so what the hell would he say to her if she asked him what his intentions were? Come right out and tell her the truth, that he was dying to go to bed with her granddaughter? Or lie through his teeth, and tell her they were planning to get married soon? No matter how you looked at it, their living together didn't look good.

Another alternative popped into his head, and he played it safe by pretending ignorance. "I'm not sure I know what you're getting at, Mrs. Underwood."

"Mercy, or Gran, remember?"

"Sorry, Gran. I can understand why you'd be worried about Jill, you being her grandmother and all, but I still don't see what that's got to do with me?"

"Let me put it this way—Jill's twenty-three and as smart as a tack about a lot of things, but she doesn't have your kind of experience. That's why I can't understand what possessed you to hire her."

Still confused, Jackson blinked. "Because she can balance my checkbook, type, file, and answer the phone."

"Surely those aren't the only reasons. Are they?"

"Well, she's not half-bad on the eyes first thing in the morning, if that's what you mean. Look, Mrs. Underwood, I mean, Gran, why don't you come straight to the point?"

"All right, I will. Why is my granddaughter working with you as a private investigator?"

"Working with me as a—"

"Now don't get me wrong; I'll admit that the only thing I know about private investigators is what I've seen on TV. And they're just acting; they're not real people like us. But some of the situations they get into have to make you stop and wonder if things like that couldn't happen in real life. So when Jill told me she was helping you solve Amanda Strickland's murder, I naturally couldn't help but be worried."

"She told you what?"

Heads turned and conversations ceased at Jackson's loud roar. Gran didn't waste any time; she grabbed hold of his arm and pulled him through the first door they came to.

"Excuse us, will you, ladies?" she said to the two women who'd been arguing inside the powder room.

Jackson waited until the pair had swished indignantly out the door before he rounded on Gran. "Just what the hell has Jill been telling you, anyway?"

"Like I said before, that she's helping you solve Amanda Strickland's murder." Gran saw a muscle twitch in Jackson's cheek, then watched his lips slowly disappear into an angry line. "Is she?"

"I don't know; I'm gonna find out," he said through clenched teeth. "But I'll tell you this much; if she is, her little ass is mine."

Champagne spilled out of a man's glass and onto his companion's designer gown as Jackson burst out of the powder room. Back across the gallery he stalked, ignoring the curious stares that patrons gave him as he searched for Jillian. He'd kill her. He'd wrap his hands around her pretty white neck and choke the daylights out of her if there was one grain of truth to what her grandmother said.

"Helping me, is she?" he said quietly, or so he thought.

The effete little character with the flowing silk scarf heard Jackson as he sailed past. Inhaling a slow breath, he turned to the man beside him. "God, now there goes a man I wouldn't mind knowing."

"When will you ever learn, Gerald?" his companion asked in a bored tone. "From the looks of him, the guy's probably straight."

"Maybe. Maybe not. One has to keep hoping, Teddy."

Jackson spied Jillian down a short hall, coming out of the gallery owner's office. She looked up, saw him, saw the look on his face, and quickly closed her beaded evening clutch.

"Hi, how did you and Gran—"

"Save the bullshit, sweet cakes," he said, grabbing her arm and propelling her ahead of him back into the gallery. "You're coming with me."

Gerald and Teddy saw them coming and stepped out of their way.

"Wh—where are we going?"

"Home. By the time I get through with you, honey, you're gonna be so tied up in knots you won't know what to think."

"See?" said Teddy. "He's straight."

Gerald, with the scarf, bit his trembling lower lip. "God, all that passion, all that fire, and he's even into bondage. Teddy, it just breaks my heart."

Fury was furious, Jillian decided. Standing at a safe distance across the room, she winced as Jackson slammed and locked the loft door. Another time her silent attempt at levity might have made her laugh, or even smile, but not this time. She knew Fury's fury was directed at her. He hadn't said one word on the way home; he'd just cut her off with a growl whenever she had opened her mouth.

Well, enough was enough. She couldn't stand the

suspense any longer. "Correct me if I'm wrong," she said, "but I've got the strangest feeling that you're upset."

"Upset? Me?" He closed the distance between them at a slow, menacing pace. "Now why would I be upset?"

Nobody's dummy, Jillian backed away from him. If he suddenly decided to explode, the last place she wanted to be was near him. "Well, I don't know. That's why I asked you. Did Gran say something?"

"Your grandmother—dynamite lady she is, too—said quite a lot. Real eye-openers."

"Like wh—what, for instance?"

"Well, like how you told her you were helping me solve the Strickland murder."

"She told you that?" Jillian's nervous laugh held an ample amount of fear as she took another step backward. Her legs touched one of the sofas, making her gasp as she plopped down. She held her clutch bag close to her chest in much the same way one of Count Dracula's victims might cling to a cross. "I wonder why on earth she'd say something like that?"

"Beats me. She's your grandmother; I was sorta hoping you could tell me."

"Well, my grandmother's not exactly like other grandmothers. She's different. Kind of hard to pin down."

"A lot like her granddaughter. Something the matter, Jill?" Jackson stopped in front of her, forcing her to shrink farther down into the sofa.

"No," she said on a croak. "No, nothing's the matter."

"Then why are you acting like there is? Like you're afraid I'm gonna do something to you."

She cringed. "Are you?"

"I don't know. I haven't made up my mind yet. I heard that you've been meddling in my business. Of course, I don't know this for sure, not firsthand, but it'd be rude, not to mention downright disrespectful, if I doubted a lady like your grandmother. She's a good woman, salt of the earth; what reason would she have to lie?

"But say I was sure," he said. "You know, hypothetically speaking. Say I did find out that you'd gone behind my back, meddled in my business, maybe even damaged the reputation it's taken me ten years to build up. Wouldn't you agree that I'd have a pretty good reason to—what did you say earlier? Oh, yeah—to get upset."

His legs straddling Jillian's knees, Jackson leaned forward and grabbed the sofa, his hands braced on either side of her head, their faces mere inches apart. "If I was certain of that, honey, let me tell you, I wouldn't hesitate one minute to wring your neck!"

Jillian swallowed. "I think I might be able to explain, Jack."

"Explain? For you to be able to explain, Jill, means you've been doing it. Have you?"

"Well . . . sort of."

Jillian was hauled to her feet before she even felt Jackson touch her.

"You idiot! You dumb, stupid little nitwit! What the hell do you think this is, anyway, some kind of game? Jesus Christ, people connected with Wyatt are dropping like flies out there."

"But it's not what you think," she said, wincing.

Jackson ignored her. "You could get yourself killed!"

With the slow evaporation of Jillian's fear her body grew stiff. "Well, so could you, buster!" she said, wrenching free of his hold.

"Come on, get serious, Jill. I carry a gun, remember?"

"Big deal! So you carry a gun. Tell me something, Jack. Why didn't you use that tinker-toy pea-shooter you've got stuck in your pants when Evelyn's husband jumped you?"

A nerve twitched near Jackson's eye. "That's a low blow,

Jill. Throwing Evelyn's husband at me at a time like this is no way to fight fair.''

"Well, you're the one who started this fight, Jack, not me.''

"Wrong, sweetheart. You started it.''

"Me!''

"Yeah, the minute you stuck that pretty little nose of yours into my business. Jesus, if your grandmother hadn't opened her mouth tonight, I never would've known what was going on.''

"That's right, you wouldn't. And if you'll calm down a minute and think back, you might just remember that you're the one who asked me to help you in the first place!''

A study of righteous indignation down to the heels of his boots, Jackson glowered. "Yeah, well, I didn't mean for you to take me seriously. But you know something? It's a damn good thing I found out now, instead of later, just how good you are at keeping secrets.''

"What's that supposed to mean?''

"To quote your grandmother: 'You got yourself a winner *this time*'? That's what it means.''

"Huh?''

"Who was he, Jill?''

"Who was who?''

"The other guy. The one your grandmother was talking about.''

Jillian, concentrating very hard, managed to recall, and rather vaguely at that, part of their short conversation with Gran.

"Well?'' Jackson said.

"I honestly don't—'' She broke off, the answer washing through her in a painful wave. "She must have been talking about Brad.''

"Okay, who is he?''

Jillian averted her gaze, not wanting Jackson to see her

expression. "Nobody really. Just some guy I dated in college."

" 'Just some guy'? You sure he wasn't a lot more than 'just some guy'? You ask me, he must've been someone pretty special if your grandmother met him."

"That was an accident, kind of like the way I met your parents. She only met him one time, too, when she went up to Denton to visit me. I never knew—that is, she never let on that she didn't like him."

"Did you?"

"Did I what?"

"Like him—this Brad character we're talking about?"

"I can't see where that's any of your business."

"Well, I sure as hell can."

Wanting to end this difficult conversation, Jillian glanced at her watch. "Look, it's late. If you don't mind, I think I'll go to bed."

"But I do mind, sweet cakes." Jackson reached out and gently grabbed her arm as she started past him. "We're gonna get this thing settled."

"There's nothing to settle. I'm not going to tell you about Brad. Why should I? You haven't said word one to me about all the other women in your life."

"What other women?"

"Well, for starters, there's Monica and Caroline and Cynthia and Beverly, and all the others who've been calling and leaving messages for you and who you've never bothered to call back."

"But Monica, Caroline, and the rest don't mean anything to me. And they sure as hell didn't leave me with the hangups that Brad gave you."

"I don't have any hangups. Especially not over the likes of Brad Palmer."

Jackson's snort held no amusement. "You could've fooled me."

"I don't!"

"You sure as hell do, Jill. You won't go to bed with me. If that's not a hangup, I'd like to know what is."

"To quote a couple of things you said earlier, Jack, 'that's a low blow' and 'you're not fighting fair.'"

"Sorry, but as someone once said, 'All's fair in love and—'"

"No, it's not! Not this time. And you want to know why? Because I say it's not. Just who do you think you are, anyway, standing here, questioning me about Brad? What right is it of yours to meddle in my life?"

"It's my right, dammit, because I love you!"

Jackson flinched, surprised by his own answer.

Stunned as well, Jillian stood very still. "You what?"

"I didn't say that. Did I? No. No, I couldn't have said that."

"You did, though."

"No, I didn't."

"Yes, you did. I heard you."

"Unh-unh," Jackson said, shaking his head. "No, I know I didn't. You must've misunderstood me."

"I'm not hard of hearing, Jack. And I'm not hallucinating. I definitely heard you say, 'I love you.'"

"Are you sure?"

"I'm positive."

Frowning, Jackson scratched the back of his head. "Wellll, come to think of it, maybe I did."

"There's no maybes about it. You said, 'I love you.'"

Jackson rubbed a finger under his nose and nodded. "Okay, so I said it. Big deal. Still don't do me much good, does it?"

"What's that supposed to mean?"

"You figure it out, sweetheart. It means that no matter what I say, you still won't go to bed with me."

"Who said I wouldn't?"

Jackson looked at her for a moment, and then swallowed nervously. "You saying you will?"

"Yes."

"Really?"

"Yes."

"Now?"

"I guess so."

"'I guess so,'" he mimicked. "I swear, Jill, you've got the worst sense of timing of anyone I've ever— Why in the sweet name of heaven didn't you say something before now?"

"I don't know. Maybe because I didn't think you'd be interested."

"Interested! Jesus Christ! I've been sleeping with my feet hanging off of this lumpy sofa for the better part of a week instead of upstairs in bed with you, and only because you didn't think I'd be interested?"

Jillian considered her answer, then said, "Yes."

"Shit! I'm interested, okay? I mean, I'm *really* interested."

"All right."

"You want me to write out a statement and have it notarized? I'm not kidding, Jill."

"I know you're not. I believe you."

Still, they just stood there looking at each other, neither one of them moving a muscle, both aware of the doubt and uncertainty the other obviously felt.

Jackson broke the tension by taking a deep breath. "So what's stopping us?"

"I don't know."

"Something is, you know?"

Jillian nodded.

"Now's not the right time; that's what's stopping us."

"You're the one with all the know-how—are you sure that's it?"

"You got a better answer?"

"No, not really."

"Then, that's gotta be it."

"What are we going to do about it?"

"Wish to hell I—" Jackson broke off, stiffening at the soft, pathetic whine he heard upstairs. They had been so preoccupied with themselves that neither had noticed the absence of Moose and Rusty.

"My God!" Jillian said, thinking the worst as she raced up the stairs behind Jackson.

Jackson reached the bedroom first and froze at the one sight he had never expected to see.

Jillian rushed past him, then she, too, froze.

"Well, I'll be damned," Jackson said.

Moose sat in the middle of Jackson's rumpled bed, looking innocent and somewhat confused by their sudden appearance. Rusty lay on the floor with his long tongue hanging out one side of his mouth, too exhausted to even move.

"What's happened?" Jillian asked, falling to her knees beside the prone setter. "What on earth have they been doing?"

"You mean, you don't know? Damn, Jill, I know you're innocent, but I didn't think you were stupid."

Jillian peered up in surprise at him. "Are you saying that these two have—"

"Yeah, that's exactly what I'm saying." Jackson studied both dogs and shook his head. "Good thing we weren't here. We might have had to throw cold water on them. Oh, well, looks like at least one of us guys finally hit it lucky."

Jillian stared back at the setter in disgust. "I never thought I'd have to say this, but I'm ashamed of you, Bertrand Russell Fletcher."

Rusty whined as Jillian rose to her feet, then trained a pitiful look on Jackson.

"Don't listen to her, boy," Jackson said, taking Jillian's place beside the setter. "She's just a little upset. Stunned, too, like me. Hard to believe the two of you actually got it off, considering Moose is almost twice as big as you are. Damn near wore you out, didn't she?"

"Honestly, Jack, how can you crack jokes at a time like this? Just look what they've done to the bed." Jillian grimaced when Moose hopped down to the floor and licked both Jackson and Rusty. "Ugh! If I didn't know any better, I'd say she was proud of herself for seducing Rusty."

"Dogs don't seduce each other, Jill; they haven't got that much sense. They just react to natural instincts. Moose was in heat, and Rusty sensed it, and being a normal healthy male, he gave her his best shot."

"I should have expected that kind of answer from you," Jillian said, chafing under Jackson's amused grin. "Well, go ahead and gloat. Gloat all you want; I don't care. Have a good laugh at what those two have done. But while you're laughing, you might want to consider this: Unless you've had Moose fixed—which I seriously doubt—in a few weeks, she's going to have a litter of puppies."

The grin on Jackson's face faded and moved to Jillian's.

"Puppies?" he said.

"Mmm-hmm. Just think, you'll get to hear the pitter-patter of all those little feet. All those big little feet. If I were you, Jack, I'd start stockpiling my newspapers. You're going to need them."

# CHAPTER 18

Monday, May 12

Jackson laughed as he watched the tall, lanky young man lope across the parking lot. The kid looked no different from some of the other teenagers in Dallas, who were currently going through a Roper, Prep, Rambo, or Punk faze. In other words, just plain weird.

But when the kid opened the passenger door of the Pontiac and climbed inside, the shocking disbelief of recognition set in.

"Randy?" Jackson asked. "Good God, what have you done to yourself?"

"Got my hair cut," his little brother said, running his fingers through what remained of his dark-brown hair.

"What the hell with, a lawn mower?" The one-inch spike growing like a paintbrush out the top of the kid's head looked bad enough in Jackson's opinion, but Randy had made it look worse by leaving the back so long that it flipped over the collar of his wrinkled shirt. He had also shaved a wide strip around his ears to show an earring. "Since when did you start wearing Momma's earring? Or did Treeva Lynn loan you one of hers?"

"It's not theirs, it's mine," Randy said. "I bought it. Lady put it in when she pierced my ear."

Jackson stared for a long, silent moment, then shook his head. "No offense, little brother, but you look like shit."

"Lay off, will ya, Jack? You sound just like Daddy."

"You mean he's seen you looking like this and let you live to tell about it?"

Randy examined the toe of his unlaced red high-top. "Yeah. Knew when I had it done it was gonna piss him off, but I didn't have no other choice."

"What did Momma say?"

"Nothing. She just sorta looked at me like you did, then shook her head and turned around and walked off. Treeva Lynn laughed so hard she started crying."

"If you knew nobody was gonna like it, what in God's name did you have it done for? The new-wave, punk, unmade-bed-look the latest craze in Mesquite, or something?"

"No, I had to get my ear pierced and my hair cut like this so I could audition for a commercial out at Las Colinas. Just for your information, I got it, too."

"A commercial, huh?" Jackson inhaled deeply. "You're nineteen years old, Randy; when are you gonna grow out of this acting thing?"

"Never. There's good money in it. Real good money."

"Not a lot of hard work either, from what I hear."

"Then you heard wrong. It's hard work, believe me. But see, doing the commercial gave me the chance to try out for a new movie they're gonna start filming here soon. Gonna be on location down in Waxahachie and up in McKinney part of the time, when they're not shooting out at the Las Colinas studios."

"When is this?"

"Later on this year, I think. By that time, my hair'll be a lot longer. At least I hope it will."

"You saying you got the part?"

"Don't know for sure yet. Gotta go back in a day or two

to read for the casting director again, but it sure looks
good."

"My baby brother, the movie star," Jack said, shaking
his head in amazement.

"Could be." Randy grinned, pleased with himself.

They sat outside the Town East Shopping Mall in
Mesquite. Meeting Randy at the loft had been out of the
question because Jackson didn't want Jillian to know what
was going on. After last Saturday night, when he discovered she'd been sticking her nose where it didn't belong,
he knew someone would have to keep an eye on her so she
wouldn't get into trouble. He couldn't very well be in two
places at once—like this morning, when she had gone to the
supermarket and he had to go see Frank before starting his
surveillance on Cherise Northrop—so he'd called Randy.

"You got anything planned between now and the time
this movie starts?"

"Nope, not a thing. Except try to keep out of Daddy's
way, I guess. Why?"

"I'd like you to do some work for me."

"Work? What kind of—Hey, wait a minute. If this has
anything to do with following some tom-catting husband
around, I can tell you right now, I ain't interested. Last dude
I tailed for you caught me and damn near broke my nose.
Finally got a chance to try out for a real speaking part in a
movie, I can't afford to have someone mess up my face."

"Don't worry, I promise she won't lay a finger on that
handsome nose of yours." Randy's heart, however, was
another matter, Jackson realized, remembering how sus-
ceptible his little brother was to a pretty face.

"She?"

"Yeah. Jill Fletcher, my secretary."

"Your secretary, huh?" A grin slowly appeared at one
side of Randy's mouth. "She the same Jill Fletcher Treeva
Lynn was telling me about?"

"Yeah. I'm gonna be real busy for the next couple of days and I want you to sorta baby-sit with her."

Randy's grin widened. "Oh, now I get it."

"Get what?"

Randy nudged his elbow into Jackson's ribs. "Come on, Jack. You know."

"No, I don't. I swear, Randy, you've been hanging around Treeva Lynn too long; neither one of you makes any sense. What are you talking about?"

"Shacking up," Randy said, "with your secretary. That's what."

Jackson's confusion vanished. "Who the hell told you that?"

"Treeva Lynn."

"Treeva Lynn! How'd she find out?"

"Momma told her to call you early one morning, and when she did, Jill answered the phone. Treeva Lynn just put two and two together and—"

"Okay, that's enough. I get the picture." Jackson inhaled a deep breath, hoping it would steady his nerves. "Do me a favor, would you? Next time you see our little sister, tell her that Jill and I are not shacking up."

"Then what's she doing living with you, if you're not shacking up?"

"Her place got shot to hell the other night when someone came gunning for me."

"No kidding!"

"No, no kidding."

"Wow!"

"Seeing as how what happened was mostly my fault, I felt I had to make it up to her, so I moved her into the loft. But that doesn't mean we're shacking up."

"If you say so," Randy said.

"I do, so you can just wipe that stupid grin off your face. And don't you dare breathe a word of this to Momma or

Daddy." Knowing his folks, his mother in particular, they'd start sending out the wedding invitations.

"Don't have to," Randy said. "They already know. Treeva Lynn told them."

"Jesus, that girl's getting to be as bad as Wanda about spreading family gossip."

"You're telling me," Randy said, nodding. "Sometimes I wish we didn't even have sisters. They're more trouble than they're worth."

"You can say that again," said Jackson. "So, will you do it?"

"Do what?"

"Keep an eye on Jill for me?"

"Yeah, sure, why not? Got nothing better to do."

Hoisting the two heavy grocery bags onto her hips, Jillian managed to insert her key into the loft door. It hadn't taken her long to realize that living in the West End had its share of drawbacks; the biggest being when it came time to do the weekly grocery shopping. She had to drive halfway across town to the Lakewood Village Shopping Center on Gaston Avenue to get all the things she wanted. Of course, there were supermarkets closer than Gaston, but they tended to cater more to cheap wine drinkers than to those who preferred eating well-balanced meals.

"Here, let me give you a hand with those," a strange voice offered as she entered the loft.

The tall, skinny young man coming toward her looked like he'd just stepped out of a punk-rock video. "Wh—who are you?" Jillian asked, suddenly apprehensive.

"Randy," he said, taking both bags from her. "Jack's brother."

She studied him closely and, recognizing a faint family resemblance, breathed an inner sigh of relief. "Yes, of course you are! Your sister, Treeva Lynn, mentioned your name the other night, when Jack took me to dinner at your mom and dad's restaurant.''

"Is this all the groceries?"

"No, there's a lot more bags out beside the freight elevator. Where's Jack?"

"He left a while ago to go see our cousin Frank."

"Your cousin?"

"Uh-huh. You put these away; I'll go get the rest."

"So, you're Jack's little brother," she said when he had returned with the last of the bags.

"Yeah." Randy grinned. "And you're his secretary."

"Among other things. Right now it looks as though I'm the chief cook and bottle washer."

"He make you do all the cooking and cleaning around here?"

"No, I was just kidding. Actually we take turns."

"I was just gonna say, you got the bad end of the deal."

"No, Jack did. Ask him. See, I love to cook, but he doesn't like a lot of the things I fix. I suppose he's more of a meat-and-potato man, while I'm your basic quiche and soufflé person."

"Meat and potatoes. Yeah, that sounds like Jack, all right. Where do you want me to put this?" Randy asked, holding up a can of soup.

"Over in that cabinet, I guess. One of these days, when I can find the time, I'm going to rearrange the cabinets. I'd like to rearrange the whole kitchen. Just tear it all out and start over."

"Why don't you?"

Jillian laughed. "Well, for one thing, I don't think your brother would like it; it's his loft, not mine. And for another, I don't have the money."

"You might not, but he does."

"Yes, I know."

"If I were you, I'd go ahead and do it. Jack wouldn't care."

"You don't know your brother as well as you think, Randy. He doesn't like people interfering." Jillian could testify personally to that. After what had happened the other night, he had warned her to keep her nose out of his business. The fact that she hadn't, that she'd done a considerable amount of snooping since his warning, was something she hoped he'd never discover. She didn't intend to keep him in the dark forever, of course; she would tell him, if and when the right time ever rolled around.

Once all the groceries were stored away, they settled themselves on the sofa with a tall glass of ice tea. "What brings you to the West End on a busy Monday like this?" Jillian asked.

"Jack, call— I just dropped in to see how my big brother was getting along. We Furies are kind of a close-knit bunch."

"That's interesting," Jillian said, deadpan. So, Jackson had called him to come over, huh? No need for her to ask why; it obviously had something to do with her.

"Yeah, we're so close, I'm still living at home with the folks," Randy said.

"Are you still in school?"

"No, I got fed up with hauling books around, so I went out and got myself a job instead of going on to college."

"What do you do?"

"Anything and everything. I can sing, dance, play the guitar and drums. Up until a few weeks ago, I was a night-duty room-service waiter at the Adolphus Hotel." Seeing Jillian's confused blink, he added, "But I quit that job when I got the commercial. Hope to be going to Waxahachie soon on location, if I'm lucky enough to get a part in the new movie."

"You're an actor? Jack never said anything about having a movie star in his family."

"That's 'cause he doesn't. Yet. So far, all I've done is a few commercials. That's how a lot of the big stars got started, you know. One of these days, I intend to pack my bags and head out for New York or Hollywood."

"Sounds to me as if you've got your future all planned."

Randy gave a nodding shrug. "Guess that all depends on how you look at it. Right now, I'm just baby—uh, I'm not doing much of anything."

"Mmm." The blush creeping up Randy's neck, coupled with his refusal to look at her, told Jillian that *baby—uh* had to mean baby-sitting. And she, obviously, was the baby he was sitting.

She glanced at her watch. "Goodness, would you look at the time. You'll have to excuse me, Randy. I've got to go change."

"You planning on going somewhere?"

"Mmm-hmm," she said, heading for the stairs.

"Mind if I tag along?"

"Yes, Randy, I mind very much. I'm not in the habit of letting strangers watch me change clothes."

"I didn't mean that," Randy said with a sheepish grin. "I meant, can I tag along with you later on, after you've changed."

"Oh. Well, I was just going to"—*For heaven's sake, Fletcher, get yourself out of this one. Think of something*—"go to the library." That sounded reasonable enough. "But shouldn't you be here when Jack comes back?"

"No, he knows I come and go when it suits me."

"Okay," she said. "Suit yourself. I won't be but a minute."

The public library was a very big place, very easy to get lost in, she thought as she climbed the stairs. If she played her cards right, maybe she could lose Randy and then get on with her business.

Holding a Styrofoam cup of coffee in one hand and a half-eaten hamburger in the other, Jackson sat in his Pontiac, watching the building across the parking lot through a rain-drizzled windshield. He had been tailing Cherise Northrop for hours now, following her from dress boutique to shoe store to dry cleaners to florist to printers, waiting, hoping she would slip up and do something. So far, she hadn't done a thing that looked even remotely suspicious. Just another widow trying to go on with her life as usual.

Damn, he hated surveillance. Good weather or bad, it made no difference; he hated it. Sitting on his butt for hours at a stretch was not his idea of doing constructive work.

However, this time he'd had something to do while Cherise had been otherwise occupied. He'd gotten the Xeroxed copies of the funeral guest books from Frank and had sorted the attendees into three categories—those who had attended both Amanda's and Wyatt's funerals, those who had attended Amanda's but not Wyatt's, and those who had attended Wyatt's but not Amanda's. Studying the lists now as ketchup and pickle juice dribbled down his shirt, no one name in particular leaped out and grabbed him.

Maybe it wasn't supposed to. Maybe not everyone signed both guest books.

Slowly Jackson uncoiled from his slouched position, thrusting his hamburger and coffee cup back inside the sacks. He reached for the Xeroxed pages beside him, intending to compare some signatures, but he stopped when he saw Cherise emerge from the printer's shop. Something was wrong. Even at a distance he could see that she looked upset. What the hell was going on?

Cherise hurried to her Mercedes, jumped inside, and took off.

"All right!" Jackson said, starting the Pontiac. "Now maybe we'll see some action."

"What are we stopping here for?" Randy asked, following Jillian into Sanger-Harris. "I thought you said we were going to the library."

"We are." Jillian calmly collapsed her umbrella, shook some of the rain off of it, and unbuttoned her raincoat. "I just remembered; I need to get a couple of things here. We won't take but a few minutes."

"Sure you won't, Randy thought. If she was anything like his sisters, her idea of a few minutes would be more like a few hours. He couldn't understand why women couldn't just go in a store, buy what they needed, and then leave again. He couldn't understand why they had to dawdle around and pick through every sale rack they came to, examine each piece of jewelry the store had in stock, and compare one price tag with another until they found what they considered a good bargain. Men didn't care about bargains and stuff like that, but then men were different. He figured it probably had something to do with hormones.

Seeing the wispy little bras and bikini panties draped on the shapely store mannequins, Randy came to a sudden stop. "You didn't tell me you were gonna buy underwear."

"I didn't?"

"No, but I wish you had. You don't really expect me to hang around here and wait for you, do you?"

"Why not? I won't be but a minute," Jillian said.

"I know, but being around this stuff, looking at it, it makes me uncomfortable."

"Then go look at something else, Randy." Jillian smiled at him and walked away.

Randy watched her select a skimpy black-lace teddy and

a skimpier black-lace garter belt off a rack and head for the dressing room. The thought of how she would look wearing them made sweat pop out on his upper lip. The thought of his brother taking the garter belt off of her, first one stocking, then the other, then the belt itself, made Randy sick with envy.

"Hey," he said, reaching out and grabbing the arm of a passing sales clerk. "That girl that just went into the dressing room."

"Yes, what about her?"

"I came in with her, but I just remembered I gotta go check out something in—in—uh, somewhere else. When she's through—when she comes out of there, tell her I said to wait for me, okay?"

Jackson watched Cherise enter the ground-floor unit of one of the many generic apartment houses near the Southern Methodist University campus. What should he have expected, that she would go into mourning and act like a respectable grieving widow now that her husband was dead? Not good old horny Cherise. Her husband had been cheating on her and she knew it. Still, it was something of a surprise to find out that she'd been cheating, too.

He sat in his Pontiac, watching the building, waiting, hoping something would happen.

Something did.

In less than five minutes a loud, shrill scream came from the apartment's open window. Jackson jumped out of the car and raced across the rain-slicked street, dodging oncoming cars.

When he reached the apartment, he paused to flip the safety catch on his revolver. Holding the weapon firmly in both hands, he lifted a leg and kicked down the door. It tore loose from the hinges and slammed to the floor with a loud thud as he leaped inside the apartment.

"Freeze!" he yelled from his crouched stance.

Dressed in nothing but stockings and a ruby-red garter belt, Cherise took one look at Jackson and, with another bloodcurdling scream, threw her arms around her bare breasts. Caught in the humiliating throes of embarrassment, Collins grabbed a cushion off the couch beside him. It managed to shield his well-filled pink-lace panties, but unfortunately left his hairy chest and pink bra still exposed to Jackson's view.

"What the hell—" Jackson slowly lowered his gun.

"Fury?" Collins said.

"Collins?" Jackson said.

"Walter?" said Cherise.

"Well, now that we've got the introductions out of the way," Jackson said, "maybe somebody'll tell me what the hell's going on here. No, scratch that. I can see for myself what's going on. Whoa, kinky too."

"It's not what you're thinking, Fury," Collins said.

Cherise stiffened. "It's not?"

Slightly flustered, Collins shot her an apologetic look. "Well, yes, it is, darling. But it's not what he thinks."

"Hey, I'm not blind, you know," said Jackson, getting to his feet.

"No, of course you're not," said Collins. "But things aren't the way they look."

"The hell they're not," Jackson said. "I know women's underwear when I see it. Gotta admit, though, I've never seen it over so much hair before."

"We can explain—about everything," said Collins.

"I sure hope so," said Jackson, " 'cause I'm kinda confused. Oh, not about the setup here—that's plain as day—but about the two of you. Together. Did Northrop know?"

"No," both Cherise and Collins said in unison.

"No one knew," Collins said, inching closer to Cherise, "until today."

"Today?" said Jackson. "You mean 'cause I found you out?"

"No, because of my wife. I asked her for a divorce earlier today, and she agreed to give it to me. She knows now that I love Cherise and that I want to marry her."

"And live happily ever after, sharing each other's underwear, right?"

"It's not a laughing matter, Fury," Collins said. "Cherise and I have been in love for years, but we could never do anything about it."

"Why not?" Jackson asked. "What stopped you?"

"My wife," Collins said. "Her husband. Our respective children. Our positions in the community. Plus a number of other things."

Like not enough space in the dresser drawers for their lingerie, Jackson thought. Jill needed to meet this pair. The three of them had a lot in common.

"So you waited for Northrop to nuke himself on the freeway," Jackson said, "and then you decided to make the big leap, is that it?"

"No, that's not what he means," said Cherise.

"Yes, it is, darling," said Collins. "Let's be honest. Jon's sickness was the one thing that's kept us apart all these years."

*Jon's* sickness? Jackson wondered, shaking his head dubiously.

Cherise winced and nodded. "Yes, you're right. It's funny, you'd think after all these years I wouldn't have any trouble admitting it." She looked at Jackson. "My husband—I mean, my late-husband—was addicted to gambling. But then, I suppose you already know that."

"Yeah," said Jackson.

"I wanted to leave him," she said. "God knows, I would

have if I hadn't been so afraid. I consulted a psychiatrist shortly after our last child was born—that's when Jon's gambling really got bad. I had to go alone, of course, because Jon refused to go with me. He wouldn't admit he had a problem, and no one could tell him differently. The doctor advised me not to leave him until he showed some signs of improvement. He said that if I left him when things were so bad, Jon might do something destructive. I just couldn't live with that on my conscience."

"And then I fell in love with her," Collins said, wrapping his arm around Cherise's shoulders. "For years I'd believed she was a cold, hard, manipulative woman. God, I was so wrong.

"At Presidio's company Christmas party two years ago, I found her in a room by herself, crying. I asked her what was wrong, and it was like a dam opening up; it all came spilling out. Jon's gambling, his blatant affairs with other women, the stress Cherise had had to live with. Everything. I only wanted to reassure her, offer her a little comfort, but when I touched her—I don't know, something just happened. One thing led to another and, well, we became lovers."

"True love conquers all," Jackson said, unimpressed by their little melodrama.

"You don't believe me?" Collins said.

"I might buy part of it, but I'm not stupid enough to buy it all. Not until I've got a few more questions answered. You want to give me a hand with this door, Collins? Wouldn't want somebody to walk by and see me holding this gun on you. They might get the idea that I was taking advantage of you ladies and call the cops. You don't want that, and neither do I. Yet."

Jackson grinned at the look of rage on Collins's face. The lawyer tossed his modesty and his protective cushion aside and moved toward the fallen door. They had a lot of explaining to do, but Jackson had the time to listen.

• • •

There were times when you had no other alternative than to be deceitful, Jillian told herself as she slipped out of the department store. She felt a little guilty for deliberately losing Randy, but he was a big boy; he could take care of himself. So could she, for that matter. Right now, the last thing she needed or wanted was some post-adolescent baby-sitter getting in her way.

She crossed the street and as the crowd of pedestrians began thinning out, she caught sight of a familiar-looking woman standing beside a strange man in front of a travel agent's office window. Slowing her pace, she studied the woman. Blond, slightly on the dumpy side, speaking with a loud New York accent.

"Evelyn?"

Evelyn turned, blinked at Jillian, and then smiled broadly. "Hi! How are ya?"

"I'm fine, how are you?"

"I couldn't be better," Evelyn said.

"Then things between you and your husband have, uh, improved?"

"Have they ever. Harry, turn around here, I wantcha to meet somebody."

Wearing an open-collared shirt that exposed his pale skin and gold chain, Evelyn's husband pushed his thick-lensed glasses higher up the bridge of his nose and gave Jillian a wide gap-toothed grin.

"This is the girl I was telling you about," Evelyn said. "You know, the one that works for that private detective of Millie's?"

"Yeah." Harry extended his hand. "Nice to meet you, Miss, uh,—"

"Fletcher. Jillian Fletcher." She took hold of his hand and shook it. Feeling weakness in his grip, rather than brute strength, she wondered how a wimpy guy like this could have beaten Jackson to a pulp. From the looks of him, he couldn't hurt a fly.

"Harry, do you mind if I ask you a question?" she asked, her curiosity getting the better of her.

"All depends on what it is," Harry said seriously, and then he laughed. "No, just kidding. Go ahead, ask away."

"I know this may sound a little strange, and it's really none of my business, but where were you Monday, a couple of weeks ago?"

"What day of the month was that?" he asked his wife.

"Don't you remember?" Evelyn said. "It was the twenty-eighth."

"Oh, yeah. Our anniversary." With a wistful smile, he wrapped his arm around Evelyn's plump shoulders and gave her an affectionate hug. "I surprised my best girl here by taking her to Hawaii."

"Then you weren't in Dallas that Monday?"

"No, we left town on Friday, the twenty-fifth," Evelyn said, blushing. "Just got back a couple of days ago, and now he's talking about us going on a Mediterranean cruise. Won't be as good as Hawaii was. Most wonderful honeymoon a girl could ever have. Made up for all the bad times, didn't it, Harry?"

"I certainly hope so, pumpkin," Harry said sincerely. "That answer your question, Miss Fletcher?"

"Yes. Yes, it does, thank you."

"What did you want to know where he was for?" Evelyn asked.

Jillian hesitated, mentally groping for a believable answer. She couldn't tell them the truth, that she thought Harry had been the one who attacked Jackson; they would think she was crazy. "Oh," she said finally, "I was just curious. When I saw the two of you standing here, I thought your husband looked kind of familiar. I was mistaken. I've never even met him before. It must have been someone else."

"Yeah," said Harry, "must have been."

They chatted awhile longer, then Jillian wished them good luck, meaning it sincerely. Turning, she headed for the *Dallas Morning News* building a few blocks away. No matter how hard she tried to dismiss it, she couldn't shake the feeling that the attack on Jackson was somehow tied in with Amanda's and Sterling's murders.

A fuzzy image flashed through her thoughts as she drew near her intended destination. A short, fat bald man with a gold chain around his neck. The image grew sharper, and she realized that the fat wasn't really fat at all, but actually muscle.

"No," Jillian said, shaking her head in denial. A woman walking beside her looked at her curiously and hurried on ahead. "No, not him."


"Whoa. Back up just a minute," Jackson said, feeling anger slowly overtake his frustration. The session with Cherise and Collins in their not-so-secluded love nest had been bad enough—it had left him without a murder suspect again—but he hadn't expected this. "You did what?"

Randy hung his head. "I lost her."

"How? Where in hell did y'all go?"

"Like I told you, to the library. But on the way, she sorta decided to stop off at Sanger-Harris."

"Is that where you sorta lost her?"

"Yeah."

"Dammit, Randy, if you'd stayed here like I told you—"

"I know, I know, none of this ever would've happened. Okay, so I screwed up. I'm sorry. But how was I supposed to know she was gonna get herself lost? Geez, the way you're carrying on you'd think I planned it or something. Which I didn't. At the time, I didn't see any harm in leaving her by herself. I mean, how much trouble can a woman get into trying on lingerie?"

"Quite a lot, by the looks of it."

"Well, it's not my fault," Randy said defensively. "They got laws against men going into ladies' dressing rooms, you know. If I'd followed her when she went to try on that black garter belt and that other whatever-they-call-it, they'd have arrested me, thrown me in jail, and I never would've got to do another commercial, let alone make a movie. Anyhow, if you were so worried about what she was gonna do, why didn't you stay here and keep an eye on her yourself?"

Jackson swallowed hard. "Did you say black garter belt?"

"Yeah, I think that's what they call it. Looked kinda like one of Momma's girdles, only smaller and made out of lace instead of elastic."

"That's a garter belt, all right," Jackson said. "And the other thing she tried on?"

"It looked kinda like the top half of one of Momma's slips sewed on to a pair of Treeva Lynn's panties. It was black, too. And made out of lace."

"Jesus," Jackson said with a groan, slowly shaking his head.

"What's the matter?"

"A black-lace teddy."

"Is that what you call it, a teddy?"

"Yeah." Jackson knew, as surely as he knew his own name, that Jillian and her sexy underwear were going to drive him crazy. The way it looked now, he'd probably get carted off to the funny farm before he ever got to see her actually wearing any of it. He'd lost count of the times he'd gone into the bathroom, just to shower and shave, and found her bikini panties, bras, teddies, and slips hanging all over the place. It was a wonder he hadn't cut himself and bled to death.

"Hi, what's going on?" Jillian asked, entering the loft at that moment.

Jackson felt a major pain settle in his groin as he watched her cross the room and toss her large purse and shopping bags onto the sofa. His hackles rose at the thought of what the small Sanger-Harris bags contained.

"Where the hell have you been?" he asked.

"Just shopping," Jillian said brightly. "Didn't your brother tell you?"

"Yeah, he told me, all right. He told me that he lost you, too."

"He lost me?" Jillian turned her amused, quizzical expression on Randy.

"I think I better be going now," Randy said.

"That's what he said," said Jackson, ignoring his brother's movement toward the door.

"Well, we did get separated, but I was never lost. What's all this about, anyway?"

"You," Jackson said. "That's what it's about."

Randy reached the door and waved his hand sheepishly. "You two take it easy, okay? Been real nice meeting you, Jill."

Like Jackson, Jillian ignored him. "Me? I didn't do anything, except buy some art supplies and other things. If anyone got lost, it was Randy. When I came out of the dressing room, he had already left."

Slowly Jackson turned and gave his brother a withering look. With a pained grin, Randy shrugged and hurried out of the loft, slamming the door behind him.

Jillian was the picture of confused innocence when Jackson turned back to her. She smiled, picked up her packages, and headed toward the stairs.

"Not so fast," Jackson said. "Come back here a minute."

"I'm just going to go put these away."

"They can wait. Come here."

"But, Jack—"

"Come here." He spoke quietly, provocatively, his gray eyes sleepy and teasing rather than threatening.

Jillian felt a twinge of uneasiness as she slowly walked toward him. She knew Jackson could be a little misguided at times, but he wasn't stupid. He had probably figured out that she had done a lot more than just shop. But if he hadn't, she would have to be on her guard and handle him very carefully.

"So, you just went shopping."

"Yes." Jillian repressed the urge to flinch when Jackson lifted his hand and moved it slowly toward her. It was silly to think he would hit her, she decided. He wasn't the type to strike a woman. Yell, holler, rant, and rave, yes, but never hit.

Jackson curled his hand gently around her neck. "You didn't do anything else?"

"No. Well, after I bought my oils and a couple of brushes, I did walk around for a while, window shopping. Why?"

Jackson raised his other hand and cupped her face, his thumbs resting lightly on the veins in her neck. Her rapid pulse told him that she was nervous. Good, he thought as he lowered his head, let her stay that way for a while.

"Remember what I told you the other night?" he whispered, his lips grazing the corner of hers.

"No."

"Yes, you do. Think back. Remember I told you to keep your pretty little nose out of this case. Out of my business."

"Oh, that."

"You did, didn't you?"

The husky timbre of his voice made Jillian's knees go rubbery. Feeling his lips nibble their way down her throat, she dropped her purse and bags to the floor and wound her

arms around his neck. "Mmm, what do you think?" she
asked, purring like a contented cat.

"I think," Jackson said, slipping his arms around her
waist, grasping her buttocks, and molding her hips firmly
against his, "you've been meddling again."

"No, I haven't."

"Yes, you have. Come on now, tell me the truth."

"Jack, don't be this way. Not now. Why don't you just
forget it? Better yet, why don't you shut up and kiss me."

He did. Long and leisurely, letting his tongue glide
playfully over the crease of her lips. He felt them open, but
went no farther than the ridge of her teeth. As her arousal
continued to increase, as she molded her lush curves against
him, he fought to keep his emotions under control. Jesus, he
deserved a medal for this.

After a time, he asked, "You horny, Jill?"

"Yes," she said breathlessly.

"Wanna go to bed and make love with me?"

"Yes."

"Really?"

"Yes, Jack. Yes."

"Admit that you've been meddling again, sweetheart,
and we will."

"No."

"No?"

"Uh-huh, no."

"Aw, Jill, you really disappoint me." With a click of his
tongue, he loosened her arms from about his neck and
stepped back.

"Jack?"

"Sorry, sweet cakes. Sure would've been fun, us going to
bed together."

"Jack!"

"What can I say? You had your chance, but you blew it."
Smiling at her astonished expression, he turned and started

to walk away. "The way I see it, you're too old and much too pretty to get a spanking, but you still gotta be punished for meddling. Don't worry, you'll get over it."

"You—you rat! You got me hot— Uh, you did that to me on purpose."

"Hey, if it bothers you so much, why don't you do what I've been doing? Go take a cold shower."

Jillian picked up a sofa cushion and threw it at him. "You dirty, no-good rat!"

Three more cushions and a big ceramic ashtray followed a smiling Jackson into the kitchen.

# CHAPTER 19

Tuesday, May 13

Thomas Wolfe was right, Jillian decided as she stepped out of the elevator. You can't go home again. However, in this case, it wasn't home she was going to; it was her old office.

Only three weeks ago, she'd walked down this same hall with all her personal possessions in tow, for what she thought was the very last time. She'd felt both angry and relieved. Now she felt somewhat exhilarated, ready to face head-on any obstacle she might encounter.

As Jillian quietly entered the comptroller's office she saw that obstacle, Miss Shaw, hovering over a new clerk. Her replacement? Probably, she decided, seeing the girl's face redden with embarrassment at something Miss Shaw said to her.

Miss Shaw hadn't changed at all, and probably never would, she decided. Three weeks ago, that might have been her standing there, getting chewed out. Three weeks ago, she would have had to take it. But not now. As an ex-employee, she was not subject to Miss Shaw's tyrannical supervision, so if the old witch decided to give her a hard time, she wouldn't hesitate to give it right back.

Miss Shaw glanced away from the cowering clerk and did a double take when she saw Jillian. The initial look of surprise on the woman's middle-aged face quickly evolved into a suspicious frown. She muttered something to the young clerk, who scurried away to her desk, and then started toward Jillian.

"What brings you back here, Jill?" asked Miss Shaw.

"Business," Jillian said and, without further preamble, took hold of Miss Shaw's arm. "We need to talk. Let's go in your office where we can do it in private."

Once inside the glass-partitioned cubicle that was no bigger than a closet, Miss Shaw turned on Jillian. "Now you look here, if you've come back here hoping I'll hire you again, you're—"

"Sit down and be quiet, Miss Shaw."

"What!"

"You heard me. I haven't got much time, so just park it and shut up."

Miss Shaw looked shocked and more than slightly indignant, but she did as she was told.

"Now then," Jillian said, "just to set your mind at ease, I did not come back here in the hope of your reinstating me. I've already got another job. I got it the day after you fired me, as a matter of fact."

"Th—that's good to hear, Jill."

"Yes, I can see you're really tickled pink."

"Jill, you've changed," Miss Shaw said. "You didn't used to be so—so belligerent."

"I prefer to think of myself as being assertive, rather than belligerent. Look, let's cut out all this catty little chit-chat and get down to business, shall we? Like I said before, I haven't got much time. I need some information and I want you to help me get it?"

"Information?"

"Yes, and before you ask, it's not about the company." Jillian sat down in the chair across from Miss Shaw and leaned forward, resting her elbows on her knees. "I'm working for a private investigator now, and we—"

"A private investigator? Really?" Miss Shaw actually sounded impressed.

"Yes, Fury Investigations."

"I've never known anyone who worked for a private eye before."

"Neither did I. Until I ran into Jack."

"Jack? You call your boss by his first name?"

"Yes, but that's not important," Jillian said, chafing under Miss Shaw's knowing look. "Oh, all right. Yes, it is important. Darn it."

"Sounds like it might be serious."

"It could be. I don't know. Yet. I mean, I've only known the idiot for three weeks, and all we've done most of that time is argue. But that's beside the point. I'm not here to talk about Jack; I'm here to get you to help me with this case we're working on."

"Well, if it doesn't cause a conflict— What case?"

Here goes nothing, thought Julian, and took a deep breath. "Do you remember reading or hearing about that young socialite who was murdered in her apartment a few weeks ago? Amanda Strickland?"

Miss Shaw's eyes widened. "You're working on that case?"

Jillian nodded.

"But I thought her fiancé, Wyatt something-or-other, murdered her."

"Sterling Wyatt did not kill her. Someone else did."

"But the police—"

"I know," Jillian said, "but they arrested the wrong man." In somewhat vague terms, she explained a few of the details about the case. She didn't elaborate on some of the more personal aspects, deciding it was none of Miss Shaw's business that she'd moved in with Jackson because her apartment had been destroyed by an unknown gunman.

"So I decided to come back here," she concluded, "where it all started. Where I ran into Sterling. He said he was here to see Mr. Taggart, but Mr. Taggart said he didn't know anything about an appointment. If I could just talk to his secretary, or get a look at his appointment calendar—"

"You think Mr. Taggart's lying?"

"Somebody is. And it's not— It wasn't Sterling. Would you help me? I mean, I know you have a lot to do, what with all the responsibilities you have here, but would you at least consider giving it a try?"

Miss Shaw chewed thoughtfully on her thumbnail for a moment, and then heaved a decisive sigh. "Lord knows, I may be pounding the pavement myself if anyone finds out, but"—she suddenly grinned, girlishly—"yes, I'll help. What is it you want me to do?"

Blocks away in the West End, Jackson entered his loft. "Jill!" he yelled, wiping his grease-covered hands on a dirty rag. "Had another race with Marsha's ex a few minutes ago. This time I blew the engine in the Pontiac. Gotta phone for a tow truck."

Moving to the foot of the stairs, he listened for Jillian's response. Fat chance of that happening this soon, he thought. Aside from the occasional monosyllabic grunt to indicate that she'd heard him, Jillian hadn't said more than ten words to him since yesterday. Anyone would think they were an old married couple instead of a pair of not-yet-lovers.

Jackson had a hunch her silent treatment had nothing to do with him turning her on and then turning her down. More than likely, she was pissed at him because he hadn't found Wyatt's killer yet. By the sound of it—or rather the lack of the sound of it—today's forecast promised more of the same.

The woman didn't know how tough it was, trying to find a killer with nothing to go on. Hell, finding a needle in a haystack would be easier. Fifteen years in this business hadn't given him second sight. Hemorrhoids from sitting surveillance for hours on end, heartburn from drinking one cup of coffee after another so he wouldn't fall asleep and lose a suspect, an intimate relationship with every late-night radio disc jockey in town maybe, but no ESP.

Okay, so he was stumped. So he didn't know who had carved up Amanda Strickland, or blown a hole in the top of Wyatt's head, or who had fed enough strychnine to Northrop to choke a horse before they turned him loose on the freeway. Neither did Hank, for that matter. Both did agree, however, that it was a miracle Northrop hadn't taken anyone else with him when he'd lost control.

"Jill, did you hear me?" Jackson yelled, wiping off the last of the grease. "Jill! Are you up there?"

The echo of his voice faded, leaving only the sound of Moose's and Rusty's heavy panting.

"Oh, shit!" Fearing the worst, that in his absence she'd packed her bags and left him, Jackson sprinted up the stairs, taking them two at a time. Although he found both the bedroom and bathroom empty, relief coursed through him when he saw her things scattered about the room.

Then his anger returned, and he stalked back down the stairs. "Damn her. If she's done what I think she's done, I'm gonna be the one that's pissed. Told her not to leave the loft. Warned her she'd be asking for trouble if she went off snooping on her own again. But does she listen? Hell, no."

Sprawled side by side on the cool hardward floor, the dogs watched Jackson search through the desk, opening one drawer after another, flinging papers aside without a thought to the order in which Jillian had put them, all the while muttering obscenities and threats beneath his breath. Rusty bared his teeth in a wide yawn, then leaned over and licked Moose's jaw. With a soft whine, the Great Dane rubbed her head against the setter's.

"Bad enough she's so hardheaded she can't understand plain simple English, but why did she have to go and hide my damn phone book?" Jackson turned at that moment to see the dogs' affectionate exchange. "Come on, you two, cut that out. Wasn't once enough?" He jerked open the bottom left-hand drawer. "Dogs acting like a couple of newlyweds. And in front of a man who hasn't had any in— What the hell?"

On top of the *Yellow Pages* lay a thick manila file folder. Jackson pulled it out of the drawer and opened it. Inside he found Xeroxed copies of dated newspaper clippings, a receipt for three hundred dollars made out to Jillian from a place called Coiffure d'Anglaise, and a number of typed and handwritten notes. "She's done all this on her own?"

His need for the phone book forgotten, Jackson moved toward the sofa and sat down. Within seconds of reading the first page, he became engrossed in Jillian's notes.

Miss Shaw slowly replaced the receiver and then looked at Jillian.

"Well, what did she say?" Jillian asked.

"I don't know how this will be of any help to you," said Miss Shaw, "but Diedre swears that his calendar was clear that entire morning. He didn't even get back in town until three that afternoon when he had an appointment with Mr. Williams from Tulsa, Oklahoma. She'd never even heard of Sterling Wyatt until the police questioned her about him."

"Is that all?"

"Well, no. She did say that she left the office around twelve-forty-five that day. Something about a last-minute cancellation that her dentist had."

"Then anyone could have walked into the office while she was out, and she would never have known about it."

"Yes, I suppose so, but it doesn't seem likely. I've known Diedre Stevenson for years. She's very conscientious about not leaving her desk unattended. The office, either, for that matter."

"Not even on her lunch break?" Jillian asked. "On a very slow day?"

A frown of uncertainty crossed Miss Shaw's brow. "Well, under those circumstances, no, of course not."

Jillian bit her lower lip, considering her options. "I'd still like to talk to her. Ask her a few questions."

"You might be wasting your time," Miss Shaw said on a dry chuckle. "Besides being conscientious, Diedre is extremely loyal. Especially where you-know-who is concerned."

"That mother-hen type, huh?"

"That's putting it mildly."

"Would she lie for him?"

Miss Shaw looked at her and shook her head. "I honestly don't know."


"Any man," Jackson said, shaking his head as he closed Jillian's file, "who would laugh at a woman when she had proof like this has got to be an idiot. Well, Fury, that's exactly what you are. You actually had the nerve to call her four-sided triangle theory ridiculous."

He was the one that was ridiculous, he realized, not Jillian. While he'd wasted valuable time and let the trail get cold chasing down one false lead after another, he should have done like Jillian and gone back to the beginning. Like any well-seasoned P.I., she'd followed through on a hunch and, from the looks of it, by golly, she'd hit paydirt. Either she had a natural instinct for the P.I. business, or she was just downright lucky.

Jackson suddenly stiffened, remembering that Jillian wasn't in the loft. God only knew what she'd been up to while he'd been reading her report, he decided, leaping to his feet. Probably out trying to find the son of a bitch.

No, not trying to find him, Jackson amended as he hurried out of the loft. Jillian already knew where he was. And after reading her case notes, so did he. Now if he could only get to her before she got herself into serious trouble.

His adrenaline pumping, Jackson raced out of the warehouse and jumped into his Pontiac parked at the curb. He turned the key and stomped down hard on the accelerator, but nothing happened.

Across the street at Harrigan's Irish Pub a group of renegade tourists in town for a church-choir convention stood on the elevated loading ramp trying to decide what to have for lunch. The sound of Jackson slamming out of the Pontiac startled them, and they turned from the blackboard-printed menu. Listening to him call the car every foul name they'd ever heard, and a few names they hadn't, they watched him throw the keys at the windshield and then take off down the street at a dead run.

"You won't see young men acting like that in Tuscaloosa, Mildred," said one blue-permed grandmother.

"No," agreed her companion. "Chances are, you'd see worse."


Jillian entered the bright, sunny office, expecting to find Diedre Stevenson seated at her desk. The company president's private secretary, however, wasn't there.

"Terrific," she mumbled to herself, "now what do I do?"

No, what would Jackson do? she wondered. Would he take advantage of the woman's absence and do a little preliminary snooping while he had the chance, or would he play it safe and wait for Diedre to come back to the office? That was her problem; she wasn't Jackson.

Hearing a tempting little voice inside her head, she shifted her eyes toward the desk. Diedre Stevenson's appointment calendar lay on top, opened and inviting. For a moment, Jillian considered the consequences that might occur from her actions and weighed them against the importance of what she might find.

"Oh, what the heck," she said finally, and pushed herself away from the door.

Just as she reached the edge of the desk, the door connecting the outer office to that of the company president's private inner sanctum eased open.

"Immediately," she heard Garner Taggart say.

"Yeah, I know, like yesterday, right?" said another voice, obviously male.

"Right. And this time, if you know what's good for you, you won't screw up. I want those two out of my hair for good."

*Those two!* Jillian wanted to turn around and run, but curiosity kept her immobile. Surely Taggart wasn't arranging to have her and Jackson murdered!

Suddenly her curiosity vanished in the face of cold reality. Good Lord, if Taggart was planning their murders, the last thing she needed to do was hang around and find out.

Jillian began moving slowly away from the desk, her eyes riveted to the partially opened connecting door. Blindly she groped behind her for the other door that would lead her to safety. The connecting door opened wider and panic jolted through her as the two men came into view. The short, muscular bald man beside Taggart caught sight of her just as she noticed the gold chain around his neck. Jackson's attacker? Of course, he had to be.

"Speak of the devil," Muscles said.

Taggart jerked his head around and looked at Jillian, his initial expression of mild curiosity evolving into uneasy recognition and settling into outright anger. "Get her," he said. "Don't let her get away."

Muscles leaped toward Jillian and grabbed her so quickly that she didn't have a chance to think, let alone move.

"What the hell are you doing here?" Taggart asked.

Jillian didn't answer; she could only stare at Taggart. No wonder those eyewitnesses had mistaken him for Sterling, she thought. Aside from the differences in their ages and facial features, he looked enough like Sterling to be his brother. His pale-blond hair, his tall, leanly muscled body, and even the shape of his head were painful reminders of the gentle man she'd met and known so briefly.

"I said, what are you doing here?" Taggart repeated.

"Tell your gorilla to get his hands off me," she said, struggling to free herself, "or I'll scream."

"Go ahead and scream, you nosy little bitch," Muscles said. "Scream all you want. No one's gonna hear you, 'cause these walls are soundproof. Right, boss?"

For a moment Taggart glowered in silence at Jillian. "Get her into the office," he said finally. "My secretary's due back soon and I don't want her asking any questions."

With a menacing chuckle, Muscles shoved Jillian into the connecting office. Struggling to free herself, she looked over her shoulder and saw that Taggart had followed them. A feeling of impending doom constricted her chest when Taggart turned the door's dead-bolt lock.

Jackson slid out of the elevator sideways as soon as the door began to open.

"Shit!" he said, realizing he now faced the impossible decision of which direction to take. One corridor led to the left, while another led to the right. Well, when in doubt, first go right, he thought.

He took off down the hall in a long-legged sprint, passing a water fountain and the men's restroom. At the first set of glass doors he came upon, he burst through them and found himself in what looked like a bookkeeping department. Unfortunately, his sudden entrance startled the woman who had just emerged from a small side office and she dropped her armload of computer printout sheets.

"What the devil—" Miss Shaw began.

"Sorry," Jackson said, and then stopped her with an outstretched hand when she made to bend over and pick up the sheets. "That's gonna hafta wait. I'm trying to find a girl. Has one been through here in the last half hour or so?"

"A girl?" Miss Shaw straightened and gave him a deadpan look. "If you'll bother to look around, young man, you'll see that this office is full of girls."

Jackson scrutinized the office with its staff of fifteen. "No, I don't see her here," he said. "Look, she's tall—maybe just a couple of inches shorter than me—dark hair, blue eyes, early twenties. Real pretty. Have you seen her?"

Miss Shaw knew in an instant that he was talking about Jillian. Always the cautious sort until she had all the facts, she chose to remain silent.

"Well, does a girl like that ring any bells?" Jackson asked, unable to suppress his mounting anxiety.

"It's possible," said Miss Shaw. "A lot of people pass through this office all the time."

"Oh, come on, give me a break, lady. This is important. I don't have time to play twenty questions with you. I gotta know now. Wait a minute. Maybe you'd know her name. It's Jill. Jillian Fletcher. I think she said she used to work on this floor." Seeing the woman stiffen and blink, he hurried on. "Like I just said, it's important that I find her. She may be in a lot of trouble."

"Are—are you Jack?" Miss Shaw asked cautiously.

"Yeah, Jackson Fury."

"May I see some identification?"

"Identifi— What the hell do you want to see my I.D. for?" At his angry shout, all work in the office stopped. "Just tell me if Jill's been here or not."

"Show me some identification first and then maybe I will."

"Jesus!" Jackson dug his wallet out of the hip pocket of his pants and flipped it open to show her his driver's license. "There, does that satisfy you?"

"Yes, it does, thank you," said Miss Shaw, sensing the conspicuous stillness that had fallen over the office. She glanced around Jackson's broad shoulders and saw fifteen pairs of eyes trained on them, lip-reading, if not actually listening to, every word they had said.

"All right, that's enough, ladies. The show's over. You all have work to do, so let's see if we can't get some of it done before five o'clock rolls around." Then to Jackson, as she began moving toward her office, "Come with me. They've heard enough as it is."


"What are you going to do to me?" Jillian asked Taggart, her voice steady and cool despite her fear.

"What do you think?" Muscles said.

"That's enough, Moreton," said Taggart. "I can handle her now."

"You sure?"

"Yes, I'm positive. You go on and take care of Fury like I told you."

"Whatever you say, boss." Muscles shot Jillian a menacing smile as he headed out the door.

Taggart turned the dead-bolt lock again and moved back to his desk. In that brief instant, Jillian realized—too late— that she should have listened to Jackson. If only she had stayed at the loft like he'd told her to do, she wouldn't be in this mess. What on earth had possessed her to believe that she could question Diedre Stevenson right under this cold-blooded killer's nose? She should have realized that there was a chance she might run into the man. After all, Diedre was his secretary; they worked right in the same office, for heaven's sake.

At that point, another reality hit her; hit her hard. Good Lord, he was planning to kill her and she didn't even have a gun.

Okay, so she didn't have a gun. She did have something almost as effective, if used properly. Her wits.

"I wonder what's going through that devious little mind of yours," Taggart said, studying Jillian's pensive expression. "In your place, I suppose I'd be trying to think of a way to save my neck. Well, go ahead and think all you want, Miss Fletcher, but it won't do you any good."

"You really want to know what I'm thinking?" Jillian asked, irked by Taggart's overbearing, egotistical tone. "I'm thinking that Amanda did the right thing when she dumped you to marry Sterling. You're not only half the man he was, you're an animal to boot."

"All things considered," Taggart said, "that wasn't a very smart thing for you to say. In fact, it was downright stupid. Pity, too. You look so intelligent."

"That's a little like the pot calling the kettle black, isn't it?"

"Oh, is it?"

"Yes, it is."

"In what way?"

"For one thing, the police know for certain that Sterling didn't commit suicide. They know he was murdered."

A muscle twitched in Taggart's face, making one brown eye narrow menacingly for a mere second. "Don't stop, Miss Fletcher. Go on. This is beginning to sound very interesting."

• • •

Jackson exploded out of the comptroller's office and took off at a dead run down the hall. Third office on the right after the elevators, what'shername had said. Or had she said it was the third office on the right near the end? Hell, it didn't matter. He'd try them all if he had to.

Just as Jackson raced past the elevators, he saw a man appear at the other end of the corridor. Even though a good thirty feet separated them, he reminded Jackson of someone—short, dumpy, sort of built on the lines of a miniature steamroller. Drawing closer, Jackson saw the gold chain around the man's neck.

Shit! he thought, coming to a sudden stop. It was the same little jerk who'd tried to beat him to a pulp in Collins's basement garage.

"Hey, you!" Jackson called out as he started forward again.

Muscles recognized Jackson and bared his teeth in a snarl. "Fury. Just the son of a bitch I was looking for."

"Funny, I wasn't looking for you," Jackson said. "But now I'm glad I found you. I believe I owe you one."

Itching for a good fight, Muscles chuckled and flexed his arms. "By the time I get through with you, you ain't gonna owe nobody nothing."

His years in the Navy Shore Patrol, handling mean drunks and doped-up sailors of every size and shape, had taught Jackson a thing or two about self-defense. He was also reminded of something his petty officer had once told him. "You can get more with a kind word and gun than you can with just a kind word."

When less than three feet separated them, Muscles took a swing at Jackson. Jackson swerved quickly to the side and grabbed hold of the outstretched arm. Pulling it down, back, and then up with a rapid twist, he pivoted sharply and shoved Muscles's face into the wall. His snub-nose slipped easily into his hand and he pressed it into the man's neck.

"Better give up while you still can," Jackson said. "Me and this gun I'm holding are gonna make damn sure you don't win this one."

Muscles chuckled. "That's what you think."

Lifting his free hand to the wall, Muscles pushed hard and sent Jackson stumbling backward across the corridor. The snub-nose flew out of Jackson's hand as he hit the wall and landed somewhere in the shadows.

The fight was well under way when Diedre Stevenson emerged from the Xerox room a few feet away. Seeing Jackson block with his left and punch with his right, and hearing the sickening crunch of knuckles against jawbone, the wrinkles on her face vanished in open-mouthed horror.

"Stop it!" she screamed, throwing papers into the air as she ran toward them. "You leave Mr. Moreton alone!"

Drawing back his fist, Jackson started to hit Muscles again, but Taggart's secretary reached out, grabbed his arm as it moved forward, and found herself thrown bodily into the other man.

"For Christ's sake, lady," Jackson said, pushing her roughly aside with his forearm. "Stay out of this."

"Leave Mr. Moreton alone!"

"Lady, you're gonna get—" The punch Muscles delivered to Jackson's jaw interrupted his spoken thought.

"Oh, my God!" Diedre said. "If the two of you don't stop it this minute, I'm going to go call the police."

Her threat, of course, fell on deaf ears. With a worried oath, she hurried into her office. The phone kept slipping from her grasp as she tried to pick it up. Finally getting a grip on it, she began to dial, but she froze at the sudden, muffled scream she heard coming from behind Taggart's door.

# CHAPTER 20

Jillian had no control over her scream; it was a natural reflex that happened when she saw Taggart pick up the letter opener on his desk. Granted, the blade wasn't as big as the butcher knife he'd used on Amanda Strickland, but she knew it could do just as much damage.

"You're actually going to kill me," she said, backing away from him.

"You don't leave me much of an alternative, Miss Fletcher. I didn't want it to come to this. In fact, I've tried everything I could to avoid it. Unfortunately, Moreton didn't succeed in scaring you badly enough when he shot at you in your apartment, and he botched up the warning threat when he attacked your boss, Fury. I'm sorry, but I can't afford to have you meddling in my life any longer."

Taggart's confession didn't surprise Jillian; she had already suspected that he had been behind both attacks. "But why kill me?" she asked. "I mean, you're already living with two murders on your conscience; aren't they enough? Do you have to add another?"

Although Taggart didn't say anything, an odd look appeared on his face. Jillian saw it and a fleeting thought registered. She inhaled a slow breath.

"No, not just two murders, three. You killed Northrop, too, didn't you?"

Taggart shrugged and took another step toward her.

"Why?" she asked. "Why did you kill him?"

"For a lot of reasons, the main one being that he was trying to blackmail me."

"Blackmail you? Why on earth would he want to blackmail you."

"Like you, he kept getting in my way. And he knew too much about Amanda and me. The fool actually thought I'd be willing to pay him to keep quiet about it."

A quick glance out the corner of her eye told Jillian that she still had a few more feet to go before she could reach for the door. The chances were better than even that Taggart would get to her before she could unlock and open it, but that was a risk she would just have to take. In the meantime, she had to keep him talking, had to keep him preoccupied so she could at least try to escape.

"What about you and Amanda?" she asked. "I know you killed her, but why? It's obvious that you were in love with her at one time. She was your mistress, for heaven's sake."

"She was much more than my mistress," said Taggart. "She was my wife."

Jillian came to a momentary halt, stunned by his admission. "Your wife?"

"Yes."

"But wasn't she going to marry Sterling?"

"Yes, she was."

"Good gracious! And at the same time, she was having an affair with Northrop."

"You know an awful lot about her personal life."

Apparently not everything, Jillian thought, retreating another step. "That sort of thing gets around."

"Like what, for instance?"

"What do you mean, like what?"

"Like, what did you hear? No, let me be more specific. What do you know? What do you think you know?"

Left with a few more inches to go before she could reach for the door, Jillian had little alternative but to answer him. "Well, for one thing, I know now that you loved her. You've said as much yourself by admitting that you married her."

"Yes, I loved her. Strange as it may seem, I still do."

"Then if you loved her, why did you kill her?"

"Oh, no. You're the one with the answers, not me, remember?"

"Well, I don't really have that many. Not as many as you have, obviously. And most of mine are based on nothing more than intuitive speculation."

" 'Intuitive speculation,' " Taggart said with a thoughtful nod. "I like the sound of that. It shows you have a degree of intelligence. Too bad you'll never have the chance to develop it." He took another step toward her. "As much as I've enjoyed our little chat, I think we've wasted enough time."

Jillian watched Taggart toss the letter opener into a trash can, then begin to move toward her menacingly. Realizing she could put off the inevitable no longer, she took a deep breath, held it, and dived straight for the door.

The dead-bolt lock gave way instantly and she yanked the door open. The woman seated at the outer-office desk shot her a frightened look and dropped the phone she was holding. Jillian opened her mouth, intending to plead for help, but instead of a plea, she screamed again when Taggart grabbed her from behind. And she continued to scream, calling out to the one person she wanted most at this moment, even as Taggart pulled her back inside the office and slammed the door.

• • •

Jackson smashed his aching fist into Muscles's jaw at the same moment he heard Jillian call out his name. He knew he had no more time to lose. With what little strength he had left, he stepped back and delivered a savage kick into his opponent's groin. Something he should have done in the first place, he realized as he watched the man crumple to the floor in a heap.

"Iron jaw, but glass balls," Jackson said, out of breath as he scooped up his gun on his way to Taggart's office.

"I tell you, they've all gone crazy around here," Diedre Stevenson was saying into the phone. "They're trying to kill each— Oh, my God!" Her piercing shriek punctuated Jackson's sudden entrance.

"Where is she?" Jackson asked.

"Wh—wh—who?" asked Diedre.

"Jill, the girl who just screamed, you idiot, that's who!"

"Oh, God!" Clutching the phone to her bosom with one trembling hand, Diedre pointed to the connecting door with the other.

"Is that the police?" Jackson nodded at the phone Diedre held.

With a frightened wince, Diedre nodded timidly.

"Good. You tell them Fury said to get hold of Hank McPherson in homicide and to send him over here on the double. He'll know what to do."

Diedre could only stare at Jackson in confusion as he stumbled past her desk, then she jerked the receiver back up to her ear. "D—did you hear that? Oh, thank God. Now do you see what I mean? You've got to do something. He's one of the crazies who've— What do you mean he's not crazy?"

Gripping the snub-nose in both hands, Jackson kicked open the door and hurtled into Taggart's office. He dropped to one knee and took dead aim, ready to fire at the first

threatening thing that moved. But the sight of Jillian and
Wyatt's double made him freeze. The man held her in front
of him, his arm wrapped tightly around her neck. Jackson
knew he couldn't get off a clean shot without possibly
hitting Jillian.

"Let her go," he said, his voice harsh and raspy, his
finger curling around the trigger.

"No." Shaking his head, Taggart took himself and Jillian
one step backward. "You shoot me and, so help me God,
I'll make sure I break her neck before I die. Now throw that
gun down and get out of here."

"I can't do that."

"Then what happens to her is your fault."

"Wait!" Jackson yelled as he saw Taggart's arm close
tighter around her neck. He noted the terrified look on her
face and, silently begging her forgiveness, he slowly raised
both arms. A twist of his wrist flung the snub-nose on the
floor between them.

"You know you don't have a chance of getting away with
it this time, Taggart," Jackson asked. "The police are on
their way over here right now."

"So you say."

"It's the truth; I'm not lying. Your secretary phoned them
herself; they should be here any minute."

Taggart winced. "Doesn't say much for Diedre's loyalty,
does it? Well, what the hell. I've already killed three; in the
end, two more won't make much difference. They can only
execute me once."

"But why Jill?" asked Jackson. "She's different. She's
never done anything intentionally to hurt you."

Taggart's chuckle held more bitterness than mirth. "Different? You've certainly got that right."

Jackson gave Jillian a quick, questioning look.

"Amanda was his wife," she said, and gasped when
Taggart tightened his hold.

"Wife?" Jackson looked at Taggart. "She means ex-wife, doesn't she?"

"No," said Taggart. "Amanda and I were never divorced. She died— I—I killed her on our eighth anniversary."

"Eight years," Jackson said, thinking that they had a ghost of a chance if he could keep Taggart talking until Hank arrived. He cast Jillian a quick, hopefully reassuring look. "Amanda would've been what," he continued, "seventeen, eighteen when you married her?"

"Eight—eighteen," Taggart said, unaware that Jackson had heard the wistful note in his voice and could see the faraway look in his eye. "The most beautiful eighteen-year-old girl I'd ever seen. I couldn't believe it when she said she'd marry me. Couldn't believe that she could love me as much as I loved her. In the end, I was right. She didn't love me. She just used me to get back at her mother.

"But you don't know about her mother, do you? Lucky you. The old bitch died in Europe a couple of years ago; that's where she took Amanda when she found out we were married. Amanda wasn't as independent then as I first thought. When Momma snapped her fingers, Amanda jumped.

"You'd think in eight years, Amanda would've found time to divorce me, but she didn't. I suppose that's what gave me the hope that we might be able to make something of our marriage. I even moved my company here from California when she came back home to Dallas. I wanted to be near her."

Taggart paused to take a deep breath. "I worked my ass off for that woman, trying to be something, somebody she would be proud of. And the whole time I knew what she was doing, who she was doing it with. It hurt like hell.

"When I finally went to see her and told her I'd been in

Dallas for some time, I asked her to have dinner with me. Just for old times' sake. We went out, and funny thing is, it was okay. At first. But she'd changed. Living with her mother, she'd become just as selfish as the old bitch.

"We'd been seeing each other for about a month, and I thought things were going well. We were getting back to where we once were, feeling about each other the way we once did—or so I thought. And then she told me she wanted a divorce so she could marry Wyatt. I didn't want a divorce; all I wanted was her to give us more time, but she wouldn't listen. She said that marrying me was the biggest mistake she'd ever made, that all she wanted was out, that she was going to try to put the past behind her forever, and then she told me she never wanted to see me again.

"What choice did I have? I knew I wasn't getting anywhere with her, so I agreed. I agreed to keep quiet about it, too. For her sake. That's what you do when you love somebody, when you want them to be happy. Even if their happiness is at the expense of your own.

"When I learned she was having an affair with Northrop, Wyatt's partner, I saw it as my ace in the hole. I guess I thought if I could get Wyatt out of her life, I still might have a chance. I knew he wasn't the kind of guy who'd put up with his wife, let alone his fiancée, being unfaithful to him, so I arranged for him to find Amanda and Northrop together. It worked, too, because he broke up with her the same night.

"When I went to her apartment the next day, I only wanted to talk to her, be alone with her for a while, see if I could reason with her one last time. I didn't intend to kill her. I swear to God I didn't. But she never gave me a chance. The minute I walked in the door, she started yelling at me, accusing me of standing between her and happiness with Wyatt. I never knew she had such a wild, uncontrollable temper. I tried to calm her down, but she started throwing things at me, screaming at me as she ran into the kitchen. I followed her and, I don't know, maybe if I hadn't she'd still be alive today. She'd gotten hold of a knife. I didn't want her to hurt herself or me with it. So I tried to reason with her again. Told her that if she'd put it down I'd leave. She didn't listen. She came toward me and somehow I managed to grab hold of her arm. We struggled and the knife slipped. I couldn't stop it. It sliced her neck. I guess it was really sharp. And the next thing I knew she was lying on the floor covered in blood.''

"Yeah, then you stuck the knife in her chest just to make it look good, right?'' Jackson said. "I don't buy it, Taggart. None of it. You suckered Wyatt into coming here to your office, cooked up some lie about being out of town on business while you went to her place, disguised yourself to look like him, then you planted your blood covered raincoat and gloves in his garbage can. That ain't no accident. That's pure, premeditated murder.''

"But it wasn't,'' Taggart said. "All right, yes, I got him up here under false pretenses. I had to. I didn't want him to show up at Amanda's place and spoil what little chance I thought I had left. Don't you see? I had to talk to her alone, without any interruptions. That's why I told Diedre I'd be out of town. I didn't want her trying to phone me or buzz me on my pager. And I only wore a raincoat like Wyatt's because I was afraid Amanda wouldn't let me past the front door if she knew it was me. She'd made it clear that she never wanted to see me again.''

"After it happened, after I killed her, I knew I had to get away from her. I couldn't face what I had done. But as I was leaving, one of her neighbors, I guess, saw me. She called out to me, called me by Wyatt's name, and I knew then that

I had a chance of not getting caught. I drove straight to White Rock Lake, found the alley behind Wyatt's house, and threw my raincoat and gloves in his garbage can. I destroyed the coat in his closet later. Then I heard that the police had arrested him and charged him with murder."

"And the day he was released from jail," Jackson said, "you went back to his house and you killed him with a karate chop across the back of his neck. Then to make it look like suicide, like he hadn't been able to live with his guilt, you took a gun and blew his brains out."

"Yes."

"Smart move, Taggart. Very smart. Too bad you didn't quit while you were ahead. You'd have been completely in the clear if you hadn't killed Northrop." Jackson knew his accusation was a long shot. Seeing Taggart sneer he knew his long shot had payed off. "Why'd you do it?"

"He knew about Amanda and me. She probably told him we were married, and he must have put two and two together and realized I was the one who'd killed her. And Wyatt. He said he wouldn't go to the police and tell them what I'd done if I'd give him a million dollars. Not all at once, though; he was going to be generous and let me pay it out ten thousand at a time. He called me, told me he wanted to meet with me, and I went. I gave him the first installment in an envelope, and spiked a drink I'd ordered for him with a stiff dose of strychnine."

Feeling her anger mount, Jillian decided she'd had just about all she could take. She was tired of having this maniac's hands on her, tired of listening to his soap opera of a love life, and fed up with waiting for Jackson to be the big hero and get her out of this mess. Some hero. She could tell by the expression on his face that he was so enthralled with Taggart's story that he had forgotten the man was trying to strangle her. Oh, sure, he'd said the police would be here any minute, but the way things were going she could be dead by then.

Well, darn it, she didn't want to die. Not like this. And by golly, she wasn't going to die. Not without first putting up a good fight.

Instead of struggling, however, Jillian did just the opposite by pretending to faint. She released a soft, fluttering sigh, worthy of one of her grandmother's worst gothic heroines, and slumped to one side.

For a moment, both men just stood there, startled by Jillian's unexpected move. Taggart moved first, dropping his arms in an attempt to support her so she wouldn't slide to the floor. Jackson launched into action by diving headfirst across the room. His body slammed hard into Taggart's, knocking Jillian aside. The two men rolled over the back of a couch, overturning it, and fell to the floor.

Jillian clambered to her feet and would have run out of the office if her conscience hadn't stopped her. As much as he might deserve it, she just couldn't leave Jackson.

Out of the corner of her eye, she saw the snub-nose lying on the floor. Her fear of guns made her hesitate for a split second, and then with a grimace, she started toward it.

Knuckles were crunching against bone and grunts from painful blows were coming from behind the overturned couch when she reached down and picked up the gun. She took hold of the butt like one might handle a dead rat, then slowly righted the weapon. Funny, it didn't feel as threatening as she had imagined it would. Why, her forefinger fit perfectly around the trigger.

The resulting explosion put a hole in the wall just above the couch and made Jilliam scream. Jackson's bruised and bloody head popped into view. He looked at her, saw she was holding his gun, saw the hole in the wall behind him, and quickly ducked again.

"Uh, freeze," Jillian said in a timid, unsure tone.

"Freeze!" Hank shouted as he leaped into the office, aiming his gun directly at her.

With a frightened squeak, Jillian tossed Jackson's gun aside and threw her arms into the air. "Don't shoot me, please! I didn't hit anyone."

# CHAPTER 21

"Ouch!" Jackson flinched and jerked his arm away from Jillian. "Dammit, that stuff burns like hell!"

"Honestly, Jack, the way you're behaving, you'd think this was major surgery instead of just a little first aid. You can be such a baby at times." She gently dabbed her alcohol-soaked cotton ball around the deep cut on his arm, cleaning away the last of the blood and carpet fuzz that had accumulated in his wound.

"Guess I ought to be grateful you're not using my vodka again."

She sat back to examine his injury in the bright lamplight, then reached for the gauze and tape. "You're just lucky Taggert's letter opener didn't cut you any deeper. If it had, you'd be in an emergency room right now getting this taken care of. Whatever possessed you to jump him when you knew he was holding a weapon, anyway? Were you trying to be a hero, or something?"

"Well, I had to save my girl from the bad guys, didn't I?" A smile tugged at Jackson's lips as he watched the light and shadows play across the curve of her smooth cheek. He wanted to reach out and touch her, but he resisted the urge. Knowing Jillian, she just might take a notion to pour the whole damn bottle of alcohol on him. Or worse, finish the hatchet job Taggart had started with the scissors she was holding.

"Bad guy, singular," she said.

"You forgetting the preppy, gold-chained jerk?"

"Preppy, gold-chain— Oh, you mean Muscles."

"Who?"

"Muscles. Here, hold this a minute." She placed a thick gauze pad over the cut on his arm and covered it with his hand.

"That wasn't his name, was it?"

"Probably not, but it was the only one I could come up with that seemed to fit him."

Jackson considered her remark for a moment and then accepted it with a shrug. A mistake, he realized, feeling most of his abused joints protest. "Seems to me," he said, wincing, "that his name was Martin, Moreton. Something like that. Damn, I never was so glad to see Hank's boys show up and cart him off to jail in all my life. I couldn't have handled another fight with him. Guy was one mean little fu— I mean, he was quite a handful."

Jillian smiled as she turned to reach for the gauze strip and adhesive tape. Jackson was changing. For the better, too. Give her a little more time and she'd break him completely from his street talk.

"One thing I gotta know," Jackson said.

"What's that?"

"How'd you get to be so smart?"

Jillian fluttered her lashes innocently. "Well, when I was a little girl, I ate all my veggies and went to bed on time like my mother—"

"No, I don't mean that, smarty pants. I mean, how'd you know Taggart was our man?"

*Our man.* Jillian liked the sound of that. "Well, who else could it have been?" she said, unwinding a roll of gauze around his arm.

"How the hell should I know? That's why I'm asking you."

"Think back for a minute. Remember my first day here, when you came back from the jail after having that little talk with Sterling and his lawyer?"

"Yeah."

"You told me that Taggart had told the police he didn't have an appointment with Sterling."

"So?"

"So, somebody was lying. And I knew that it wasn't Sterling."

Jackson waited for her to elaborate further. When she didn't, he asked, "That's it? You're telling me you knew from the very beginning that Taggart did it?"

"Well, no. There were other things. Little things, details, that really didn't mean anything at the time. Like the day I saw Taggart walking down the street. It was the same day Sterling was released from jail. He must have been on his way to Sterling's house. Anyway, it was raining and, from a distance, he sort of reminded me of Sterling. When his hair was wet, it was a much darker shade of blond than when it was dry. A lot like the shade of Sterling's hair. That's probably why Amanda's neighbors were so positive they had seen Sterling coming out of her apartment. Taggart could almost have been Sterling's fraternal twin brother, you know? And, too, there's the fact that he was at Amanda's funeral. He sat in the pew beside me."

"He did what!"

"He sat in the pew—"

"Why didn't you tell me that before?"

"Because, like I said, at the time, I didn't think it was significant."

She cut off a piece of adhesive tape and fixed it to the gauze strip. "You'd told me to keep my eyes and ears open for anyone who looked or acted suspicious, and all Taggart did was offer me his handkerchief. Nothing at all suspicious about that in my opinion."

"So all you really did was follow up a hunch, right?"

"Well, no. It was actually a little more involved than that. I guess it has a lot to do with feminine intuition, but you wouldn't understand about that."

"Feminine intuition, huh. Like maybe a three-hundred-dollar trip to a beauty shop that's so exclusive it's not even listed in the phone book?"

"Oh, you know about Coiffure d'Anglaise, do you?"

"Yeah, I saw the bill. Nearly had a heart attack, too. Nobody lays out that kind of cash for a simple shampoo and set, Jill. Nobody who has to work for a living, that is."

"But I got a lot more than just a new hairdo, Jack. You'd be surprised at what Amanda told her hair stylist, manicurist, and masseuse."

"After this case, I doubt if I'll be surprised at anything. But three hundred bucks—I sure hope you're not expecting to get reimbursed for that."

"Of course I do. I was on company time, doing company work."

"Aw, now, Jill—"

"Aw, now, Jack, it was a legitimate business expense. The information I got at Coiffure d'Anglaise got me headed in the right direction. Which is a lot more than you managed to accomplish."

"Now wait just a damn minute. I was going straight by the book, following the most logical suspects. It wasn't my fault they all turned out to be false leads."

"If you'd listened to me in the first place, you'd never have gotten sidetracked. I told you there was a third man involved, and you just laughed at me."

"Yeah," he said grudgingly. "Sorry about that. You were right, and I was wrong."

"Maybe next time you'll pay closer attention."

Jackson looked at her for a long moment. "Is there gonna be a next time?"

Jillian blinked, then turned her head, not wanting him to see the blush creeping into her cheeks. "What do you think?"

"I think I hope there will be a next time. We make a damn good team, don't you think?"

Slowly she nodded in agreement. "When we're not arguing. Isn't that what you meant to say?"

"Sometimes arguments can lead to nicer, uh, encounters." With a sexy, lopsided grin, he ran a hand up her arm and let his fingers slide around the curve of her neck.

"Now, Jack," Jillian said as he began pulling her head down toward his, "you're in no condition to be doing what you're doing."

"Wanna bet?"

Like so many times before, the moment their lips touched, fireworks seemed to go off inside their heads. Jackson heard the purr vibrate in Jillian's throat, felt her body mold itself against his, and knew he'd be a fool not to take immediate advantage of the situation. He deepened the kiss, pushing his tongue gently past her lips and tasting her inner sweetness.

Moments of mindless pleasure passed, and then Jillian turned away. She buried her forehead against his shoulder. Jackson, too aroused to quit, began nibbling on the lobe of her ear.

"We can't do this, Jack," she whispered.

"Yeah, we can."

"No, we can't."

"Yes, we can. We almost did once before."

Jillian lifted her head to study his drowsy expression. "And look what happened to us that time."

"Just forget that one, sweetheart; I swear it won't happen again."

"How can you be sure?"

"Simple," Jackson said. "Taggart and his hired preppy gun are locked up good and tight in jail, and as far as I know, there's nobody out there gonna start shooting at us. Why don't you just relax and let nature take its course?" He flicked a glance up at the loft. "Wanna go someplace where it's more comfortable."

"Like where?"

"Like upstairs. To bed."

Her brows arching in question, Jillian sat up. "Do you honestly believe that a man in your condition should risk trying to make it up those stairs?"

Jackson released a disappointed sigh and stared at the ceiling. "I knew it. The one and only time I managed to luck out, we got interrupted. Now, when I'm certain nobody'll bother us, she's not in the mood." He looked at Jillian. "So what you're saying is that I should scratch this one too, right?"

Jillian blinked once, twice, then allowed a smoldering warmth to soften her gaze. Without a word of what she intended to do, she lifted her hands and slowly began to unbutton her blouse.

Jackson blinked once, twice, then his eyes widened in disbelief. He looked up from her enticing cleavage and saw that she had lowered her head to his.

"Tell me something, Jack," Jillian said, her lips a mere whisper above his, "where does it itch?"